MONTEZUMA'S FIRE
A Sheriff Lansing Mystery

MONTEZUMA'S FIRE
A Sheriff Lansing Mystery

Micah S. Hackler

SPEAKING VOLUMES, LLC
NAPLES, FLORIDA
2023

Montezuma's Fire

ISBN 978-1-64540-719-5

TO THE MEMORY OF MY SON
MICAH STUART HACKLER
(1975 – 2022)

Acknowledgments

This past year was tough for me, both physically and emotionally. I am truly thankful for the three blessings that kept me going. My faith in God. My beautiful wife, Olivia, who makes my life wonderful. And my writing, which gives me a reason to get up every morning.

As always, I thank George Sewell and Dan Baldwin. We shared our dreams around campfires. We lived our lives, encouraged each other, and made those dreams a reality. *The Factory* lives on.

Thank you to the readers of my novels, especially those who take the time to review them and who provided critiques. Even the rough ones.

Thank you, Kurt and Erica Mueller. You and your phenomenal staff at Speaking Volumes continue to provide all the exceptional help and support I could ever hope for.

Prologue

"You must leave, *mi corazón,*" Juan Huerta said, tears stinging his eyes. "You must go far away."

The village of Tetlapayac sat in the foothills of Cerro El Rosario. Like so many towns of Tlaxcala, it was ancient. Its traditions and superstitions were ancient as well. Far older than the traditions and religion introduced by the Spanish.

As the village's old adobe brick walls and buildings crumbled away, the new cinderblock houses, though utilitarian, were far from pleasing to the eye. Huerta's own shack sat high on a hill, at the end of a dirt street, overlooking the other houses. While other yards boasted concrete block walls, Juan's fence was no more than sticks woven together by vines.

The father straightened the folds of the doll's multicolored dress . . . so very similar to the dress his daughter would have worn for her *Quinceañera.*

"Fernanda, you must understand, it is not safe for you here. Not any longer."

His daughter's dark eyes flashed, but she said nothing as she clutched the porcelain doll. She had possessed it since she was a small child. It was the only memory she had of her mother.

"Others in the village suspect us . . . suspect you. I see how they stare. I hear their whispers. They think I don't, but I do."

His daughter said nothing.

"Miguel Santos has family in Nogales. They own a *mercado de artesanias.* Tomorrow he will take you and your doll there. Maybe someone kind will bring you to the United States. Maybe you will be safe there." His tears flowed freely now.

"Fernanda, remember, always, how much your father loves you."

If Fernanda had been capable, she might have cried too. Such emotion was beyond her. But she understood what her father was telling her, and she knew what she ultimately had to do.

Chapter One

"We still don't have an ID on that hit-and-run," Jack Rivera said, stepping into Sheriff Cliff Lansing's office. He sat in a chair in front of the desk before taking a sip of his coffee. "The State Police couldn't find any matching fingerprints, and no one's reported a missing person."

"I'm not surprised about the prints," the sheriff admitted. "The Medical Investigator guessed she wasn't more than twenty. Obviously, she hadn't been in trouble with the law."

"Never will be, either."

"Yeah," Lansing agreed, sadly. "The Examiner's office found something else. Even though the girl was definitely hit by a car, it looked to them like the body had been moved. The blood pooling didn't match our accident photos."

"So, this might be more than an accident?"

Lansing shrugged. "The guilty party might have moved the body to make sure it was found."

"Why bother?"

"Who knows?" Lansing stood. "We need to show the girl's photo to the farms and ranches east of the Apache Reservation." He glanced out his window. "You know, coming back from Aztec last week, I drove right past that area . . . must have been the day before they found the body."

"Too bad you didn't catch the guy dumping the body . . . You know, there's a chance she was visiting Navajo Lake," Rivera observed, standing as well. "We should post the photo and our contact information on the marina bulletin boards."

"Good idea. Be sure copies are hung on the San Juan County side as well."

"Right."

The two men headed to the day room to refresh the coffee in their mugs.

"Don't forget," Lansing said. "I'm leaving here at ten. Tina's flying in from Phoenix and should arrive in Albuquerque around one."

"How long has she been gone?"

"Almost two months. She'd still be in Mexico if school wasn't starting next week."

"Yeah. I know all about when school starts. Deedee's in first grade this year. I don't know who's more excited . . . her or her mother."

"She's excited about having the house to herself?"

"Naw. She's going to work part-time at the IGA."

"A little extra spending money never hurt." Lansing filled his mug, then his Chief Deputy's.

"Speaking of money," Rivera said, nodding to his boss to thank him for the fill-up. "How could Tapia afford all that radio time for his campaign ads?"

John Tapia was Lansing's opponent for the upcoming Democratic primary election for sheriff.

"The Cattleman's Association is backing him. They weren't happy when I got Felix Esteban's operation shut down."

"That doesn't make any sense. Wasn't he buying stolen cattle?"

"Whenever he got caught red-handed, he always paid the rightful owners for their losses. But they also knew he would look the other way when they tried to sell watered stock."

Watered stock was the practice of getting steers to drink lots of water just before a weigh-in for a sale.

"The sellers also knew Esteban employed fake buyers to drive up the cattle prices during the auctions," Lansing concluded. "They all made out like bandits. Now the San Phillipe ranchers have to go to Farmington or Santa Fe to unload their cattle."

"I can see why they're not happy with you."

"Getting Tapia elected won't bring Esteban back. He still has three more years on his sentence. They just want to punish me."

"Do you think he has a chance?"

"No," Lansing shook his head. "He's been on the Segovia City Council for eight years. Before that he was with the police department, so he does have law enforcement experience. But I don't think anyone outside of Segovia even knows who he is."

"His commercial was pretty nasty."

"Well, like Twain said, 'There are lies, damn lies, and statistics.' And Tapia used all three in one ad."

Chapter Two

Lincoln Baca sat in his truck, both hands on the steering wheel. He had the wheel in a death grip, squeezing to the point that his hands hurt. He took deep breaths and stared hard at nothing.

He was angry. He was frustrated. He was lost.

Since he was five years old, he wanted nothing more than to be a wildlands firefighter. In high school, he was no great athlete. But he managed to find a firefighter's fitness manual and began training. What held most candidates back was the rigorous physical test they had to pass to be certified. The weekly exercises were a challenge to master and applied to both men and women.

The "burpee" was the hardest exercise to master.

From a standing position, the trainee had to squat, then jump straight up with their arms fully extended above their heads. On landing, they again squat and extend their legs to a plank position, hands on the ground directly below the shoulders, body straight. After a single push-up, the candidate recovered to a squat position to repeat the jump for another burpee.

Doing a single burpee was tough. Qualification required the candidate to do 25 burpees, followed by a half-mile run—three times. Interspersed were explosive squat jumps, 10 yards of overhead walking lunges (twice), and more push-ups.

There were also certifications for CPR, chainsaw operations, and driving.

Baca became a qualified firefighter at the age of twenty. One of the youngest ever hired on by the Black Mesa Pueblo Crew, he lived his dream job for only eighteen months. On the first night of the Cerro

Grande Fire, he allowed himself to be spooked. Trying to move down the steep slope too quickly, he tripped and fell.

After tumbling fifty feet, he slammed against the trunk of a tall pine, breaking his collar bone and the humerus of his left arm. Eight weeks in a cast left his arm weak and his shoulder frozen.

Even after three weeks of intense physical therapy, he still couldn't lift his left arm above his head. With no muscle strength, a push-up was impossible.

A single mistake had forced him to start his training all over. Until today.

He paid no attention to the other cars coming and going from the hospital parking lot. He was only aware of the words the doctor spoke to him earlier that morning.

"I'm sorry, Lincoln. I'm afraid we found the reason for your head-aches." Dr. Lopez, the neurologist, placed scan images from an MRI on the lighted board. "You have a tumor." He pointed to a dark spot that appeared in several pictures.

"Is it cancer?"

"We don't know. We have to do a biopsy to find out."

"You mean, cut open my brain?"

"The location of the tumor makes it inoperable. No. I'll drill a small hole in your skull and insert a needle. I'll remove a sample and examine it under a microscope."

"Okay," Lincoln said quietly. "Then what are we going to do?"

"If it's benign, we don't need to do anything. If it's cancer, we can do chemotherapy, radiation therapy, or even a combination of both."

"My hair will fall out, right?"

"Most likely."

"Can't we just cut the tumor out?"

"No. As I said, the tumor is inoperable."

"Well, will these therapies work?"

"There are more and more cancer survivors every year. We need to schedule the biopsy. The sooner the better. After that, we'll decide what to do."

"I visit my uncle at the Senior Citizens Center all the time. I see what those poor people look like after their cancer treatments. All they do is get sicker and sicker until they finally quit coming to the center . . . because they die!"

"These are old people to begin with. You're young. You won't suffer as much. I highly recommend the therapies."

"And if I don't get the therapy?"

"If the tumor is cancerous, you're going to die. I can guarantee it. And whether you pursue the therapy or not, I think your firefighting days are over."

Not be a firefighter? That thought was as bad as the prospect of dying.

During his convalescence, he had become surly. He hated being treated like an invalid. His mother complained about his attitude daily. He separated himself from his family by taking long walks. He visited his Great Uncle Eluterio at the senior center two or three times a week. Anything to get out of the house.

He borrowed money from his sister to fix his truck. Once he got the cast off his arm, he wanted to be independent again.

Now what?

"How long do I have?"

"Weeks, months, even years if you take the therapy."

Lincoln stood and headed for the door. "I'll let you know."

"Let's at least do the biopsy."

"Why? If it's cancer, I'm not doing your treatment. If it isn't cancer, it doesn't matter."

"Lincoln," the doctor said, stopping him. "I brought this for you to read." He handed Lincoln a pamphlet.

"What is it?"

"It's a description of what to expect if you have a brain tumor. It also discusses the different therapies and their effects. There's a whole section on what might happen to you if the tumor gets worse. You need to pay attention to that part . . . especially if you choose not to pursue treatment."

"Thanks."

Lincoln started his truck and backed out of his parking spot. He needed to tell his family what the doctor said. Later, though. He didn't want to go home. Not yet anyway.

Chapter Three

According to the Arrivals board, Southwest Flight 5843 from Phoenix was ON TIME.

Lansing glanced at the wall clock: 12:55. He had fifteen minutes to get to Gate B7. That was plenty of time. With only one terminal, the Albuquerque International Sunport was relatively small compared to other airports. Lansing wasn't much of a traveler though. The only other airport he'd been to was the Phoenix Airport, which, with three terminals, he considered a nightmare.

Tina Morales suggested they could meet at the baggage claim, but the sheriff insisted he would greet her at the gate. She had been gone for seven weeks. He couldn't believe how much he missed her. They had talked nearly every day, usually in the evenings when there would be no distractions. But only hearing her voice made him long for her even more.

Tina's trip that summer was dedicated to learning as much as she could from Naomi Sanchez, her grandmother. Tina's abuela was in her nineties, and the chemistry teacher was afraid Naomi's vast knowledge as a *curandera*, a type of witch or *bruja*, would soon be lost. Tina had studied under her for years. She knew there was so much more she could learn. Her grandmother was an expert *yerbera* who could point to any plant and explain its use for good or evil. It was her abuela's influence that pushed Tina into studying chemistry and becoming a chemistry teacher.

He watched out of the window as the blue-painted Boeing 737 came to a stop next to the jet bridge. A few minutes later the first passenger entered the terminal. Lansing couldn't believe how impatient he felt.

"When are these people going to get out of the way?" he thought.

Tina finally emerged, hidden behind a large man wearing a cattle-man's hat.

Lansing gingerly picked his way through the arrivals, refusing to simply wait for the schoolteacher to reach him. They immediately embraced and he planted a kiss. Unknowingly, they blocked others trying to exit. An elderly woman readily pointed that out.

"Sorry," Tina said, pulling her man to the side. "Oh, we need to be careful with this." She indicated the straw bag tote she was carrying.

"What's that?"

Tina opened the bag and removed a porcelain doll. Twelve inches tall, it wore a colorful dress long enough to cover the feet. The face had finely painted features that were hauntingly beautiful.

"I didn't want to ruin her by stuffing her in a suitcase. She's much too precious for that."

Tina cradled the doll as if it was an infant. The two began working their way through the terminal toward the escalators. The baggage claim was on the bottom level.

"Where did she come from?"

"Originally? I don't know," Tina admitted. "My abuela and I visit-ed a *mercado de artisanries* in Nogales. They had handicrafts from all over Mexico. There must have been a thousand different dolls."

There were numerous dolls distinctively Mexican. The most famous was the Maria doll, a rag doll named after the most popular girl's name in Mexico. But there were other cloth dolls, the Lele, Dönxu, Frida Khalo. There were also other porcelain dolls like the Lupita doll.

"But Izel is special. I had never seen anything so exquisite."

"Izel?"

"The shop owner said Izel was Aztec for 'unique.' I couldn't agree more."

Lansing thought the teacher's attitude toward the toy was a bit obsessive but said nothing. "What did your grandmother think of Izel?"

"I don't think she liked her. She frowned when I bought her, but she never said anything."

It was a short wait once they reached the baggage carousel. Tina pointed out a bag once it came around to them. Lansing picked it up.

"You ready?" he asked.

"Oh, no. I have two more bags."

"Two?"

"I had to stock up when I was in Mexico. One bag has dried plants, seeds, and cuttings you can't find in New Mexico."

"The other one?"

Tina smiled. "Presents!"

Chapter Four

Jeremiah Black sat in the doorway of his 10-foot travel trailer and smoked a cigarette. He knew it would be a long week. It was Monday evening, and he was already tired. Part of his weariness was from working eight hours as an auto mechanic. The rest was because he hadn't completely recovered from the all-night service that ended at dawn on Sunday.

The small adobe house he called his "church" stood several feet away. It needed to be swept, mopped, and cleaned in general, though there was no hurry. The next service wouldn't be until Saturday evening. He had opened the door to his ministry only four weeks earlier. He depended on word-of-mouth to announce his presence.

Seven people actually attended his last service. Counting himself, the fireman, and the drummer, the small church accommodated the ten with no problem. Jeremiah was confident it would hold twice that many. Twenty would be the most he would want to attend. For now, anyway.

His goal was not to have a large congregation. And he accepted the fact he needed to work an outside job to support his plans. Many ministers did.

Four years in the army taught him vehicle maintenance. Auto repair was his vocation. When he returned to his Oklahoma home outside Tulsa he was introduced to the Native American Church by Harper Stillwell, his future wife. The NAC cured him of his drinking problem. After that, the church became his avocation. The experience was so profound, he resolved to become a church minister, though that wasn't the title normally used.

"Healer" was a more accurate term. Over his ten years in the church, he had heard other terms used: orator, physician, Priest of the Sun, Prayer Leader. But the term "roadman" was the official title used.

It took eight years before Jeremiah Black became a roadman. His dedication cost him his marriage. His disagreement with established doctrine drove him from the church.

The doctrine was specific. The Native American Church was strictly for Native Americans. NO exceptions. If an individual wanted to join the church, they had to prove they were at least one-quarter Native American. That had to be proven, not through DNA testing, but through marriage documents. (The use of DNA for any purpose, even ethnic studies, was discouraged by tribal leaders.)

The NAC had been around since the 1880s. After one hundred and twenty years, its membership was 250,000, barely six percent of the four million Native Americans in the 2000 census.

For Jeremiah, the point of contention was the use of peyote during church ceremonies. The NAC maintained that peyote was a sacred plant. The Great Spirit gave it specifically to the indigenous people for their use alone. (Some tribes like the Lipon and Mescalero Apache, however, viewed peyote as a tool of the devil and refused to endorse its use.)

The church fought individual states for years for the right to use peyote in their ceremonies. In 1965 the federal government ruled against the states and declared that Indians and Indian tribes had the right to use peyote in their services. However, in 1967 the federal government declared mescaline, the hallucinogen compound found in the peyote, a Class I drug. Now only Indians were allowed to possess, transport, and use the plant/drug.

Jeremiah Black believed, as did many others, that the use of peyote should not be restricted to only Indians. Peyote wasn't a recreational

14

drug. It was medicine. Its use combined with the religious practices of the church (an amalgam of Christianity and Indian traditions) could be a powerful healing tool . . . for anyone. It worked for him.

The Native American Reform Church, as Black called his ministry, was open to all. He knew, eventually, there would be a battle with the authorities over non-Indians using peyote. He also knew there were a dozen organizations that would defend him. For the moment he wanted to keep his church and its philosophy out of the spotlight.

Initially, he would seek only Indian members. Located just north of Segovia, he was within a hundred miles of a dozen reservations and Pueblos. With legitimate attendees initially, he would expand the congregation gradually. His intent was to show his church, his philosophy, and his incorporation of peyote in his ceremonies, would never be a threat to anyone.

Black's property was near Rio Cohino. His adobe church sat between the river to the south and a paved, county road to the north. A dark red SUV caught his attention as it crept along the road. The driver must be looking for something, he casually thought.

Black didn't give the vehicle another thought as he finished his cigarette, grinding the butt into the ground. The adobe church, formerly a private residence, had a full bath. The roadman finished the last bite of his hamburger, then grabbed a towel and clean clothes from his trailer. He knew a shower would invigorate him.

Chapter Five

"Hola, Councilman," Paul Trevino said, standing. He grabbed John Tapia's hand and the two men did a modified hug and chest bump.

"Glad you called me, cuz," Tapia said. "It's been a long time."

"Sit down. Sit down." Trevino indicated a chair across the table from where he was sitting. "What are you drinking?"

"Just iced tea. I have to maintain an image, you know."

Trevino signaled to the waitress. "Iced tea for the councilman and I'll have another cervesa."

Ernesto's Restaurant and Sports Bar was not particularly busy. A small knot of men had gathered at the bar. Only two other tables were occupied in the dining area.

"Are you still living in Las Cruces?"

"No. I'm in Santa Fe, now."

"How's Diane?"

"I have no idea," Trevino said, frowning. "She walked out with the kids and took me for every penny I had."

"I'm sorry to hear that."

"Yeah. Thanks." There was no hiding his bitterness.

"So, what are you doing in Segovia?" Tapia asked, changing the subject.

"My new job with the state. Department of Agriculture. I get to do a lot of traveling. Mostly I work with university extension services."

"What do you know about agriculture?" The councilman said, a slight frown on his face. "We both grew up here in town."

"Oh, I don't know anything about farming or ranching. I'm what you call a facilitator. Some people just need help. I put them in touch with people and programs who want to help them."

"A lot of money involved?"

Trevino smiled. "There can be."

"Why am I not surprised? You always said, 'Money isn't every-thing. It's just way out in front of whatever's in second place.'"

Trevino shrugged before taking a sip of his newly arrived beer. "And you don't believe that? You figured out a long time ago how things work. You married rich. Now you're a politician. Beats working for a living."

"You know some of us actually believe in public service."

"Okay, okay," Trevino nodded. "You believe in public service. Is that why you're chasing after the county sheriff's job? You want to serve more people?"

"I think I'm bigger than just Segovia."

"Yeah, yeah. I heard your campaign ad on the radio today. This Lansing isn't doing his job. Violent crime's up two hundred percent. Drug use is up three hundred percent. Property crimes are up three-hundred and fifty percent. No one's safe. It's time for a change."

"Where'd you get those statistics?"

"I got them from the FBI. You think I just pulled them out of my butt?"

Trevino gave his cousin a hard look. "I work for the state. Crime's up all over New Mexico. We're a corridor for the Mexican cartels. I'll bet your stats are for Segovia, not the entire state."

"You're splitting hairs. If crime's up in New Mexico, it's up in San Phillipe County."

"To hell with whose jurisdiction is responsible, eh?"

"Why did you want to get together, cuz? It isn't because you missed me."

17

Trevino held up his hand as if professing his innocence. "John, you got me all wrong. I wanted us to get together because I want to help you."

"Help me?"

"Get elected. How are your polling numbers?"

Tapia frowned. "I'm ten points behind. But the primary is only a month away. What can you do in a month?"

"You need more than doctored statistics. You need an 'October Surprise.' Of course, it will end up being an August Surprise."

"What are you talking about?"

"Lansing has a pretty squeaky-clean image, from what I hear. Maybe we can dirty it up a little."

"Like what?"

"You let me worry about that. When the time comes, be ready to use it."

John Tapia learned at an early age not to trust his cousin. He wasn't sure he was ready to change his opinion. "Exactly what do you want in return?"

Trevino took a large gulp from his mug of beer, then wiped his mouth with the back of his hand. "When the time comes, I just want you to remember me."

"Remember you? How?"

"You've always had big plans for yourself. You married a millionaire's daughter. Like you said, Segovia isn't big enough for you. I'll bet San Phillipe won't be big enough either. As you climb your way to bigger things, I want to come along for the ride."

The city councilman leaned back in his chair and thought for a long moment. He had always been pragmatic in his political approach. He even had dreams of being a U.S. congressman . . . maybe a senator.

He was in his late thirties. He had plenty of time. He had gone step-by-step. A short stint as a policeman, then elected to the city council. He needed a county-wide job before going for a state position. The sheriff's job was a perfect route to follow. Politics cost money, though. Something he didn't have a lot of. Fortunately, his father-in-law did.

Tapia nodded his head slowly. "Okay, Paul. If you think you can help with my campaign, I promise I'll remember you. You staying at your mom's place?"

"Of course."

How long are you in town?"

"I'm leaving in the morning. I'll get in touch with you as soon as I can."

Chapter Six

"So, what are your plans?" Simon Baca asked.

The conversation around the Baca dinner table stopped when Lincoln announced he couldn't return to the Black Mesa Wildland Firefighters . . . for physical reasons. It was Lincoln's father who broke the silence.

Lincoln looked up from his plate of food. The corn and beans had grown cold, as had the goat meat. All the former firefighter had done was push the items around with his fork.

"I don't know, Dad. I haven't thought that far ahead."

The elder Baca frowned. "Well, you need to. Linc, you're twenty-one. You should be living in your own place."

Pauline shot her husband a dirty look from across the table. Her son had been out of his arm cast for only three weeks. He wasn't in any shape to work let alone move out.

"I know I need to move out," Lincoln growled. "You've mentioned it enough!"

It was Simon's turn to shoot a dirty look. This one was at his son. "You need to come with me in the morning. The pueblo road department is always looking for help."

"Shoveling gravel to fill potholes?"

"I started out doing that," his father said. "I'm running the heavy equipment now. You can work your way up, just like I did."

"What happens if I tell you I'm not interested?"

"What happens if I tell you that you have to pay rent if you want to live here?" Simon snapped.

"Simon!" Pauline scolded angrily. The mamma bear instinct to protect her cub had crept in.

Lincoln suddenly stood, fed up with the confrontation.

"Lincoln," his mother pleaded. "Please, sit back down and finish eating."

"I'm not hungry." He tried not to sound angry.

"How much longer is this physical therapy going to take?" Simon asked, softening his tone.

"I don't know," Lincoln admitted. "Till I get better, I guess."

"Son, you can stay here for as long as it takes," Pauline said calmly. "Isn't that right, Simon?"

The patriarch frowned.

"Simon?" his wife pushed. "Isn't that right?"

He turned his head to avoid his wife's stare. "Yes. Linc can stay here as long as he wants."

Joy, Lincoln's sister, sat silently at the table during the whole exchange. She hated that her family was arguing, cringing at the harsh words. At eighteen, she knew what she would do for the rest of her life. She was well on her way to becoming a pottery maker of note, just like her mother. Pottery making was a well-established industry in Santa Clara Pueblo and some pieces fetched prices in the thousands of dollars.

She stood and began clearing dishes from the table. "Linc, can you drive me over to San Ildefonso in the morning? Mamma and I need some fresh clay."

"Yeah, sure," her brother readily agreed. At this point, he was glad to contribute anything he could to the family. "What time? I have therapy at one."

"Let's go early. Right after breakfast."

"Can do."

Lincoln slouched back to his bedroom and flopped onto his bed. He pushed away the thought of telling his parents about the tumor. He knew he would need to tell them . . . eventually. Just not tonight.

He thought about his girlfriend, Serita. He worried about how she would take the news.

Chapter Seven

Dinner was finished and the dishes were washed. Lansing followed Tina back to the bedroom, where she lifted the heavy bag loaded with presents onto the bed.

"Do you need help with that?"

"No, no, mijo," she said to Lansing. "I've got it."

Once the bag was flat, she flipped the clasps and splayed it open. Lansing looked over her shoulder at the contents.

"You're not going to unload all that on our bed tonight, are you?"

"Don't worry. I'm only grabbing one thing."

Digging through the contents, she found the plastic bag she was looking for. Pulling it out, she turned to Lansing and held it flat. "This is for you. I'm sorry I didn't have time to wrap it properly."

Lansing was intrigued. Tina had said nothing about getting him a present. She never even asked if he wanted anything. He took the offering. It was vaguely shaped like a shirt, but much heavier.

He reached inside and pulled out a leather vest. The lining was brightly colored like a Mexican blanket. The buff-colored leather was smooth and elegant with no fancy leather embroidering. It had a collar and lapels. The buttons were dark brass.

"Do you like it?"

"I've never seen anything so beautiful!"

"Try it on!" Tina squeaked, excited at his approval.

Lansing slipped it on. It hung on him as if he had been measured.

"Does it fit?"

"Like a glove. How'd you get it so right?"

She put her arms around him. "I've held you enough times, I should know what would work."

"How did you know I wanted one?"

"You've mentioned them before . . . Besides, what do you get the man who has everything? You're not the type for a silver-encrusted belt with a two-pound buckle.'

"True."

The cellphone in his pocket began to ring.

"Excuse me," he said. Flipping it open, he noticed the caller ID. "Lansing, here. What's up, Phil?"

Deputy Phil Peters, the night dispatch, responded. "Sorry to bother you at home, Sheriff. It looks like we have another hit-and-run."

"Can't the night patrol handle this?"

"You were asked for, specifically."

"Who asked for me?"

"Police Chief Aquino, San Juan Pueblo."

"If it's on his reservation, can't he handle it on his own?"

"Sorry, boss. I'm just passing on his request."

"Alright. Where can I find him?"

Peters relayed the information.

Lansing closed the clamshell and turned to Tina. "Looks like we'll have to postpone our romantic evening."

"It won't be the first time." She stood on her toes and gave him a kiss.

He started taking off the vest.

"What are you doing?"

"I didn't want to ruin this the same day I got it."

"It's leather! It can take a little punishment. Besides, you're supposed to wear it, not leave it hanging in the closet."

"Okay," he conceded. "It'll probably be a bit cool out there anyway."

Chapter Eight

It was dark by the time Lansing reached the turn-off for Highway 285 south of Artiga. After crossing Rio Cohino, he took a right onto a county road. He could see the flashing lights ahead. He parked his patrol unit behind a deputy's SUV. There was also a Pueblo police unit and an ambulance.

"Hi, Sheriff." Deputy Jake Redwine nodded at his boss.

"Jake," Lansing said, looking around. "Are we on the reservation here?"

"I'm not sure. There aren't any signs."

A dozen roads entered San Juan Reservation. There were only four signs positioned on major roads that told drivers they were entering Pueblo lands. County roads weren't significant enough to warrant signs of their own.

Police Chief Joseph Aquino approached. "Good evening, Cliff."

Lansing shook the extended hand. "Joe." He looked over Aquino's shoulder. "What do you have?" He noticed a blue tarp stretched over a body.

The police chief gestured for the sheriff to follow him.

"Young lady . . . late teens, early twenties . . . found off to the side of the road."

Lansing followed. "And your office responded because she was found on the reservation."

"We're not sure the body's location is the accident scene. That's why I wanted you here."

They reached the blue tarp and Aquino signaled to the paramedic to lift it. There was a young Hispanic, maybe Native American, female lying face-up, a slight trickle of dried blood at the corner of her mouth.

Wearing dark shorts, the knees were bloodied and skinned up as if she had fallen forward. Her arms were against the side of her body. She had obviously been positioned.

"Any ID?" the sheriff asked.

"She had nothing on her," Aquino observed. "She doesn't look familiar, so I don't think she's from Ohkay Owingeh." The police chief used the Tewa name for San Juan Pueblo.

Lansing knelt and used his flashlight for a closer look.

"Obvious hit-and-run," the policeman continued. "We haven't touched anything, but it looks to me like she was hit from behind."

Lansing checked one arm, then the next.

"Did you notice these thin, red bruises on the wrists?" he asked.

Aquino bent over for a closer look. "No, I hadn't seen those. What are they?"

"It looks like her hands were bound together by wire." He thought for a moment. "No, a zip tie." He stood. "Are we on Pueblo land here?"

"Just barely."

"I have to agree with you, this is not where the crime took place."

"Crime?"

"Until we know better, we need to assume this person was run over intentionally."

"You're saying she was murdered?"

"Until we know differently, yes." Lansing checked his watch. "It's nearly ten. Do you mind if I bring in my forensic experts?"

"Please, do. Are we going to call this a joint investigation?"

"Sure, unless you want to call the FBI to report a suspicious death."

"I'll have to inform them eventually . . . but I'll hold off as long as I can."

"Good man," Lansing nodded. He turned to Redwine. "Jake, call dispatch. We need to get forensics out here, pronto."

"Yes, sir."

The sheriff pulled out his cell phone.

"Hi, Cliff . . . Are you almost finished?"

"Looks like it's going to be a long night, Tina. Don't wait up for me."

"O-o-h!" she whimpered in protest.

"Sorry."

Closing the phone, Lansing immediately thought about the hit-and-run in the northwest corner of San Phillipe County. He could only hope this second death was not connected.

Chapter Nine

Slipping her feet under the covers, Tina found the sheets cool and soothing.

It had been a long day. First, there was the drive from her parents' house in Sun City West to the airport. Then the car she used for seven weeks had to be returned to the rental car center. There was loading the luggage onto the shuttle. At Terminal Four she used a Sky Cap. She had no interest in standing in line with such a load.

The two-and-a-half-hour drive from Albuquerque to the ranch could have been tedious, but she spent the time telling Cliff about everything she did. Back at the ranch, he grilled steaks while she started laundry. When she gave Lansing his present, she had been up for twelve hours.

She was actually glad when he called and told her to go to bed. She wasn't in the mood for anything "romantic," and could barely keep her eyes open.

Tina moved items around and placed her memento, Izel, in the center of her dresser, in front of the mirror. She turned off the light on the nightstand. As her eyes adjusted to the darkness, she thought she saw the momentary greenish-yellow flash of a lightning bug from across the room.

She rubbed her eyes and looked again.

Only darkness.

"You're just tired," she told herself. Number one, how could it get into the house, and number two, what the hell was a firefly doing on the ranch. As far as she knew, there were no fireflies in the entire state of New Mexico.

Exhaustion took over. She would have to ponder lightning bugs another day.

Tina was only vaguely aware of the bed jiggling. She didn't wake up. Her subconscious made an assessment. She was in hers and Lansing's bedroom . . . in bed . . . asleep. Cliff had been somewhere doing sheriff stuff and now he was getting in bed. That's why the bed moved. But it moved very little because he didn't want to disturb her.

"What a wonderful man!" was the last thing she thought.

***

Tina Morales woke at 6:30. She sat up and noticed her partner's side of the bed had not been slept in. She could hear the shower running so she knew Lansing was home. At least she hoped it was Lansing.

She swung around so her feet hung over the side of the bed and stretched. She still felt incredibly tired . . . almost weak. The travel the day before must have really taken a toll.

Standing, Tina felt unsteady. Glancing around the room, something wasn't right. Lansing's clothes from the night before were draped over a chair. She expected that. The curtains were still drawn. Tina's survey of the room stopped at her dresser. Izel wasn't where the teacher had left her.

Morales frantically looked around the room. Her search stopped at the nightstand on Lansing's side of the bed. Somehow, the doll had migrated there from the dresser.

"Why would Lansing put her there?" she thought, as she moved Izel back to her original position.

Over breakfast, Cliff explained as much as he felt appropriate about the night before. In general, Lansing was reluctant to talk about his work. On-going investigations needed even more restrictions. Tina knew better than to push for more details.

The morning conversation was about how glad they both were that Tina was finally home. Lansing was especially happy Tina was fixing their food again. She had spoiled him. He admitted he was tired of the Las Palmas Diner breakfasts.

Lansing pooh-poohed Tina's suggestion that he take a nap before going to work.

"That's why God gave us coffee," he said gesturing with a raised mug.

Clearing the dishes from the table, Tina's question was almost an afterthought.

"By the way, why did you move Izel from the dresser?"

"What do you mean?"

"You moved her from my dresser to your nightstand. This morning."

"That doll was on my stand when I came in. I was wondering why you put it there."

Morales almost said, "I didn't" but reconsidered. Did she move it herself? In the middle of the night, she thought Lansing was getting into bed. He hadn't.

Was her sleep so deep she didn't realize what she had done? Or had she placed it on Lansing's side, only thinking she put it on the dresser? She had been so tired before going to sleep, maybe she had been confused about where she put Izel. That had to be it!

"I guess I wasn't thinking straight last night, I was so tired. I must have thought I put her on the dresser."

Lansing finished his coffee and stood. "I need to get to work."

"Lunch?"

"Sure. You're coming into town?"

"I have a suitcase full of presents I need to deliver. Remember?"

"That's right! Well, give me a call later."

"I will."

After a quick kiss, Lansing was out the door. Tina turned her attention to dirty dishes.

Chapter Ten

After putting four large plastic buckets in the truck bed, Joy Baca and her brother got into Linc's Chevy and started for Pojoaque Pueblo. The ex-firefighter decided to take Highway 30 to the south. There was less traffic than on Highway 15/285.

Joy was afraid to mention the argument at the dinner table the night before. She'd heard there was lots of work in Los Alamos after the Cerro Grande Fire. However, the topic of her brother getting a job seemed touchy at best. Instead, she asked why they weren't taking the main highway.

"I like this way better . . . and I think it's just as fast."

Highway 30 paralleled the Rio Grande. Three miles south of their home on the opposite side of the river stood Black Mesa, the last stronghold of the Santa Clara/San Ildefonso defenders.

The Spanish were driven from New Mexico during the 1680 Pueblo Revolt. The coalition of Pueblos fell apart soon after and the Spanish launched a successful reconquest in 1692. Some Pueblos put up little opposition. The Tewa people of Santa Clara and San Ildefonso resisted fiercely, making their last stand on Black Mesa. The flat-topped mount was only 300 feet above the river but had no readily accessible water.

Most of the defenders realized they could not hold out for long. Many escaped to the west, settling with the Zuni and Hopi Indians. The remaining fighters surrendered and returned to their respective Pueblos.

Fearing a second revolt, the Spanish overlords took a kinder approach to their subjects. The Pueblo Indians were no longer sold into slavery or drafted into forced labor. Their land rights and religion were finally respected. Because of the new policies, most of the escapees returned to their pueblos by 1702.

Three miles past Black Mesa, Highway 30 dead-ended into Highway 502. A right turn would take him to Los Alamos. Left took him past San Ildefonso to Pojoaque Pueblo.

All six Tewa-speaking pueblos shared a common religion and history. They migrated from Mesa Verde to Frijoles Canyon (now Bandelier Nation Monument), then to their present locations around 1250 AD.

The peoples of Santa Clara and San Ildefonso were particularly close. Their shared culture included pottery making, a tradition dating back hundreds of years. The exceptional craftsmanship was introduced to tourists in the 1880s when the Denver and Rio Grande Railroad laid track north from Santa Fe. Owning Pueblo Pottery suddenly became popular, and the craft became a lucrative business.

Santa Clara became known for its black-on-black pottery, but the technique originated at San Ildefonso by Maria Martinez. She was already an established artisan. Around 1910 her husband was working for archeologists. They discovered beautiful shards of black-on-black pottery. Intrigued, they asked Maria if she could duplicate the process. After several attempts, she had perfected the style by 1919.

The technique spread to Santa Clara and was now used by the Baca family. Both Joy and her mother specialized in black-on-black pottery.

Driving past San Ildefonso, Lincoln wondered why Santa Clara seemed so compact while her sister Pueblo was spread out. Much of Santa Clara's population lived within a mile of the Pueblo municipal buildings and elementary school . . . easy walking distance. San Ildefonso, not so much. The municipal buildings and post office were along a nearly three-quarter mile stretch of road. Most residents had to drive a mile or more for services.

The Baca's drive to Pojoaque was necessary to obtain white clay for pottery making. After hundreds of years, the Santa Clara and San

Ildefonso artisans had mostly depleted their own quarries of white clay. Pojoaque had plenty of clay . . . for sale.

Pojoaque was unique among the Pueblos. It had ceased to exist three times since 1680. Before the Spanish returned, for safety, the Pojoaque residents abandoned their homes and scattered to other pueblos. Five families resettled the pueblo in 1706.

The second time, Pojoaque was destroyed during the 1837 revolt against Mexico. The residents once more escaped to other pueblos. The pueblo was repopulated after the 1846 Mexican American War. It was recognized by the U.S Government as one of New Mexico's nineteen established pueblos in 1858. In 1863, all the pueblo governors traveled to Washington D.C. to receive a silver-tipped Lincoln Cane. The Lincoln Canes, still used today, symbolized each pueblo's independence and sovereignty.

By the late 1800s, however, Pojoaque had been decimated by drought and disease. In 1870 the population was only 32 persons, too few to continue traditional religious ceremonies and dances. In 1900, the last Cacique (religious leader) passed away and the governor left for outside employment, ending Pojoaque's existence for a third time.

In 1924, the year Indians were given the right to vote, the Pueblo Lands Act was passed confirming each Pueblo title to its lands. At the time, very few Pojoaque families still lived in the pueblo.

It was the Bureau of Indian Affairs that helped bring Pojoaque back one last time. In 1933 the BIA advertised for Pojoaque tribal members to return to their ancestral home or risk losing the independent pueblo forever. Many families responded. When the Indian Reorganization Act was passed the next year, Pojoaque was once again recognized as a fully functioning pueblo.

Chapter Eleven

Passing under Highway 15/285, Lincoln reached the stop sign at the service road. In front of him was the Cities of Gold Casino, one of Pojoaque's many lucrative businesses. The pueblo property was adjacent to the busy Santa Fe to Taos highway. The tribal planners took full advantage of easy access for travelers.

Turning right onto the service road, Lincoln would have headed into the Pojoaque Business District. Starting with the casino, the mile-long stretch of road boasted a motel, RV park, eight places to eat, shopping, a supermarket, two gas stations, the tribal courts, and a cultural center. With a tribal population of less than two thousand, unemployment was non-existent. In fact, they were one of the biggest employers south of Segovia.

Lincoln had been to Pojoaque a few times. He always marveled at how new everything looked. He had to remind himself nearly all the buildings were recent. The pueblo had been abandoned so many times there were no buildings left that could boast continual habitation.

"We'll turn left at the stop sign," Joy had instructed.

Lincoln had never been to the clay merchant before, so he needed the directions.

Following the road into the heart of the reservation, they turned left after passing a church, then right onto the Old Pueblo Road. At the first dirt road, they took a left.

At the end of the long road, they passed a large adobe-styled house. Just past the house was a tin-roofed barn. A single hand-painted sign said, "CLAY FOR SALE."

"I take it this is the place," Lincoln said, bringing his truck to a stop.

"Yup," Joy said, getting out. "Come on. I'll need help."

Lincoln grabbed the buckets from the truck bed and followed his sister into the barn.

There were two men inside, an old man and a teenager. Most of the barn was filled with whitish-grey rubble.

"Clay?" the old man asked, not getting up from his chair.

Joy nodded.

"It's three dollars a pound. How much do you want?"

"I need fifty pounds."

"Ah, good," he said, noticing Lincoln. "You brought your own buckets." He motioned toward the teen. "Give them to Nate. He'll fill 'em for you."

Nate took the buckets and set them down next to the rubble pile. Using a coal shovel, the teenager started dumping clumps of clay into two buckets. The clay was hard and dry. It had been pulled from the ground using a pickax. The jagged chunks varied in size. There were pebbles and baseball-sized clumps.

Clay began as rocks, often granite. After millions of years of chemical erosion, the rocks melted into fine particles that accumulated in place or were deposited in rivers. The quality of the clay determined what it could be used for. Coarse, sandy clay was used in making bricks and tiles. Other clays were used for terracotta, flowerpots, earthenware, stoneware, and ceramics.

Ceramics needed a finely ground clay that could be fired at high temperatures. This was the kind of clay Joy needed.

Nate moved the buckets to a scale. Each held fifteen pounds. He filled up the third bucket and partially filled the fourth. The total came out to fifty-three pounds.

"Grandpa, you want me to take out three pounds?"

"Naw, that's okay." He turned to Joy. "That'll be a hundred and fifty."

Joy handed him an envelope. "Grandpa" quickly thumbed through the bills, then nodded again at his grandson. "Load them in the lady's truck, Nathan."

"Yes, sir."

Once the Baca's were back on the road, Lincoln asked, "How many pieces can you make from fifty pounds of clay?"

Joy shrugged. "After adding the pumice binder, maybe a hundred. Mamma could tell you better."

Lincoln knew making ceramics was a long, laborious process. His grandmother, mother, and his sister would spend days on a single piece. He didn't have the patience or, he was sure, the talent to tackle such a task.

He felt a dark depression descending on him. He couldn't make pottery. He couldn't be a firefighter. He couldn't do anything, not that it mattered. He was going to die anyway!

Chapter Twelve

Tina Morales sat on her bed and stared at the porcelain face of Izel.

Tomorrow, Wednesday, would begin three days of in-service prep for the new school year. There were a dozen things the chemistry teacher needed to do first. One of those things was to decide what to do about Izel.

Overnight, Tina's infatuation with the Mexican doll had evaporated. She couldn't explain it. It wasn't because she feared the doll, or that it made her uncomfortable. She simply had a feeling Izel didn't want to be with her.

"Maybe you need to belong to someone younger, Izel," Tina said out loud. "Is that it?" As she spoke, she unconsciously rubbed a bruise on the inside of her wrist. It was new and she couldn't remember where it came from.

The doll made no response to her question.

"Okay, then. It's settled. I know a little girl who will love to have you."

Tina turned her attention back to the presents spread across the bed. Gifts for teacher friends were set to one side. She would bring them to the high school the next day. The other pile was for the wives and children of Lansing's deputies. That pile was returned to the suitcase so she could carry them to her car.

She still gave Izel special treatment. She carried the doll separately in the same straw tote bag she used on the plane.

***

Deedee Rivera squealed with delight at the sight of Izel.

"What do you say, Deedee?" Sue Rivera prompted.

"Oh, thank you, Miss Tina! She's beautiful." Deedee hugged the doll as she ran back to her room.

The Rivera household was the teacher's last stop.

"I love this hand-embroidered blouse," Sue said, holding it up to admire it.

"I'm glad you like it," Tina smiled. "Is Deedee ready for school next week?"

"Oh, she can't contain herself. She's more excited about that than Christmas, I think. We both can get out of the house now."

"Yes, Cliff told me you have a job at the grocery store."

"Just part-time, but it beats sitting around an empty house."

"I know what you mean," Tina agreed. "I need to go. Meeting the sheriff for lunch."

"Well, thank you so much for thinking of us," Sue said. "You didn't have to do this."

"It was my pleasure!"

***

Lansing stood inside the door of *Paco's Mexican Cantina* waiting for Tina. He greeted her with a big kiss before he said a word.

"What was that for? Not that I'm complaining."

"I'm just trying to catch up for all the kisses I missed while you were gone."

"We also have a romantic evening to catch up on, as well," she observed.

"You don't have to tell me twice." He turned his attention to the hostess. "Table for two, Maria, please."

"Right this way," Paco's daughter said.

37

After being seated, they both asked for iced tea. They also ordered lunch, Taco salads.

"Did you get everything delivered?"

"I certainly did. Jack's daughter loved Izel."

"Izel. That doll in our bedroom? I thought it was supposed to be something special."

"She is! It's just that . . ." She paused, trying to find the right words. "I think she wanted to be with someone else. Someone younger."

" 'She' wanted to be with someone else?" Lansing gave his partner a strange look. "Izel? The doll?"

Tina nodded.

"The doll told you this."

"No, of course not," she admitted. "It was just a feeling I got this morning. It didn't feel right that I should keep her stuffed away in our bedroom. She needs to be with someone who could appreciate her more. That's all."

Lansing nodded. He didn't care one way or the other. He never understood the teacher's infatuation with the toy to begin with.

Chapter Thirteen

Jeremiah Black was installing the rebuilt carburetor in a '64 Chevy Impala Lowrider. Carburetors were rare, phased out by manufacturers by 1990. The car itself was a bright and shiny blue with fine pinstripes. No dents, no scratches, no missing exterior chrome parts. He was almost afraid to touch the car.

The Cherokee Indian had little experience with Lowriders or Chicano society. The culture supposedly began in Southern California in the late 40s and spread from there. The Segovia Hispanics took exception to that claim. They considered the Lowrider their idea, so much so, Segovia was called the Lowrider Capitol of the World. They were equally offended at being called Chicanos. Chicanos were from Mexico. New Mexican Hispanics claimed Spanish descent.

"Hey, man," a voice called from behind him. "I hear you're a preacher."

The mechanic turned to look at the speaker. It was the owner of the car, a Hispanic man no more than five foot four inches tall.

"Yeah, sort of. You know you're not supposed to be in the work bays."

"That's okay, man. I know the owner."

Black hadn't been around a lot of Latinos. There were a few in Oklahoma. He'd met more in the service. And there were always plenty when he made his trips to southern Texas. As far as he was concerned, they were just people like anyone else. They just had funny accents.

"What's a 'sort of' preacher?"

Jeremiah returned to his work while he talked. "It means I didn't go to a seminary or get officially ordained. I'm more like a shaman."

"Oh, so you're an Indian."

"Yeah."

"You from around here?"

"Oklahoma."

"I see," the man said, nodding, not really "seeing" anything. "That's my car, you know."

"Yeah. I saw you drive it in."

"It's got real good hydraulics. Wanna see?"

"I'm kind of busy right now."

"Sure, I understand." He looked around, looking for something to talk about. "They call me Chaparro. That means 'Shorty.'"

Jeremiah nodded, not looking up from his task.

"So, you're like a Baptist or a Methodist?"

"Non-denominational . . ."

"But if you're a shaman, is that like being a witch doctor?"

"No . . . nothing like a witch doctor."

"What's the name of your church?"

"How old are you?"

"What kind of question is that, man? I'm thirty. What of it?"

"You ask a lot of questions like you're a teenager or something."

"I'm just curious, man."

Jeremiah stopped to size up his inquisitor. He didn't sense anything disingenuous about the Hispanic. He was just annoying.

"It's called 'The Native American Reform Church.'"

"So, like it's just for Native Americans?"

"Sort of."

"You like to say that a lot, don't you? Sort of."

The mechanic smiled. "Yeah, sort of."

Chaparro thought for a moment, unsure about the Indian's response, then smiled as well. "Okay, man. Like I get it."

"I should be done here in about fifteen minutes. You can settle up in the office if you want."

"Sure, man. Thanks." Chaparro started to walk away, then stopped. "What's your name?"

"Jeremiah."

"Okay . . . See you later, Preacher Man."

Chapter Fourteen

Broadcast Ad, KRAR Radio, Segovia, New Mexico:

NARRATOR: *FOR EIGHT YEARS OUR COUNTY HAS SEEN A SIGNIFICANT LOSS OF CONFIDENCE IN OUR SHERIFF'S DEPARTMENT. A VOTE FOR JOHN TAPIA CAN CHANGE THAT.*

FOR EIGHT YEARS VIOLENT CRIME HAS INCREASED BY TWO HUNDRED PERCENT. A VOTE FOR JOHN TAPIA CAN CHANGE THAT.

DRUG USE IS UP BY THREE HUNDRED PERCENT, PROPERTY CRIMES BY THREE HUNDRED AND FIFTY PERCENT. A VOTE FOR JOHN TAPIA CAN CHANGE THAT.

ONE FORMER DEPUTY SITS IN PRISON FOR DRUG DEALING AND MURDER. CORRUPTION IS OUT OF CONTROL UNDER THE CURRENT REGIME. A VOTE FOR JOHN TAPIA WILL CHANGE THAT.

JOHN TAPIA: *THIS IS JOHN TAPIA. I HAVE BEEN IN PUBLIC SERVICE MY ENTIRE ADULT LIFE. I HAVE BEEN A POLICEMAN. I HAVE BEEN ELECTED TO THE SEGOVIA CITY COUNCIL TWICE. I HAVE A PROVEN RECORD OF ACCOMPLISHMENT. SAN PHILLIPE COUNTY DESERVES A MAN OF INTEGRITY AND HONESTY TO SERVE AS SHERIFF. THAT'S WHY I AM ASKING FOR YOUR VOTE IN THE DEMOCRATIC PRIMARY ON SEPTEMBER FIFTH.*

SAN PHILLIPE COUNTY DESERVES BETTER. VOTE FOR ME, JOHN TAPIA, FOR SHERIFF.

NARRATOR: *PAID FOR BY THE COMMITTEE TO ELECT JOHN TAPIA FOR SHERIFF.*

"So, Ernie," Tapia asked, turning down the radio, "what do you think of the new ad? We just cut it this morning."

Segovia Police Chief Ernesto Solano leaned back in his chair. He had known John Tapia for fifteen years, seven of those when the city councilman was still a police officer. Solano thought the man had been useless in both positions. He expected, if the man was elected to be sheriff, he would be just as worthless there.

He also hated it when Tapia called him "Ernie." That was a privilege reserved for friends. The two men were not friends.

"Do you think they mention your name enough?"

"I needed people to remember who to vote for. It's pretty much the same as my first one, but the other ad only mentioned my name twice. I also added the line about that deputy that got busted for drugs. It fits nicely with the corruption angle."

"Let me point out it was Cliff Lansing who busted his own deputy. And the man is not corrupt, no matter how many times you shout it."

"Listen, Ernie, when I get elected you and I need to have a solid working relationship. I want to do another ad in a couple of weeks. I was hoping I could mention that I have your endorsement."

"You mean 'if' you get elected. Police Chiefs have to stay nonpolitical, that way we get to hold onto our jobs no matter who's running the city. So, that would be a big NO! I won't give you an endorsement."

"You know, I wouldn't be sheriff forever," the councilman said coyly. "I have plans for bigger things than San Phillipe County. I've got my eyes on a state-level position. As I move up, I certainly won't forget the people who helped me along."

"I'm sure you won't," Solano snorted. "If you'll excuse me, councilman, I have work to do."

Tapia stood. "Well, Chief, I'll check back in a few days . . . after the next polling numbers come out. You may want to reconsider your position."

"Be sure and close the door when you leave," the police commander said, not looking up from the papers on his desk. "And don't let it hit you in the ass," he mumbled under his breath.

Chapter Fifteen

When the man offered her a ride, Mandy Gomez thought he seemed nice. Lit only by the dome light of his SUV, he appeared to be about forty . . . maybe younger. Not bad looking, though she wasn't interested. She just needed to get home. After working eight hours at the burger place, then having to shop for herself and her mother, she was tired.

The walk from the grocery store to the trailer park was over a mile. On a normal night, that wasn't an issue. Tonight, she was carrying four plastic bags that got heavier with every step. The bag with the gallon of milk was the worst.

When the SUV pulled over and the driver offered her a ride, she thought it was a prayer answered. There was little traffic on the streets. Typical for a late Tuesday evening in Taos.

The man got out and walked around his red Chevy to open the door for her. Mandy placed her bags on the floor of the back seat, then got into the passenger side.

"You need to go straight for three blocks, then take a right," the twenty-year-old said.

"Sounds good."

"I can't tell you how glad I am you stopped to help me."

The driver just smiled and nodded. The car started picking up speed. Mandy looked out the window and watched as they passed the turn.

"You missed my street!"

She turned and looked at the driver who now held a gun that was pointed at her.

"What are you doing?"

"Sit back and relax . . . we're just going for a little drive."

"Why? Where are you taking me?" she screamed.

The driver ignored the questions.

Mandy could only whimper as the houses and streets went by. They were heading out of town. Why and where she didn't know. She did, however, expect the worst.

The last of Taos disappeared. Ten minutes later, the SUV turned on-to a deserted road and came to a stop. The driver shut off the engine and turned off the headlights.

"Open the glove compartment," the driver ordered. "And take out one of those zip ties."

Mandy did as she was told.

"You know how those things work?"

Mandy nodded quickly, tears streaming down her face.

"Make a loop, put it around your wrists, and pull it tight with your teeth."

The frightened girl fumbled with the tie. Her hands were shaking so badly she couldn't slip the loose end through the locking head.

"Do it!" the man growled. "Quit screwing around, or I'll shoot you right now!"

"I'm trying!" she cried. "I'm trying, really!"

The girl took a deep breath and steadied herself. Letting out her breath slowly, she successfully managed to insert the plastic strip into the lock. She put her hands through the loop, then pulled the loose end with her teeth.

"Tighter!"

Mandy whimpered as she felt the thin plastic tie dig into her flesh.

"Don't worry," the driver said, putting his gun into the side pocket of his door. "I'm not going to rape you."

Somehow, Mandy didn't feel reassured.

The man got out and walked around to the passenger side. Opening the door, he reached inside and pulled Mandy's tennis shoes off, then her socks. He turned and threw them into the darkness of the high desert. He grabbed the young lady and jerked her out of the cab.

As he pulled her around to the front of the vehicle, Mandy guessed they had stopped at one of the new subdivisions west of town. The road was paved, but there were no houses.

The two finally stopped thirty feet in front of the truck.

"Stand right here," the driver ordered. "Don't move until I tell you to."

Mandy did as she was told. Behind her, she heard the engine start and the street around her was illuminated by the headlights.

"Alright," the man yelled, sticking his head out the window. "Run!"

"What?" Mandy screamed, turning to look at her tormentor.

"I said, RUN!"

Mandy turned and began running down the middle of the street. Her bare feet smacked against the asphalt. She heard the engine roar behind her. She thought running in the rock-strewn desert would hurt her feet. That idea was overridden by the thought that if she didn't, she would be hit by the SUV.

She veered toward the black desert . . . but too late.

Her last thought was of her mother . . . who she would never see again.

Chapter Sixteen

Chief Deputy and Undersheriff Jack Rivera walked into his boss' office with a large paper bag. He walked straight up to Lansing's desk and set in front of him.

"What's this?" Lansing asked, more perturbed than curious.

"It's that damned doll Tina gave to Deedee."

"What's wrong with it?"

"I have no idea, but my little girl woke us up screaming last night. By the time we got to her room, she had her covers pulled up over her head and she was shaking like a rattle on a snake. It took Sue and me twenty minutes to calm her down.

"When she finally quit sobbing, we asked her what was wrong. She said she was afraid of the lady."

"What lady?"

"I have no idea." Rivera plopped into a chair in front of the desk. "Sue and I sure as hell didn't see anything."

Lansing opened the bag and peered inside, then looked up at his deputy. "What does the doll have to do with it?"

"I don't know. Probably nothing. But that stupid doll was the only thing that was in her room."

"So, it might not have been the doll?"

"It doesn't matter. I'm not going through another night like that. We brought her to bed with us. I didn't get any rest after that." He sighed. "Her feet are cold and that munchkin kicks like a mule."

Lansing chuckled. "Okay, so, do you think something's wrong with the toy?"

"I don't care. I just don't want it in my daughter's room. I don't want it in my house."

It was the sheriff's turn to sigh. "Alright. I'll take it back to Tina."

"Thanks," Jack stood. "Now, I'm going to drink a gallon of coffee so I can stay awake."

"Before you go . . . Have we heard anything about that DB from the pueblo?"

"Danny Cortez was conducting interviews with nearby houses. You can ask him if anything's turned up . . . Do you want me to call Albuquerque about the autopsy?"

"No. I'll handle that, thanks."

***

Tina was already sitting in a booth when Lansing got to the Las Palmas Diner. He slid in opposite her.

"What's in the bag?"

"It's your doll." Lansing signaled to Kelly, the senior waitress, that he needed a cup of coffee.

"What's wrong with it?" the teacher asked, grabbing the bag and opening it.

"Nothing. The doll's alright."

She pulled Izel from the paper sack for inspection. "Deedee didn't want it?"

"Jack and Sue didn't want it."

"What? Why not?"

The sheriff explained the conversation with Jack Rivera earlier. Tina listened.

"So," she finally said, "the Rivera's don't think there's anything wrong with Izel, but they don't want her in their house."

"That's it. I guess you have to take her home."

Tina thought about the situation. She was still trying to decide what to do when their burgers arrived. Halfway through her meal, she asked, "Do you know someone else who might want her?"

"What? You don't want the thing either?"

"Like I said yesterday, Izel doesn't want to be with me." Unconsciously, she rubbed the bruise on the inside of her wrist. "I mean, if no one else wants her, of course, I'll keep her."

Lansing took a bite of his jalapeño burger. After chewing and swallowing, he wiped his mouth. "I know a little girl up in the mountains . . . Edie Gonzalez. I think she's four. She might like a new doll."

Tina smiled. "You really think so?"

"All I can do is ask."

Chapter Seventeen

Joy Baca and her mother stood next to the four, white buckets. Pauline was surprised when her children showed up with fifty pounds of clay. There was enough material to keep both artisans busy through the rest of the year, maybe longer.

The clay had to be soaked in water and cleaned several times, then sifted for pebbles and other foreign materials. It had to be dried completely and pounded into fine dust. The dust would be mixed with "filler" material to prevent cracking when fired. The Baca's used volcanic tuft, but sand or even crushed pottery shards could be used.

"We will only use part of one bucket at a time," Pauline observed.

"Why?" Joy had envisioned going into mass production, cleaning all the clay at one time. They would have plenty of material to work without wasting their time on preparations.

"Because what we do is sacred. This clay is a bounty from the earth. It is harvested the same way we harvest the crops from the fields." She noticed the doubtful look on Joy's face, so she elaborated.

"When the corn is ripe, it is gathered, but we don't eat it all at one time. It is stored. Saved for when we need it. And in prayer, we thank God for the blessing. That is how we will treat this gift. Besides, there is no hurry. Craftsmanship . . . good craftsmanship . . . takes time.

"When you were younger and the pots you made failed, why was that?"

"I was in a hurry," Joy said, sheepishly.

"So, patience is the key. Patience and prayer."

"You're right, Mamma . . . I didn't do anything wrong by buying so much clay at Ildefonso, did I?"

Pauline shrugged. "I would think, no. Provided we use it properly."

Lincoln stepped out of their house and headed for his truck.

"Where are you going in such a hurry?" his mother asked.

"Serita's getting off work. I thought we'd go out for a burger."

"So, you won't be here for lunch?"

"Nope," he admitted.

***

Dandy's Burger was across the Rio Grande from Santa Clara Pueblo. Even though it was lunchtime, the indoor dining area was not crowded. The two sat across from each other in a booth.

Lincoln Baca and Serita Silva had been dating seriously for four months. He liked the way she lavished her attention on him while he healed from his injuries. However, they had yet to be intimate . . . sexually speaking. The biggest obstacle had been the cast on his arm. Even when the cast came off, for the first two weeks he wanted to be careful not to hurt himself.

In the previous week, though, he thought he could be more adventurous. He didn't think Serita was the smartest person he'd ever met, but she was a very attractive young woman. He was sure she wanted him as much as he wanted her.

That's when he discovered a new obstacle. Serita's virginity. Despite Joy's insistence that Serita Silva had the reputation of being loose . . . she wasn't.

She supplied plenty of hints she would never disappoint him. But she insisted there needed to be a ring on her finger before anything would happen.

Lincoln was sure his announcement wouldn't change anything between them.

"I saw the doctor yesterday," he began.

"Yeah? How'd that go?"

Lincoln cleared his throat. "Not well."

"Really? What'd he say?"

Lincoln needed to break the news gradually. "For starters, I can't be a Firefight."

"What?" she asked halfway through a bite, not hearing him. "What'd you say?"

"I said, I'm not going to be a firefighter anymore."

Serita put her burger down. "You're not going to be a firefighter?" She frowned severely as she considered his statement.

"No, I won't. But that doesn't change anything between us!"

"Of course, it does. All the girls from school . . . they were jealous of me. I was dating a firefighter."

"That doesn't change who I am . . ."

"Yes." Serita scowled as she considered her future. "Yes, it does. You won't be a firefighter."

Lincoln stared at her. "That's all that mattered to you . . . my job?"

"Don't you know anything? Your job tells the world who you are. You fought forest fires! You were a hero! Now you'll just be . . ." She didn't finish the sentence.

"I'll be what?"

"I'm not hungry!" she said, scooting out of the booth and standing. "I need to go home."

"I'll be what, Serita?" he pressed.

"I said, 'I need to go home!' "

Suddenly, Lincoln's appetite was gone as well. In Serita's eyes, he was nothing. That's what she wanted to say. She didn't ask why he couldn't be a firefighter or what was wrong with him.

"Alright," he said quietly.

Without another word, he gathered their meals and dropped them in a waste can. Serita followed him to the truck. When they reached her home, she got out without a goodbye.

As he drove off, his growing depression crashed over him like an avalanche.

Chapter Eighteen

Four-year-old Edie Gonzalez was thrilled with Izel. She thought it was the most beautiful doll she had ever seen. Both she and her mother thanked Lansing profusely. The sheriff didn't mention that little Edie would be the doll's third owner in two days. That fact never even crossed his mind.

It was late afternoon by the time Lansing got back to his office. The trip to the Jemez Mountains and the Gonzalez farm took three hours. Lansing admitted to himself his excursion was an excuse to avoid the office. He hated paperwork and loathed his meetings with the county commissioners.

The other issue bothering him was the election. Sure, he told Norman Salerno, the county attorney, and his campaign manager, that he still wanted to be sheriff. But he hated politics and politicking. Initially, Norman convinced him to do at least one radio ad, but that same ad had been playing for three months. His opponent was putting out a new radio ad every two weeks.

"I have posters scattered across the county," Lansing argued. "From Colorado to Santa Fe County. From Taos to San Juan. Everyone knows me. They know my name and what I stand for. That Segovia radio station is local. I'll bet they barely reach Cohino, and nobody west of the Jicarilla Reservation can hear them."

"Let me point out, Sheriff, hardly anyone lives west of the Jicarilla. Seventy percent of San Phillipe County lives in the Rio Cohino and the Rio Grande valleys. That's who will elect the next sheriff," Salerno argued back.

After the last pack of lies Tapia had broadcasted, Lansing agreed to correct the record. He would not, however, play tit-for-tat and put out a new ad every time Tapia did. He had a day job that took his full attention.

Once he was back in his office, Lansing read the Medical Investigator's FAX twice. In a day or two, he would receive a certified copy of the autopsy report. In the interim, he needed to share what he had learned.

"Hi, Chief. Cliff Lansing."

"Good afternoon, Sheriff," Joseph Aquino said over the phone. "What's going on?"

"The MI's office faxed me a copy of the autopsy from our hit-and-run. It was ruled a homicide. Death was caused by massive internal injuries, probably caused by being hit by a speeding vehicle."

"Well, that's no surprise."

"There's a little bit more. The woman wasn't hit once. It looked like after the initial impact, the body was run over at least one more time. And, as we both suspected, the body was moved after death."

"That means we don't know where the crime took place."

"No, we don't. Like I said, I suspect the body was dumped at San Juan to confuse us. They probably thought we would fight over jurisdiction."

"Well," Aquino said slowly. "Since the woman was not a tribal member, and the crime scene has yet to be determined . . . I would like to avoid calling in the Feds."

"I agree. I'm not sure how much help the FBI would be at this point." Lansing hesitated. "There's something else. Late last week we had a hit-and-run similar to this one."

"Where?"

"In the west part of the county, close to Navajo Lake."

"Was it a woman, too?"

"Yes."

"Do you think the deaths are linked?"

"I hope not. The deaths weren't identical. That first body wasn't run over a second time. It was only hit once."

"Was the body moved?"

"Yeah," Lansing admitted. "Our first thought was the body was placed along a busy highway so it could be found."

"Like the body at my pueblo."

"Yes, like the body at your pueblo."

Chapter Nineteen

When Jeremiah Black left the auto repair shop, he hardly noticed the dark green Lowrider that followed him. He drove down Riverview Drive till he hit Highway 15/285. That road was the busiest in San Phillipe County. The mechanic and several other cars were going the same way.

Highway 285 eventually split from 15. Traffic split evenly, half heading to Las Palmas, the rest toward Taos.

Again, the car followed Black.

The green car finally caught his attention when it also turned down the county road that passed in front of his property. He suspected he was being followed but wasn't sure.

His "church" sat 75 feet down a dirt drive from the road. His trailer was thirty feet further. His truck kicked up a cloud behind him. Coming to a stop, he watched through the settling haze as the Lowrider continue down the road, passing his turn-off.

Relieved that he wasn't about to be bothered, he got out of his truck and walked to his trailer. As he unlocked the door, he glanced up his drive. The car had done a U-turn and now was slowly driving past Black's property.

The driver must have noticed his quarry had spotted him. He quickly sped away.

The Cherokee Indian had seen too much and done too much to let the incident worry him. But that didn't mean he wouldn't take precautions.

Inside the 10 x 7 foot interior, he dug through a stack of clothes until he found a locked compartment. Inside, he found his 9 mm Beretta and his Winchester 30-30. Not protected in cases, they were dusty. He hadn't pulled them out since leaving Oklahoma.

Finding a couple of rags, gun oil, and a cleaning rod, he sat on the step of his trailer and began removing the dirt.

If the SUV happened to return, he wanted the visitors to know he could protect himself. He was sure he knew why he was followed. The lowrider he met the day before, Chaparro, didn't come across as particularly bright. Of course, that could have been an act. He could have also talked to others about their conversation.

Jeremiah had been immersed in the Native American Church for ten years. He didn't know how much the outside world knew of its practices. Some people certainly did know about the sacred plant they used during the ceremonies. Only members of the church could legally possess or use peyote. And the small, spineless cactus only grew in northern Mexico and four counties in southwest Texas.

That made the plant practically inaccessible . . . and desirable.

***

Before arriving in New Mexico, Black needed a supply of peyote buttons for his services.

It was a seven-hundred-mile drive from Broken Arrow, Oklahoma to Oilton, Texas, forty miles east of Laredo.

Christina Lopez had been selling peyote for twenty-five years. Her business supported herself, her husband, and their invalid daughter. She didn't grow the cactus. The plant only grew wild on the surrounding ranches. She had to pay for a lease on the properties to access the peyote. Some leases cost up to six thousand dollars a year, but she gathered several hundred plants on each visit.

Lopez was one of only nine authorized peyote dealers in the United States. Two more were located near Oilton. The other six operated in the Rio Grande Valley south of Laredo.

A single button of peyote sold for a quarter. Individual customers often came to Christina's and consumed the buttons on her property. Many preferred fresh plants and what wasn't eaten there was taken home for brewing tea.

Peyote buttons would go bad after several days, so Lopez dried most in the sun. She usually sold the buttons in bulk, a thousand at a time, $80 for fresh buttons, and $100 for dried. Annually, she sold 390,000 buttons. Some dealers sold up to 600,000 each year.

Sales were only made to qualified customers . . . members of the Native American Church. As a certified "roadman," Jeremiah Black's face was familiar to Lopez. When he showed up, she didn't bat an eye when he asked to purchase 4,000 dried buttons.

Mescaline, a Schedule 1 drug, was peyote's active ingredient. A hallucinogen, it took up to six buttons to produce a mild experience and as many as sixteen for a strong one. Consuming peyote was not for the faint of heart. The buttons tasted bitter and those who ate them often had to suffer through bouts of violent vomiting before the hallucinations began.

During the four services Black conducted in New Mexico, his congregation had consumed a total of fifty buttons per evening. He knew more would be consumed as their tolerance increased and the membership grew. He also knew, if he needed to, he could legally order more of the cactus by mail. That way he could avoid the sixteen-hundred-mile round trip from Segovia to Oilton.

***

Jeremiah Black was not naïve. Eventually, word would get out he used peyote in his ceremonies. It might have gotten out already. He couldn't guard his supply while he was at work, so it was securely hidden away from his property.

Dope heads and other unsavory characters could rummage through his trailer and "church" but would come up with nothing. Other drugs were certainly available on the street, some a lot more powerful than peyote. But the concept of obtaining mescaline for free had to be a temptation worth pursuing.

Still, someone might simply walk up to him with a gun and demand he hand over his stash. That was why he sat cleaning his guns. He wanted others to know he would not be intimidated.

Chapter Twenty

Great Uncle Eluterio Tafoya had just finished his dinner when Lincoln arrived at his aunt's house. The Simpsons lived across the Rio Grande in La Mesilla, not far from the future site for Santa Clara's Black Mesa Golf Course.

"You missed supper!" Aunt Marie said, closing the door behind her nephew.

"That's okay. I already ate."

"Sit down, sit down," Eluterio exclaimed. "I haven't seen you at the Senior Center."

"I'm sorry, Uncle. I've been doing physical therapy," he said, sitting at the table near his elder relative. "I'm usually so tired when I finish, I just go home and rest."

"Rest is a good thing."

"Papa, do you want some coffee?"

"Yes, please."

"Linc?"

"Yeah, that sounds good." Lincoln looked around. "Where's Uncle George?"

"He's out for his evening stroll. He always takes a walk after dinner." Marie headed for the kitchen to make coffee.

Marie, unlike her sister, did not take up pottery making. Being more of the academic type, she got a degree in education and taught at the *Kha'p'o* Community School across the street from the Senior Center. With business and accounting degrees, her husband George Simpson worked at the Pueblo Community Development Office.

"I really need to talk to you, Uncle . . ."

Eluterio's eyesight was not nearly as sharp as it had been a few years earlier. He couldn't see the expression on his nephew's face. But he could hear the stress and pain.

"What troubles you, Lincoln?"

He had tried to talk to his parents about Serita. His mother assured him there would be other girls. His father insisted his problems would be solved if he simply got a job. Hard work would occupy his mind and he wouldn't have time to wallow in self-pity.

The discussion left him depressed and angry. The anger was what stopped him from telling his parents about his medical condition.

Lincoln told Uncle Eluterio he could no longer be a firefighter. He said it was for medical reasons but didn't elaborate. Part of his distress was his girlfriend dumped him.

"I'm angry all the time, and I don't know what to do."

Eluterio listened thoughtfully, sipping on his coffee. He was quiet for a long time after Lincoln was finished. Finally, he said, "I cannot look into your soul and fix these problems. You must find the answers within yourself."

"How?"

"There was a time when young pueblo men went into the wilderness and sought guidance from the Holy Ones."

"The Holy Ones?"

"The Kachinas. Through them, the people could communicate with the Great Spirit."

"I pray to them like they were Catholic Saints?"

"No. Other tribes like the Apache and Ute people not tied to the land as we are, would send their young men on vision quests. They would fast and pray until they discovered their spirit animal . . . brought to them in a dream state.

"Our young men had such quests, seeking wisdom and guidance. But not from a spirit animal. From a Kachina, a Holy One."

"Did you ever go on such a quest?"

The old man frowned sadly as he shook his head. "I never did."

"Why not?"

"When I was young, the Pueblo was in chaos. Too much politics. Many moved north to Canjilon to escape the turmoil. The Summer Cacique acted like a dictator. Not until we had a Pueblo Constitution in 1935 did we return to the old religious ways.

"Then there was the World War. Those who didn't enlist worked to support the effort. All that time I was too busy to worry about spiritual guidance."

"Is what I need? Spiritual guidance."

Eluterio didn't say anything.

After a long pause, Lincoln asked, "How would I do a vision quest?"

Uncle Eluterio nodded, then explained what he knew.

Chapter Twenty-One

"Edie," Dorothy Gonzalez said, gently shaking her youngest daughter's shoulder. "It's almost eight o'clock. You need to get up. It's way past time for breakfast."

"Un-uh," the four-year-old whined, refusing to open her eyes. "I don't wanna."

"Why not?"

"Because I'm tired."

Dorothy checked Edie's forehead to see if she had any fever. This wasn't like her. Of her five children, Edie was usually the first out of bed. She was responsible for gathering eggs from the henhouse for breakfast, even if the sun wasn't up. Since turning four, even in winter, she did her duty. When the snow was too deep, her father carried her across the yard to pluck the eggs from beneath the chickens. Dorothy couldn't remember if Edith had ever shirked her task before.

"Do you feel alright?"

"Yes," the sleepyhead admitted. She sat up, still clutching Izel, the doll Sheriff Lansing had given her the day before.

Dorothy sat on the edge of the bed and helped Edie get dressed.

"You know, I had to send Eric out to get the eggs this morning."

"A-aw! I wanted to get them," the little girl complained, struggling to slip an arm into a sleeve.

"Well, to gather the eggs you have to get out of bed first."

Esteban, Dorothy's husband, stuck his head through the bedroom door. "Edie, your brother and I are driving into town. Do you want to ride along?"

"Edie's not going anywhere until she's had breakfast."

"Aw, mamma!"

"No arguments, little girl."

"You mind your mother," the farmer insisted. "We can go to town another day."

As Mamma Gonzalez dressed her daughter, she noticed a bruise and a small cut on Edie's neck.

"What happened here?"

"I don't know."

"Did you fall?" Edith was not a clumsy child, but living on a farm, it wasn't unusual for the four-year-old to show up with a bump or bruise from running and tripping.

"Maybe. I forget."

All the mother could do was shake her head. She scooped her youngest up and started for the kitchen.

"Can't you leave that doll in your room?"

"She wants to be with me!" Edie insisted.

"Alright, but don't get food on her."

"I won't." After her mother took a few more steps, she said, "Guess what?"

"What?"

"I saw a lightning bug last night."

"A lightning bug? Where?"

"In my room."

"How do you know it was a lightning bug? We don't even have those things in New Mexico."

"I know what they look like. I see them on TV."

"Do you think you dreamed it?"

"I don't think so." Edie thought hard for a moment. "Maybe I did . . ." she agreed with a small shrug.

Dorothy set her daughter down at the kitchen table. "You have to eat cereal this morning. The eggs are all cold."

"That's okay, Mamma. I like cereal."

Chapter Twenty-Two

Juan Sanchez looked up from his plate of eggs and beans. His wife, Naomi, sat near him at the breakfast table tearing her tortilla into smaller pieces. She stared vacantly at her cup of coffee, a troubled look on her face.

"What bothers you, *mi cariña?*" he asked.

"What?" She snapped out of her trance.

"I asked you what is troubling you."

"Oh, nothing."

The two had been married for sixty-five years. They knew each other's moods and thoughts almost better than their own.

"Is it Tina? You two talked for a long time yesterday evening."

Abuela Sanchez did not hesitate. She couldn't hide anything from her husband. "That doll she bought at the Mercado. The one she was so excited about."

"I remember."

"She gave it away . . . to a little girl she knows."

Juan shrugged, sopping a piece of tortilla in the runny yolk. "And that bothers you?"

"No. But why she gave it away. That seemed strange."

"What did she say?"

"She said the doll didn't want to be with her."

"The doll told her that?"

"Not in words. It was a feeling she got."

Juan chewed on his tortilla while he considered Naomi's words. He knew before he even married his wife that she was a *bruja*, a witch. But she was more of a *curandera*, a healer. She understood the dark arts, though, only to enable herself to fight them.

Hand-in-hand with her curative skills, she also possessed *psíquica* abilities. Her psychic skills allowed her to touch and view realms hidden to laypersons. None of their five children inherited the talent.

Theresa, Tina's mother, was a trained *curandera*, as was Tina. The psychic trait seemed to have skipped a generation, though. Tina, at times, exhibited some of her grandmother's abilities.

When Tina said "she got a feeling" about something, Sanchez knew better than to dismiss the claim out of hand.

"So, why would this bother you?"

"The girl had the doll only one night. She loved the doll when she got it. But that first night the child had nightmares. The doll scared her, and her father gave it back to Tina. He didn't want it in his house."

"Tina has the doll now?"

"She still didn't think the doll wanted to be with her. Lansing found another girl to give it to."

"There have been more problems?"

"Tina doesn't think so."

"Tina doesn't think so, but you do, don't you?"

Naomi Sanchez nodded her head. "The doll made me uncomfortable. I told her to choose a more traditional doll, but she insisted on the porcelain one."

"There is nothing you can do, is there? I mean, she is almost a thousand miles from here."

"She is as far away as the phone on the wall. And what she feels, I can feel. What she fears, I fear as well."

"Then what?"

"I must think. Maybe this evening we can walk to the church. I will light a candle to Saint Iglesia."

Juan nodded as he finished his plate of food. "We will do whatever you wish."

Chapter Twenty-Three

"*Friends, neighbors, this is Sheriff Cliff Lansing. I have had the honor of protecting the citizens of San Phillipe County for thirteen years, first as a deputy, then as your elected sheriff. Today, I am again asking for your vote.*

"*I was born and raised on a ranch just south of Las Palmas. This county is in my blood.*

"*I have an opponent in the upcoming election who has made very incorrect and exaggerated claims.*

"*There is no rampant corruption in my office. I have a zero-tolerance policy for such activity. Under my leadership, there has been only one deputy who broke the law. I arrested him. He was charged, found guilty, and now sits in prison. No other allegations have ever been brought against any other member of my team.*

"*As to the claims of increased crime in San Phillipe . . . The statistics my opponent quoted were for the entire State . . . not our county. My opponent finds facts to be inconvenient.*

"*I promise if you re-elect me, Cliff Lansing, I will continue to dedicate myself whole-heartedly to the enforcement of our laws and the protection of each and every citizen of San Phillipe County.*

"*I thank you for your past support. I hope I have earned your trust and that I can count on your support in the Democratic primary. On September fifth, vote Cliff Lansing for Sheriff.*"

Another voice followed. "*Paid for by the committee to re-elect Clifford Lansing sheriff.*"

***

It had taken Lansing and Norm Salerno an hour to draft the one-minute campaign plug, another hour to record the piece at the radio station in Segovia. The campaign manager spent an additional hour polishing up the recording with patriotic background music. The sheriff couldn't help but grimace at the sound of his own voice.

"You sound great," Salerno said, removing the recording from the player.

"I don't know. It sounds tinny to me."

"That's just the tape machine. It doesn't have any bass. It'll sound just fine on the radio. So, do I have your final approval to use it?"

"Sure," Lansing sighed, hoping he was finished dealing with his campaign.

As Salerno left, Lansing's desk phone rang.

"Lansing here."

"Sheriff, we just got a report of shots fired," Marilyn Bea, the dispatcher reported.

The sheriff stood. "Where?"

"Little Creek Resort and RV Park."

"Who made the call?"

"Danny Cortez. He was fired on."

"Is anyone hurt?"

"Not that I know of. He's on the radio right now."

"Tell him I'm on my way."

Chapter Twenty-Four

Northern San Phillipe County had become a favorite vacation destination over the years. The Cohino motels, lodges, and bed-and-breakfasts stayed busy throughout the summer months. The big draw was the Chisum and Aztec Scenic Railroad. The excursion from Chama to Antonito, Colorado took a full day and tickets were usually at a premium.

When visitors weren't riding the rails, they could enjoy hiking, bridle trails, and fishing.

South of Cohino, a five-mile stretch of Highway 15/64 was filled with seven lodges and trailer parks. The largest was Little Creek Resort. Nestled in an oxbow, it was surrounded on three sides by the Rio Cohino. It had twelve cabins and enough slots to accommodate sixty trailers and RVs. During the summer every spot was filled, with some people staying there the entire season.

Crowded onto five acres with an average of 20 persons per acre, there was little room for privacy. An argument in one trailer could be heard three trailers away. The two minimum-wage security officers could only threaten eviction from the resort. They needed the State Police or the Sheriff's office to enforce any regulations.

Deputy Cortez had been notified about a domestic disturbance in one of the trailers. A security guard had pounded on the door in an attempt to squash the commotion. He was rudely informed about his probable heritage and instructed to perform an unlikely sex act on himself. Eventually, 9-1-1 was called.

When he arrived, Danny Cortez could still hear the commotion. He stood to one side of the trailer door as he knocked and announced his presence. The fighting stopped. There was quiet for a moment, followed by the blast of a shotgun.

Following proper procedure had saved the deputy's life. Otherwise, he would have a hole in his chest matching the hole in the door. Cortez scrambled to the safety of his patrol car and immediately called dispatch for backup.

Nearby vacationers in lawn chairs immediately ran for the safety of their own trailers. Nosey neighbors from further away tried to creep closer to watch the "entertainment."

"Everybody stay back!" Cortez yelled, waving the crowd away.

The deputy's radio crackled. "Danny, Sheriff Lansing. I'm on my way. What's the situation?"

"There was a domestic fight. I knocked on the trailer door and was greeted with a round of buckshot."

"Did you return fire?"

"No. Way too many people around here for a gunfight."

"Stay where you are. I'll be there in five minutes."

The situation hadn't changed by the time Lansing arrived. Cortez was crouched next to his patrol car. The travel trailer had Texas plates and currently was quiet.

"Have you been able to talk to the occupants?" Lansing asked.

"No," Cortez admitted. "I was waiting for you. I haven't heard anything since that shotgun blast."

"So, you don't know if anyone is hurt?"

The deputy shook his head.

The door of the neighboring trailer flew open and a large man in cargo shorts and a loud Hawaiian shirt jumped out. Bending over as if he was dodging bullets, he scurried toward the officers. Overweight by at least eighty pounds, he was out of breath by the time he reached the patrol car. He plopped down on his fat bottom and leaned against the tire, sweating profusely.

"What's wrong?" Lansing asked.

The man held up his hand, indicating an answer would come as soon as he caught his breath. Finally, he said, "That maniac shot holes in my trailer!"

"I'm sorry to hear that."

"Somebody will have to pay for those repairs."

"I wouldn't advise talking to your neighbor at the moment."

"I hadn't planned to," he snapped angrily. "But you need to do something, Sheriff."

"What would that be?"

"My insurance will probably fix it, but I'll need to file a police report."

"And?"

"Well, duh! I just told you. I need a police report."

"Mister, right now I have other things to worry about. Why don't you go stand with those people out of the way?" Lansing gestured toward the small crowd that had gathered to watch. It was incidents like this that made him wonder if he really wanted to get re-elected.

"What about a police report?"

"My office is in Las Palmas. Check there in a few days. Now please go!"

"You're going to arrest that SOB, aren't you?"

"If he cooperates, yes."

The man gave a loud "harrumph" as he struggled to stand.

"Just a minute," Lansing said. "What can you tell me about those people?"

"They're a couple of drunks . . . And when they're not drinking, they're fighting."

"Do they fight a lot?"

"Is a bear Catholic?"

"What?"

"Never mind . . . It's a joke. Yeah, they fight a lot."

The commotion in the trailer started up again. It was a man yelling and items being smashed.

"Come on," Lansing said. "Let's get over there while they're fighting." Pulling his gun from the holster, he ran toward the trailer. The deputy followed. They positioned themselves on either side of the door, their backs against the trailer.

From inside, a woman was yelling. The drunken sentences were hard to understand. The only words the officers could make out was a final, "Get back!"

The man screamed "No!" followed by another shotgun blast. This one was not through the door.

Chapter Twenty-Five

August 12th was Santa Clara Pueblo's annual feast day. This year the participants performed the Harvest Dance. What should have been a joyous gathering was dampened by the flash flood two weeks earlier.

The New Mexico Monsoon Season lasted from June 15th until September 30th. The annual rains contributed to stamping out the last of the Cerro Grande Fire. After three months, the fire was declared extinguished on July 20th.

The rains did, however, cause problems. Twelve hundred acres of the Santa Clara Reservation were burned. These acres, west of the Puye Cliff Dwellings, were part of the Santa Clara Creek watershed. With no trees or shrubs to absorb the water, the creek filled quickly. The rush of water followed the creek bed through the center of the Pueblo proper, washing away the foundations of three homes. Fortunately, no one died.

Lincoln Baca was mindful of these events when he left his home on foot. His backpack held two one-quart bottles of water, an ample supply of beef jerky, and the pamphlet from his doctor.

"Where are you going?" his mother asked.

"On a hike," Lincoln said. It was an honest answer, though not a complete one.

"You'll be home for supper, right?"

"No . . . I might be gone for a few days." With that, he was out the door before she could mount any more questions.

***

The former firefighter had no specific destination. Uncle Eluterio's instructions were vague at best. Lincoln was told to let his heart guide him. When he found the right spot, he was supposed to stop there so he could fast and pray.

"How will I know when I've found the right place?"

"You will know," the uncle said.

"Will there be a sign?"

Eluterio shrugged. "Maybe."

At home, in bed, staring at the dark ceiling, Baca debated whether he should go or not.

The depression settled on his chest like an anvil. His heart beat faster. He struggled to breathe. He wanted to scream.

He took a deep breath and closed his eyes. He told himself to relax.

He cleared his mind, concentrating on his breathing. As he did, he resolved to go on his vision quest. After he made that decision, the anxiety lifted, and he soon fell asleep.

***

Once he left his house, he followed Drum Road to Highway 30. Going north would take him through Segovia . . . south to San Ildefonso. His instincts told him to cross the highway and continue west, into the heart of the reservation.

Canyon Road paralleled Santa Clara Creek on the north side. There were few houses. A mile from the highway they disappeared completely. Portions of the dirt road had been washed away by the flash flood and Lincoln found the mud sticking to his boots.

The Rio Grande plain was 5700 feet in elevation. The road Lincoln was now following gradually ascended. Eight miles further west, the dirt track would climb to 6400 feet. The rolling hills close to the Pueblo transitioned first to steep banks, then to cliffs 300 feet above the canyon floor.

Two trucks passed him. One offered him a ride which he declined.

He reached a track for four-wheelers that climbed to higher ground to the north. The dirt road would take him beyond the reservation boundary to the pumice pits. The volcanic deposits had been mined by the Pueblo Indians for hundreds of years. The rock was crushed to a fine powder for use in the making of their pottery.

Lincoln sat and pulled out a water bottle. He guessed he had walked nine miles.

The Puye Cliffs were a mile to the southwest. The reservation extended for another twelve miles to the west, but only five miles to the north.

As he sipped his water, Baca considered his options. He knew parts of the Pueblo's lands west of the cliffs had been burned. He had no interest in seeing the devastation. Two hours of hiking north would take him into the Jemez Mountains and beyond the reservation.

Stuffing the bottle into the backpack, he stood and started up the track to the north.

That was where he felt compelled to go.

Chapter Twenty-Six

Karen Baker sat in the interrogation room, her face buried in her folded arms on the tabletop. At five foot four, she hardly seemed a threat, so Lansing had the handcuffs removed once they reached his offices.

She had killed her husband with a shotgun blast to the chest. It was a homicide. That was clear. Lansing needed to determine the reason for the murder. He knew there was a fight. He heard the shouting and items being broken. He heard Karen yell "Get back." Her husband, Bill, responded with a loud "No!" just before the 12-gauge was fired.

The trailer had a single bedroom in the front, next to the hitch. The outside door was near the rear. When the shooter fired at Cortez, they couldn't have been more than a couple of feet from the door.

The trailer interior was a wreck. Empty beer cans and whiskey bottles were scattered across the floor. The husband was sprawled in the middle of the main room. The wife apparently fired from the bedroom door. The distance, just a few feet.

She dropped the gun when Lansing ordered her to. She immediately slumped to her knees and started crying.

Cortez checked the body for a pulse, though it was obvious the man was dead.

Lansing noticed Karen's crying didn't include tears.

Holstering his pistol, Lansing lifted the woman to her feet and guided her a few steps to the bed. She was a slight woman with blotchy skin. Years of drinking had faded her beauty.

"Can you tell me what happened?" he asked gently.

"We had a fight," she whimpered. "We had been drinking."

"It's ten in the morning. Do you always start drinking this early?"

"No, not always."

"I'm sorry to interrupt you . . . but what was the fight about?"

"I can't even remember."

Lansing waited for her to continue.

"But we were fighting . . . then he grabbed the shotgun and threatened me."

"I understand the resort security tried to intervene."

"Yeah, I think I heard someone banging on our door. Bill told them to go away."

"The resort called nine-one-one. When my deputy showed up, someone shot at him through the door."

Karen nodded quickly. "That was Bill. He had the shotgun."

"When I first arrived, your trailer was quiet."

"I was hiding in the bedroom . . . Bill was finishing off a bottle of bourbon. He started dozing off. That's when I was able to grab the shotgun. He woke up and started throwing things . . . threatening me. He said he was going to kill me if I didn't give him the gun."

"Why did you shoot him?"

"Like I said. He threatened to kill me. I told him to get back . . . He kept coming . . . I had to shoot him."

"So, it was self-defense?"

She blinked her eyes, surprised at the question. "Of course, it was self-defense!"

"He was abusive?"

"Damned right he was abusive."

Karen Baker couldn't understand why she had to be handcuffed or why she was being taken to the Sheriff's office.

The handcuffs were a precaution, and she needed to provide a formal, written statement at the office. Besides, she couldn't stay in the trailer. It was a crime scene.

Once she was in Lansing's patrol jeep, he had her do a breathalyzer. He wanted to measure her level of intoxication. She registered 0.000.

Flags were popping up all over the place. No tears and evidently no alcohol in her system. She obviously hadn't been drinking. The sheriff couldn't help but notice there were no bruises either. Of course, abuse came in all forms and, so far, she hadn't claimed her husband beat her.

While Karen Baker waited to be formally interrogated, Lansing called Norman Salerno.

"Hey, Cliff. I was just getting ready to call you. Your new ad will start running in the morning."

"That's good I guess, but that's not why I called you."

"What's up?"

As County Attorney, it was Norman Salerno's job to conduct all legal affairs for San Phillipe. The county itself was his client. His office represented all elected officials, employees, bureaus, offices, and commissions in court. He provided legal advice on all aspects of the law, from contracts to proposed legislation. He was not the county prosecutor. That position was held by James Lujan, the County District Attorney located in Segovia.

Lansing described the shooting at Little Creek Resort. It was obvious the wife shot her husband. She even admitted it. He now had the wife, Karen Baker, at his office for a formal interrogation.

"You haven't arrested her?" Salerno asked.

"No, not yet. There seem to be a few mitigating circumstances."

"Like what?"

"She claimed she was abused, and the shooting was self-defense."

"Is she a New Mexican resident?"

"No. She's from Texas. Does that matter?"

"Well, you certainly don't want her sneaking out of the state while you're still investigating the death. Have you sent the body to Albuquerque yet?"

"Danny Cortez is at the scene, waiting for the transport."

"What do you think? Justifiable homicide or just plain murder?"

"I want to poke around a little bit more before I recommend anything to the DA. I wasn't completely satisfied with her answers when I first questioned her."

"You can only hold her for forty-eight hours without charges."

"I know that," the sheriff snapped. "I'll call the Medical Examiner's office and see if they can expedite the autopsy."

"I don't know what an autopsy will do for you. You already know the cause of death."

"Maybe they'll find something I missed at the trailer."

"The clock doesn't officially start until you inform her she's being detained. I wouldn't say anything until you've finished the interview and she's signed a statement. That will buy you a little time."

"If I do need to hold her longer than forty-eight hours, I would think as a minimum she could be charged with involuntary manslaughter."

"Well, we both know Lujan shies away from being sued for malicious prosecution. If she has a job and a false arrest gets her fired, there could be all sorts of problems."

"I'm not going to push anything, don't worry."

Chapter Twenty-Seven

When Tina Morales showed up for the second day of teacher preparation for the new year Principal De la Cruz asked to see her, privately.

"Ms. Morales, we got an edict from the State Board of Education this summer. They really want to push STEM education."

"That's great," Tina smiled. STEM stood for Science, Technology, Engineering, and Math. She always felt those subjects needed more emphasis. "What do you need from me?"

"How do you feel about teaching physics?"

"I don't know," she said, surprised and confused. "You mean this school year?"

"Well, no," he hedged. "Not the Fall Semester, anyway. You're only teaching four classes a day. There's plenty of room in your schedule to add one more."

Tina scowled. She worked a full day. The two hours she didn't teach were occupied with grading papers and preparing lesson plans. Even then, she had to take work home.

"What happens if I say I can't do it?"

"We have to meet state requirements. A physics course must be added. If you can't handle it, that would be a problem. We don't have the budget to hire another full-time teacher."

"Why didn't you bring this up yesterday?"

"Because I thought I had another solution. I'd have a teacher from Segovia drive up every day to teach the class. Over time, though, that would be too expensive."

Tina let out a long, deep breath while she stared at the top of De la Cruz's desk. She knew she could teach a physics course. She touched on the subject when she taught her General Science course to the eighth graders. And she recognized how much of an overlap there was between chemistry and physics.

Eventually, she nodded. "Sure, I can handle a physics class. Is there anything else?"

"No, that's it. Mrs. Basa has the course proposal for you to look at. You can pick it up on your way out."

As she left, Tina stopped at the door. "I don't suppose a pay increase comes along with the additional work."

"No. This just means no one will get a pay cut."

***

Halley Basa, the school secretary, looked up from her computer. "How did it go?"

"You obviously knew about the new course. Why didn't you warn me?"

"I'm sorry, Tina. I was sworn to secrecy."

"Hmph . . . I take it you have a package for me."

"Yes." Basa retrieved a thick, manila envelope from behind her, then handed it to the teacher along with a physics textbook wrapped in clear plastic shrink wrap.

Tina held the book in one hand. It was heavy. "This looks expensive."

"All textbooks are expensive. What kills us is the state requires that we get new editions of all textbooks every five years."

"Yeah, because chemistry and physics and math all change so much," Morales said sarcastically.

"Same with English and Biology," the secretary agreed. "Though the students do tend to destroy the books after a while. They get worn out."

"Only the books that are actually opened."

***

"What's all that?" Marta Gomez asked when she intercepted her fellow teacher in the hallway.

"My new course," Tina said.

"New course? What?"

"Physics."

"You didn't tell me you were going to teach a new subject."

"I didn't know until five minutes ago."

"O-o-h. Does that come with a pay raise?"

Tina scowled at her friend. "No, it just means I get to keep my salary."

"Is that what Mr. De la Cruz told you?"

"Of course . . . and I used to like that guy."

Chapter Twenty-Eight

Lincoln Baca couldn't guess how far he had walked. After getting to the top of the cliffs above Santa Clara Creek, he followed a four-wheeler track toward the northwest. When it came to an end, he continued on his northerly trek. He followed animal trails when he could.

His hike took him up and down hills and hints of canyons. A series of steep slopes, the southern wall of the Jemez Mountains, forced him further west. Another four-wheeler track finally allowed him to travel north again. The Jeep trail followed a gentle slope. Lincoln continued up the 700-foot incline until he reached a graded, gravel road.

A sign told him he was now on State Road 565. The road ran east and west.

He stopped and took a gulp of water. He had almost finished his second bottle. He hoped there were streams with water. His quest wouldn't last long if he had nothing to drink.

At 8000 feet, the road ran along a ridgeline. The pueblo man's gut told him to continue down the other side, though there was no trail to follow. His descent through thick trees was gradual for a quarter of a mile.

Suddenly, the terrain became so steep he had to lurch from tree to tree, desperately holding on to keep from tumbling down the slope. The canyon floor was still 100 feet below him when he miscalculated the distance to the next tree. His fingertips brushed the rough bark as he fell forward. With nothing to grab, he tumbled, slid, and was knocked unconscious before he reached the rocky bottom.

***

When Lincoln regained consciousness, the bottom of the canyon was dark. Only the highest peaks caught the last rays of the sun. Sitting up was painful. He couldn't see out of his right eye. He gingerly touched it. It was sticky with blood.

Panicked, he felt around, finally finding his backpack. He took the last of his water and cleaned as much blood from his face as he could. He blinked both eyes . . . He could see. The right one was not damaged. The blood had come from a gash on his forehead.

He tried to stand. It took three tries. Once he was on his feet, he was hit with a wave of nausea and dizziness. He hoped it was from the tumble and not the tumor. With nothing to lean on, he took deep breaths until the dizziness passed.

Confident he was steady enough to walk, he glanced around at his surroundings. It would be completely dark soon, and the night air would be chilly. He pulled a jacket from his backpack and slipped it on.

He needed to find water. He was disoriented and had to decide which way to go. He turned to his right because his gut told him to. He was moving north. Five hundred feet further up the canyon, he heard water dripping. Bubbling up beneath a rock outcrop, the spring filled a stone depression that overflowed onto the canyon floor.

Lincoln couldn't believe his luck. He knelt and began scooping water into his mouth. It was cool, clean, and fresh. Drinking his fill, he washed the remaining blood from his face, trying to be careful when he touched the cut on his head. He then filled his two bottles. If he'd had a map, he would have discovered he was in Rio del Oso Canyon and this spot was called San Lorenzo Spring.

The often-dry Rio del Oso meandered for 15 miles to the northeast. The sometimes river, fed by this small spring and monsoon rains, eventually crossed under Highway 15 before it reached Rio Cohino.

Lincoln sat and thought. As he chewed on a piece of jerky, he realized he needed a place to spend the night. Staying next to the spring didn't seem safe. All sorts of animals probably visited the spot at night.

Across from where he sat was the opening to another, smaller canyon. In the growing darkness, it looked promising.

He found the base of the canyon climbed gradually higher. As it grew darker, Lincoln considered finding a flat spot to use as a bed. Two hundred feet from Rio del Oso, the canyon suddenly made an abrupt turn to the right. The canyon walls became vertical on either side.

His eyes were fully adjusted to the darkness. He could tell the canyon made a bend to the left. He decided he would follow the creek bed as long as he felt safe.

Ahead of him, the light from a fire flickered against the canyon wall.

"Wait," he thought. "Is someone else up here in the mountains?"

He had no desire to meet anyone. He was on his own personal quest. He needed to be alone.

Lincoln turned to retrace his steps . . . but was stopped in his tracks. He would have sworn he heard his name whispered. It was a voice foreign to him and at the same time familiar.

"Who's there?" he whispered in return.

There was no answer. But the glow ahead of him beckoned.

He continued cautiously. He didn't want to surprise whoever tended the fire. His steps quietly crunched the gravel beneath his feet. When the flame came into view, he stopped.

A flame no more than a foot tall danced around a flat cluster of broken rock and pebbles.

The fire was blue at the bottom, transitioning to white and yellow as it dissipated. There were no remnants of burnt wood. No ash or glowing cinders. Nothing but the bare ground. There was no one else in the canyon. No one tended the fire. No one needed to.

The firefighter stepped closer, sitting a few feet from the flame. He stared at the fire, mesmerized. After a time, Lincoln realized he had no need to go further. The flame was what he had been seeking.

Chapter Twenty-Nine

"I don't feel like cooking tonight," Tina Morales announced when Lansing walked through the door. "We need to go out."

"Okay." From the tone of his partner's voice, the sheriff knew he should tread lightly. "Is something wrong?"

The teacher ignored the question. "Do you want to change first or just wear your uniform?"

"I'd prefer to change . . . Give me a few minutes."

Lansing considered Tina Morales one of the most even-tempered persons he knew. If something bothered her, she would tell him in her own time. He knew better than to press the issue on the drive into Las Palmas.

They were greeted by one of Paco Garcia's daughters when they entered *Paco's Mexican Cantina*.

"Just the two of you, Sheriff?"

"Yes."

"Do you need menus?"

"No. We have them memorized."

They were seated toward the back where they wouldn't be bothered.

"Cerveza, Sheriff?"

"A Corona, please."

"What would you like, Miss Morales?"

"Tonight, I need a margarita."

Lansing was surprised not only by her choice of drink but the fact that she "needed" it.

"Alright," he finally asked when they were alone. "What's going on?"

Tina scowled. "I have to develop a course for a new subject."

Lansing raised his eyebrows. "What new subject?"

"Physics."

"Why?"

"It's an edict by the State Board of Education."

"For this semester?"

"No. It sounds like the school wants to implement the classes in January."

"So, you have what . . . four months? Isn't that plenty of time?"

"Cliff, that's not the point. De la Cruz is doubling my workload without any compensation."

"Couldn't they just hire a new teacher?"

"Not cost-effective. If they did, the school said I would be looking at a pay cut."

"So, work more or they'll dock your salary."

"In a nutshell."

"What does your union have to say about it?"

"The AFT? Our union rep said the requirement met the federation's guidelines."

"In other words, they don't give a damn?"

"As long as the union big-wigs get their salaries, they don't seem to care what happens to the rest of us."

"Then quit the union."

"Why? Until they change the law, they'll still deduct dues from my salary."

"Well, you don't have to work if you don't want to."

"And what am I supposed to do all day? Cliff, I love you and I love the ranch, but I'm not getting stuck out there by myself."

"So, what are you going to do?"

"Exercise my God-given right as a woman, a teacher, and an American. I'm going to develop the new course . . . make it the best one in the state . . . and bitch all the way!"

Chapter Thirty

"Where are you going?" Pauline Baca asked as her daughter, Joy, headed for the front door.

"I'm driving up to see Eric." Eric Gonzalez and Joy had dated each other during their last two years in high school. Since graduation in May, their relationship mostly continued on the phone.

"How? Your father has the truck."

"I'm using Linc's Chevy." She saw the doubtful look on her mother's face. "He said I could borrow it whenever I wanted to . . . At least as long as he didn't need it. And he's not here, so . . ." Joy didn't mention the fact that Lincoln's truck only ran because she loaned him the money to fix it.

"I thought you were helping me clean the new clay."

"I'll help tomorrow. I promise. It's just that Eric's father told him he needed to find a job. I guess there isn't enough work for both of them on the farm. He needs a set of wheels so he can get to work. I'm going to help him look."

"Couldn't his father take him?"

"No. The Gonzalezes only have that one truck and they had to take his littlest sister to the emergency room."

"Oh, my God. What's wrong with her?"

"They don't know. Eric didn't, either. She looked sick. That's all he said."

Pauline shook her head. "How long do you think you'll be gone?"

"Mom, I don't know. I'll get home as soon as I can."

"What about dinner tonight?"

"Can I call and let you know?"

"I suppose," her mother sighed. "Just be careful on those mountain roads."

"I will. Bye, Mom." With that, Joy Baca was out the door.

Pauline Baca was struck by how lonely she suddenly felt. Yes, her husband kept pushing for Lincoln to move out and she gave lip service to his wishes. Secretly, though, she relished the idea of both of her children living with them forever. There was a time when pueblo households would be filled with four generations of the same family.

Mostly, those days were gone . . . as were so many other Tewa traditions. Holding onto the old ways like pottery making seemed more important than ever. At least Joy was following in her footsteps. That was a consolation to her . . . a great consolation.

Chapter Thirty-One

Luis Sanchez knocked on the screen door. Like the bars on the windows, the door was made of strong metal that was bolted on the inside. Nogales residents knew thieves lived among them . . . thieves who needed money to feed drug habits or who stole because it was easier than working.

"*Uno momento*," Juan Sanchez called from the kitchen.

"Ah, Luis," he said, recognizing his grandson. He unbolted the door. "Come in. Come in."

Luis followed his grandfather into the kitchen.

"Luis, would you like some coffee?" Naomi asked.

"*Gracias, no, Abuela.* I need to go to work."

Luis had followed in the family tradition of making saddles. He was a fifth-generation leatherworker. Juan, his grandfather, was forced to retire at 75 because of his arthritis. But Luis, his father, and now, his son all worked in the business. Their charro saddles were popular in Mexico, though not so much north of the border. The family could care less. They were well established in their niche and comfortable with their status.

"Well, then. You came by so you must have found out something."

Being a craftsman, Luis was familiar with all the other artisans and their merchants in Nogales. It was nothing for him to inquire about where a certain piece might come from.

"Señora Santos said the doll Tina purchased came from Tlaxcala. A cousin brought it from his little town of Tetlapayac."

"That is very far," the grandmother said, knitting her brow.

"Yes. Over a thousand miles. Why is this doll so important?"

"I had an uneasy feeling when Tina bought it. Now, she claims the doll does not want to be with her."

Luis gave Naomi a doubtful glance. "The doll told her this?"

"In a way, yes."

Luis knew his grandmother dealt with the occult. He had heard rumors that Tina Morales was following in her footsteps. A true believer, these were things he wanted nothing to do with.

"I need to go." He started for the door.

"No! Wait!" She held up her hand. "I must know more about the doll."

"I cannot help you, *Abuela*," Luis insisted. "I can't just leave. It would take a week to travel down there, find out what you want to know, then travel back."

"Luis, my grandson, I would not be asking this if it wasn't important," she pleaded.

Sanchez pondered the request. "I cannot go myself, but maybe . . ."

"Yes?"

"Tlaxcala is an hour east of Mexico City. I have contacts in the capital. They might be willing to go there and make inquiries."

"How soon could they go?"

"Grandmother, please. I don't even know if they will go."

"But you will ask, yes?"

"Yes, ma'am. I will."

"And you will tell me what they say?"

"You know I will. Now, I must go." He kissed his grandmother on her forehead.

"I will unlock the door for you," Juan said, leading the way. He had sat quietly at the kitchen table, staying clear of the conversation. He knew there was little he could do, but he would help his wife in any way possible.

Luis said his goodbyes, then climbed into his truck, wondering what he had gotten himself into.

Chapter Thirty-Two

Lansing stepped into the day room to fill his coffee mug. Despite Dr. Nicholas Picado's instructions, the sheriff didn't keep track of his daily caffeine consumption. Nor did he attempt to cut back. He would consider such a move if his blood pressure went up, but for now, it was fine.

Deputy Willie Estrada was ahead of him filling her own cup.

"Oh, good morning, Sheriff." She offered to fill his cup. He accepted. "I was heading to your office."

"Is this about what you found at the Baker trailer?"

"Yes, sir."

"Good."

The two proceeded to his office. Estrada carried her coffee cup and an evidence bag.

"So, what do we have?" Lansing asked. He stood next to his desk so he could examine the bag's contents.

"These are receipts," she said, producing a large, manila envelope. "It's easy to track where they've been in the last couple of weeks."

"They haven't just been at the Little Creek Resort?"

"No, they didn't get there till last Thursday. The week before they stayed at an RV park outside Mesa Verde. Last Wednesday they spent the night at Riverside Campground east of Farmington. Their spot at Little Creek was paid up through today."

Lansing nodded. "Yeah, Mrs. Baker said she needed to leave. She had to be at work Monday . . . Abilene, Texas. What else?"

"Nothing really. I have their wallets and IDs. We impounded the shotgun and shells. There were lots of empty liquor bottles and beer cans. I didn't find anything that would contradict her claims about self-defense."

Lansing sat in his chair. "She's still in our detention cell. I didn't see a reason to put her in county lockup for just an overnight stay."

The San Phillipe County Adult Detention Center was located two blocks away. A department of the Sheriff's Office, Lansing didn't get involved with its daily operations. Roman Veneno had been the administrator for ten years and was doing a great job. He had a staff of over twenty. Most were detention officers, but there were also secretaries, maintenance workers, and cooks. It was a 24/7 operation.

The center had a 140-inmate capacity, though there was room for only 28 females. Lansing used the four cells in his building for short-term incarceration, drunks, and the like. That cut down on paperwork . . . the sheriff's nemesis.

"Did you find anything in the truck?"

Estrada blushed. "I'm sorry, boss. We didn't even look."

He gave his deputy a stern stare.

"I'll go back this morning."

"Well, if we don't find anything else and the Medical Examiner doesn't have any issues, I'll have a hard time keeping Mrs. Baker much longer."

"Will there be an inquest?"

"Always. But today's Friday. I'll probably get the autopsy results today, but there's no telling when the inquest will be scheduled. It's one of New Mexico's great mysteries. The coroner's office gets our findings along with the Medical Investigator's results. The coroner then puts on a blindfold, then throws a dart at a calendar. He might hit a date a week from now, or a month, three months, even six months away."

"Do I need to get moving, then?" Willie asked.

"Yes, you do. The coroner doesn't start throwing darts till he gets all the evidence."

As sheriff, he kept a measure of distance between himself and his subordinates. He maintained a good relationship with his staff. Even friendly. But there was no doubt in anyone's mind who was the boss. Undersheriff and Chief Deputy Jack Rivera, Lansing's longest friend in the department, knew this and never questioned the sheriff's authority.

That respect rippled down through everyone else under Lansing. Few in the department were worried about the upcoming election. No one could imagine anyone else being sheriff.

Chapter Thirty-Three

Dorothy Gonzalez knew something was wrong before she ever went into Edie's room. This was the second morning in a row the four-year-old wasn't up and ready to gather the eggs. Eric, the oldest, was tasked with waking her up. Edie didn't respond, even when he gently shook her.

"She doesn't look very good," Eric reported. "And she won't wake up."

Dorothy rushed to her child's room. Edith shared the room with her two sisters, Mary and Adonna. The two older siblings, still eating breakfast, did not appear ill . . . at least not yet.

When the mother pulled back the covers, Edie's color was ashen, and she was cold to the touch. Dorothy immediately knelt and put her ear against the child's chest. There was a faint heartbeat.

"Edie," she begged. "Please wake up!"

In response, the little girl tried to open her eyes. "Mamma?"

Dorothy bundled up the child in the bed covers and headed for the kitchen. Edie, barely aware of what was happening, still clutched Izel, the gift from Sheriff Lansing.

"Eric, go find your father," the mother ordered. "We have to go to the hospital!"

When he heard Dorothy's request, Esteban rushed to the house. His wife never succumbed to histrionics. If she requested they go to the hospital, he knew she was desperate.

"Dot, what's wrong?" he demanded, throwing open the kitchen door.

"It's Edie! She's sick. She needs to see a doctor!"

"A doctor?"

"She doesn't look good. She can't wake up and she's really cold to the touch!"

Esteban hurried over to see for himself. When he opened the covers, he could see for himself how ill Edith looked. He also saw Izel.

"Are any of the other kids sick?"

"No!"

He tried pulling the doll from his daughter's grasp. In response, she whined and hugged the doll even closer.

"She started getting sick when she got that damned doll, didn't she?"

"I don't know . . . I guess."

Esteban quickly ushered his wife and daughter out the front door. Heading to the truck, he called over his shoulder. "You kids take care of yourselves. We'll be back!"

Opening the rider's side door, he nearly lifted his wife into the seat. Without saying a word, he ripped the doll from his daughter's arms and threw it onto the sparse lawn. Edie's only protest was a whimper.

The drive to the Presbyterian Hospital Emergency Room would take an hour.

***

After filling out the paperwork, the Gonzalezes were ushered into triage. Edith's vitals were normal, though on the low side. Despite the parents' concerns, they still had to wait almost an hour before they were brought to an exam room.

For a second time, they had to explain to an ER nurse why they were there. It was another 10 minutes before the doctor came in.

Dr. Garnepudi seemed genuinely concerned about the child. He had reviewed the vitals and knew something was wrong. The blood pressure was way too low. At 93.6°, Edie's temperature barely registered in the normal range. Her pupils were slow to dilate when he shined his pen-light in her eyes.

He immediately ordered a saline drip and blood cultures. He promised the worried parents the hospital would find out what was going on.

Chapter Thirty-Four

"You want to know why I'm going to win the election?" a self-satisfied John Tapia asked, staring at the motel room ceiling.

"Why, Johnny?" his companion cooed while she traced her finger up and down his arm.

"Because I'm a people person . . . and the voters like that. They want someone they can relate to."

Tapia knew his observation about himself wasn't true. He got ahead by manipulating people. He had the ability to tell people what they wanted to hear, whether he believed it or not. His veneer of sincerity was so thick, he never came across as anything but honest.

It didn't hurt that he was tall, athletic, and handsome . . . all attributes he used to their fullest. No one in his family had ever gone to college and he was no different. He had no interest in the military, but the police academy offered similar opportunities . . . a paid education beyond high school, a respectable career, and a future. Despite his youth, he convinced the police recruiter he would be an asset to the force.

Four years in the Segovia Police Department gave him some real-world experience. It also taught him the value of power and how money influenced power. He saw that when he attended City Council meetings. They met twice a month in the evenings, and he volunteered for security detail.

Ordinary citizens brought their concerns and complaints to the council. No resolutions were ever adopted. Most concerns were deferred for later consideration, that is, unless you were well-to-do businessmen. Those concerns were always advanced because the skids were greased well ahead of time.

Tapia's life changed the night he stopped to investigate a Lexus sedan pulled off to the side of the road. A very drunk Matthew Franco was passed out at the wheel. The young officer recognized the man immediately. Franco was the founder/owner of *Magnifico's Burgers and Burritos*, a fast-food chain that stretched across the entire state.

As always, Tapia made a self-serving decision. Instead of arresting the man, the patrolman loaded the millionaire into his patrol car and took him home. He was greeted at the door by Franco's twenty-year-old daughter, Daniela.

Things moved quickly after that. Tapia began dating the almost attractive Daniela. Matthew, grateful for not getting another DUI, took a shine to the officer. One evening, Franco asked Tapia what his aspirations were.

Tapia admitted he was interested in politics. He thought a position on the City Council would be a perfect spot for him.

Franco saw two problems with the idea. Councilmen were only paid a stipend of $400 a month . . . hardly enough to live on. And Tapia couldn't be a councilman and serve as a police officer at the same time.

"How serious are you about my daughter?"

"Danny? I don't know. I haven't thought about it."

"Do you love her?"

If Tapia had been honest, he would have said, "No." He almost blurted out, "I could learn to." Self-interest kicked in. "Of course, I do."

"Have you two talked about marriage?"

"No."

"You should. I like you, John. And I owe you. I want to back your bid for the city council. If you quit the police department, I have a position for you in my company."

Tapia knew strings were attached. "What if I propose to Danny and she turns me down?"

"She won't."

With that last statement from Franco, Tapia's future was secured.

After eight years of marriage, John and Daniela Tapia had two children, two cars, a house, and money in the bank. And, after eight years on the City Council, Tapia was ready to move on.

He was reluctant to give up his position as a regional manager for *Magnifico's Burgers and Burritos*. It was great money for doing nothing. But he aspired to much higher offices. Being sheriff of San Phillipe County was just another rung on the ladder he was climbing.

He threw the bedcovers off and began looking for his clothes.

"Aw, do you have to go?"

Abbie Fontana was a secretary at Real Estate of the Rockies. Her goal was to become a certified real estate agent, a dream she had been chasing for four years. That was as long as Tapia had known her. He didn't think she was smart enough to complete all the courses and pass the state and national exams. The only thing he cared about was that she dropped everything when he beckoned. She was ten years his junior. She was pretty, petite, and disposable if he got elected sheriff.

"Sorry, Abbie. I've got a meeting tonight."

"When are you coming back to Santa Fe?"

"I don't know."

Tapia's sometimes girlfriend sat up in bed. "I know you can't make any promises about our future. But would you be honest with me?"

"Sure."

"Am I the only woman in your life besides your wife?"

"Of course, you are," he lied, sitting on the bed to pull on his shoes.

Abbie was truly the only woman he was seeing in the capital city. But a regional manager's territory covered other towns. That meant other women. Tapia was honestly proud of how well he could sell himself to the fairer sex.

She scooted closer to put her arms around him. He patted her hand.

"I need to be honest with you, Abbie. I know I'm going to be the next sheriff of San Phillipe County. I'll have to give up my position as a regional manager. That means I won't be able to make these trips to Santa Fe to see you. That breaks my heart. You are such an important part of my life."

"You're important to me, Johnny!" she said, unable to hold back her tears.

Tapia stood and turned to her, holding her hands. "I know things would be different between us if we lived closer to each other. But you have your life here in Santa Fe. I'll have to move to Las Palmas. That's more than an hour away . . . and I'll be swamped with new responsibilities."

"You won't forget me, will you?"

"You know I won't." He gently kissed her forehead. "I'll always remember you."

Chapter Thirty-Five

Joy Baca stopped her brother's truck in front of the Garcia house. She had expected Eric to be waiting for her outside. He needed to know she had arrived. Getting out of the truck, she started across the lawn made up of stunted weeds. It was the bright colors of the dress that caught her eye.

Joy walked over and picked up Izel. She brushed the dust off the porcelain face and marveled at the doll's beauty. Why was the toy so callously discarded?

Nine-year-old Adonna answered the door.

"Hi, Joy. Come in. Eric's doing the dishes."

Joy followed her into the kitchen.

"I see you are domesticated."

"Oh, hey, Joy!" Eric was drying a plate. "We're almost done."

Eric's brother, Robert, had just finished scrubbing a skillet. He set it on the stove and lit the burner for a quick dry.

Joy held up Izel. "I found this on the lawn."

"Papa didn't like it!" Adonna said. She had been in the kitchen and observed the conversation between her parents. "He said the doll made Edie sick. I saw him throw it away when they got in the truck."

"I'm ready," Eric announced. "Let's go!"

"What should I do with the doll?" She looked at Adonna. "Do you want it?"

"Oh, NO!" The girl was emphatic. "I don't like her, either!"

"Why?"

"It does things at night!"

"What things?"

Adonna just shook her head and ran from the room.

"Kids," Eric said, shaking his head. "I guess you can keep the doll, if you want."

"Really?"

"Sure. Why not?"

"Thanks."

Once they were in the truck and headed down the gravel road, Joy asked, "Where to?"

"I was wondering if we could swing by the hospital first. I'm worried about Edie."

"That's no problem."

***

The dozen parking spots next to the Emergency Room were filled. Eric recognized the family truck, so he knew his parents were still there. Joy parked across the road and the two walked in.

ER policy limited two visitors to a patient at a time. Eric requested a nurse to ask one of his parents to come out. A few minutes later Esteban came into the waiting room.

"How's Edie?" Eric asked.

His father shook his head. "The doctor said she's anemic. They're going to give her a unit of blood. He thinks that might help."

"After that are they sending her home?"

"No. They want to keep her overnight. Your mother's going to stay with her."

"Do they know what's wrong with her?" Joy asked.

"They're still running tests. They're talking about antibiotics, but they don't know what to give her yet. I mean, she's not running a fever, so they don't think she has an infection."

"I can stay here if you want," Eric offered.

"That's alright. Your mother and I have it under control . . . I know you wanted to go car hunting today. Are the rest of the kids doing okay?"

"Yeah, they're good."

"I'm heading home as soon as I know what's going on. If you beat me there, tell your brother and sisters I'm bringing pizza."

"They'll love that," Eric admitted. "Can Joy stay for dinner?"

"Of course," Esteban said, managing a smile. "She's always welcome."

Chapter Thirty-Six

Lansing stared at the contents of the handbag Deputy Estrada found in the Bakers' truck. Next to the driver's license photo was the picture of the hit-and-run victim discovered in the western part of the county. It wasn't a perfect match because of the body's condition, but it was close enough for him to pursue an investigation.

He had the desk sergeant call the San Juan County sheriff's office. Had there been any missing persons reported in the last week?

There had been two. One was a runaway from a foster home. He was found at a friend's house. The other was an 18-year-old girl, separated from friends when they went to Navajo Lake. It was assumed she had drowned, though no body had been found yet.

"Her name wasn't Victoria Sewell, was it?" Sergeant Montoya asked.

"As a matter of fact, it was," the surprised deputy responded. "Do you have news about her?"

"Yes," Montoya admitted. "But you're not going to like it."

Clem Montoya's news was only partly satisfying to the sheriff. He had a name to go with the dead body found the previous Friday. Now, however, there was the possibility the woman in his lockup was tied to two deaths.

***

"I hope you are planning to release me, Sheriff," Karen Baker snapped, when she was brought into the interrogation room. Since she was not under arrest, she wasn't required to be in handcuffs. "This has been illegal incarceration, as far as I'm concerned! You know you could be sued?"

"It wouldn't be the first time," Lansing admitted.

He directed Estrada to put Baker in a chair at the table. Lansing sat across from her with a large grocery bag. Willy stood near the door.

Lansing slipped on a pair of white, latex gloves. He reached into the bag and pulled out a handbag, placing it on the table.

"Do you recognize this?"

Baker leaned forward, looked at the bag briefly, then shook her head. "Never saw it before."

"You're sure?"

"Absolutely." Baker leaned back in the chair, folding her arms.

Lansing retrieved a photo from the paper bag and set it on the table. It was a crime scene photo of a dead girl. "How about her?"

Baker spent less time looking at the photo than she had the handbag. "No!"

"Okay . . . help me with something." He opened the handbag, removed a wallet, and took out the driver's license. He placed the license next to the photo. "Does this look like the same woman, to you?"

Baker looked at the two, then shrugged. "Could be."

"Take a closer look . . . You see, I believe this is what Victoria Sewell looked like after you hit her." He tapped the photo. "Because these . . ." He tapped the license picture. "The driver's license, the wallet, and the purse were all found with your other possessions."

"I told you! I've never seen those things before!"

"We also have receipts taken from your trailer. They indicate you spent Wednesday night at a campground east of Farmington. The next day you drove near Navajo Lake on the San Juan/San Phillipe County line, on your way to Little Creek Resort.

"You had to be on Highway 64. The same road where we found Victoria's body the next day."

"Okay," Karen Baker said nervously. "There was an accident! But it wasn't me. My husband, Bill . . . He was driving. I think he had been drinking.

"I must have dozed off. I felt the truck hit something and it woke me. Bill told me he thought he hit a deer. He stopped the truck and got out to check the damage. I asked him if I should come with him, but he told me no.

"So, I waited. He might have been gone for five minutes. That must be when he grabbed the handbag. He must have put it behind the seat when he got back in . . ."

"How did you know we found it behind the seat? All the sheriff said was we found those items with your other stuff," Estrada said from her position near the door.

"I . . . I mean," Baker thought quickly. "If it had been in the trailer, I . . . I would have seen them. So, you must have found them in the truck."

"How did you know we found it behind the seat?" the deputy asked.

"Where else could he have hidden it?"

"Under the seat," Willie offered.

"Karen Baker," Lansing said. "I'm arresting you for leaving the scene of an accident and for being a possible accomplice in a hit-and-run fatality."

"What?" Baker shrieked.

"Deputy Estrada, please read her her Miranda rights. After she's handcuffed, escort her back to her cell."

I can at least hold her on the hit-and-run, Lansing thought, *while I figure out if she murdered her husband.*

Chapter Thirty-Seven

Segovia Secure Storage was perfect for Jeremiah Black's needs. The 5 x 10, climate-controlled unit provided 24/7 protection for his peyote supply. At $60 a month, it was very affordable. Located 10 minutes from where he worked, he could slip in and out of the unit during lunch without fear of being followed.

The Road Man counted sixty-six dried peyote buttons into a gallon-sized, clear plastic, zip lock bag. The previous week he had used only forty-eight. However, two attendees assured him they would bring companions for the next service. He wanted to make sure he had enough to go around. Since the buttons didn't spoil, any extra would survive until the next week.

Sealing the bag, Black placed his wares into a nylon tote. He locked the metal box holding the peyote, then pulled the outside door closed. Making sure it too was secure, he got into his truck and headed back to work.

***

When Jeremiah got back to the car repair garage, he saw Chaparro's Lowrider parked in the lot. Black's first thought was the Hispanic was back with a complaint. What had he done wrong or didn't do? He racked his brain trying to answer the question as he locked his truck.

"Hey, Preacher Man!" a familiar voice called from the office.

The mechanic looked over to see Chaparro approaching. "Oh, yeah. Hi. Is something wrong?"

"No, man. I was wondering if, like, maybe me and a friend could come to your church on Sunday?"

"Why?" Black was wary.

"We were talking to some guys. They said these Indian Churches . . . they're special."

"How are they special?"

"They said sometimes you take . . . what did they say it was?" he asked himself. "A sacrament?"

"Lots of churches have sacraments." Jeremiah knew exactly what sacrament Chaparro meant. Black's instinct was to distrust strangers. He was mostly out of his element in New Mexico, and he knew it. He didn't know the man he was talking to, therefore, there was no reason to trust him.

"I know, man . . . but me and my family, we've been looking for a new church to go to," Chaparro protested.

"You said you and a friend wanted to attend my service."

"Oh, yeah, well . . . that's just to check it out."

Black shook his head. "I told you the other day, my church is for Native Americans."

"But I got Indian blood, Preacher Man!"

"Chaparro . . . right?"

"Yeah," the lowrider said hopefully.

"Maybe someday down the road, I'll open my doors to non-Native Americans. I want to keep my services small. I'm not ready for large crowds."

"So, you're telling me 'No?' " The man sounded indignant.

"I'm telling you 'No.' "

"I know where you live, Preacher Man!" Chaparro was angry now. "Maybe I show up Sunday, whether you like it or not."

That the Hispanic knew where he lived was not a revelation to Jeremiah. Nor was he surprised that the man knew nothing about how or when Native American Church services were conducted.

The roadman walked past Chaparro. He had nothing more to say and needed to get back to work.

Chapter Thirty-Eight

"Where do you want to go now?" Joy asked.

Baca and Gonzalez had visited all three used car dealerships in Segovia. It had taken two hours to see every car that was available. Eric had planned on buying a truck. Since he lived on a farm, that only made sense. He had seen just one truck, though . . . a Chevy. But it was only a year old, and the price was much more than he could afford.

"I don't know." He sounded depressed.

"Who says you have to buy a truck?"

"No one. But I didn't see anything I liked. I'll probably have to go to Santa Fe," he said, opening the passenger side door. "There's nothing here in town."

"I can take you," Joy offered. "I need to check with my folks first."

At eighteen and a high school graduate, Joy had a lot of autonomy. Taking her brother's car to a big city without him knowing about it, though, pushed the envelope.

"Not today. I need to get back to the farm."

Joy got into Lincoln's truck. "Do you want to get a paper to see if anyone is selling their old truck?"

"Naw. My dad always said buying someone's car was just buying their old headaches. No telling what you were getting . . . I'll just wait."

"I thought you wanted to get a job."

"I do." He pulled his door closed. "It just won't be today . . . Take me by the hospital if you don't mind. If my dad's still there, I can ride back to the farm with him."

"Are you sure?" Joy asked, disappointedly. "I don't mind driving you back. We never see each other."

Gonzalez considered the implications. Letting Joy drive him home did mean they could spend more time together. Besides, there were dozens of spots along the way where they could pull off and talk . . . and kiss . . . and maybe more.

"You're right," Eric smiled. "It's been a long time since we were together."

Joy was thrilled. "You want to pick up some burgers? We could have a picnic."

"You're driving. Whatever you want to do is fine with me."

Chapter Thirty-Nine

Lansing sipped his beer while he monitored the ears of corn on the grill. The steaks sat to one side, covered with aluminum foil, waiting their turn. Tina sat quietly in a chair, staring at the glowing coals.

"It's hard to believe I'm starting my fourth year at Las Palmas High," the teacher sighed. "Kids I taught in eighth grade are juniors now. I'm feeling old, Lansing."

"Sweetheart, you can get in line with the rest of us."

"I heard your new campaign ad driving home. You sounded pretty good."

"Thank you." He raised his beer in a cheers motion. "I hope the rest of the county shares your sentiments."

"You haven't talked about the election much. I guess you aren't worried."

"Worrying is more tedious than actually doing something. Besides, I have plenty to keep me busy."

"What would you do if you lost the election?"

He eyed his partner. "Do you know something I don't?"

"No. Of course not. It's just a question."

"It's a question I haven't asked myself. When I quit being sheriff, I hope it's on my terms."

"Then you had a pretty good day?"

"Remember the hit-and-run found near Navaho Lake last week? We have a pretty good idea who did it."

"Really? Who?"

"It was either the husband who was shot and killed this morning or his wife, who did the shooting."

"Husband . . . Wait . . . What shooting?"

Lansing explained the incident at Little Creek Resort that morning.

"When Willie Estrada searched the couple's truck, she found a purse belonging to the victim. An eighteen-year-old from San Juan County. When we questioned the wife, she couldn't give us a straight answer on how the purse ended up in her possession."

"So, you were holding her for the murder of her husband, and then you found out about the hit-and-run victim."

"We haven't charged her with the murder yet. She's claiming self-defense. We do have enough to hold her for leaving the scene of an accident. That gives us time to investigate both deaths."

"Is she going to get away with killing her husband?"

"I don't know. All I have to go on is her testimony. I need evidence if I want to prove it wasn't self-defense."

Oscar Vega came down the long drive, eventually parking in front of the bunkhouse.

He came running over.

"Sheriff, I got the spare stall cleaned out today. Can I borrow the horse trailer tomorrow? Oh, hi, Miss Morales."

Tina gave a small wave.

"Bringing home your mustang?"

"Yes, sir."

Lansing nodded. "Sure . . ." He nodded toward the grill. "I've got an extra steak if you're interested."

"Oh, yes," the ranch foreman beamed. "Do I have time to take a shower?"

"Go for it!"

As Vega ran back to the bunkhouse, Tina laughed. "You'd think it was Christmas."

"We find happiness where we can." Lansing finished his beer. "And I would be happy if someone could round me up another beer."

Tina stood. "I can take a hint."

"One of the many reasons I love you. I don't have to explain my-self."

Chapter Forty

Lincoln's first night in front of the mysterious fire was uncomfortable. The rocky floor of the canyon was hard. The fire itself gave off little heat, so the chilly mountain air seeped into his bones. His empty stomach growled, but he had resolved to begin his fast when he stopped at the fire.

At first, he tried to satisfy himself by simply staring at the dancing blue flames. Sitting with his legs crossed gave him the most secure position. He had grown up hearing it called "Indian-style." The term was deemed racist, even though it was a yoga position used by East Indians. Maybe, he thought, "Indian-style" applied to them as well as Native Americans. That way, everyone could be offended.

He dozed often. He would jerk awake and resume staring into the fire. He wanted to chant the words for the Eagle Dance. He learned them in Tewa when he was younger. He could tap the rhythm against his leg to replicate the drumbeat. The beat drove the words.

After several false starts, he gave up. It had been a long day. He was tired and his head throbbed. Curling up next to the fire, sleep overcame him.

The sun was up when he woke. The chirping birds welcomed him to the new morning. He pulled a water bottle from his backpack. Sipping sparingly at first, he realized the spring he found the day before was only ten minutes away. The high, dry mountain air had dehydrated him. He allowed himself several big gulps, then poured water into his hand to wash his face.

He looked at the fire. It wasn't there. He reached to where he had seen flames the night before, then jerked his hand back. The flames burned him. The fire was still there but it was barely visible in the daylight.

Lincoln assigned himself the task of gathering rocks to make a stone circle around the fire. He needed to avoid stomping through the invisible daytime flames. When he stood, the dizziness from the day before returned. Bending over and picking up rocks was more difficult than he anticipated.

Once his stonework was finished, he hiked down to the spring. He fought through the unsteadiness. Filling his stomach with water helped fight the hunger. He stripped down to nothing and washed thoroughly, ignoring the freezing water. He shook himself like a dog, then dressed in the same clothes. The shivers subsided on the hike back up the canyon.

With his water bottles filled and no other project to accomplish, Lincoln cleared his sitting area of any rocks and pebbles. He sat and pulled the pamphlet from his backpack. He blamed the new dizziness and headaches on his tumble the day before. Could his tumor cause the same symptoms?

The list of symptoms was near the front of the brochure. Lincoln counted a total of eleven.

Headaches were the first symptom. He knew that already.

Headaches were followed by seizures;

difficulty thinking, speaking, or finding words;

personality changes;

weakness, numbness, or paralysis;

loss of balance, dizziness, or unsteadiness;

loss of hearing;

vision changes;

hallucinations;

confusion and disorientation;

memory loss.

He had three already . . . headaches, dizziness, and personality change. The first two could also be tied to his fall. The last one Lincoln knew he had been fighting for weeks.

He stuck the medical handout into his backpack, then assumed his cross-legged position next to the fire. Closing his eyes, his unsteadiness gradually dissipated.

Sitting and meditating were foreign to him. Clearing his mind of any thoughts was a challenge. When he eventually opened his eyes, the sun had passed its zenith. He must have dozed off because he remembered nothing.

Uncle Eluterio was vague about what a vision quest entailed. Lincoln was making up his own rules as he went along. Besides, there was no one to chastise him if he was doing things wrong.

He considered exploring further up the canyon. When he stood, nausea and dizziness returned. In frustration, he plopped back down. As the canyon became awash in deepening shadows, the chill air wrapped around him. He wished he'd brought a heavier jacket.

He considered gathering wood to build a large fire.

No, he told himself. This was no ordinary fire. It was a sign from the spirit world. He should do absolutely nothing to disturb or alter the flames in any way.

Reaching into his backpack, he pulled out a bundle of sage. He had cleansed himself in the spring. It was time to purify himself. He stuck one end of the short bundle into the sacred fire until it lit. He let the bundle burn for a few minutes, then blew out the flame.

What remained was pungent, white smoke. He held the bundle in front of him with one hand, using the other to waft the smoke into his face. He then "bathed" each arm, each leg, and his torso with the vapor.

He staggered to his feet, then raised the bundle in each of the four, cardinal directions praying for the Great Spirit's blessings.

He sat, cross-legged again. He willed himself to be warm. The coolness around him dissipated. He closed his eyes. The world quit spinning as he sank into unconsciousness.

Chapter Forty-One

As Joy began to fall asleep, she thought about her day with Eric.

After grabbing burgers and drinks they made a pass by the hospital. The Gonzalez truck was gone. That meant Joy had to take her boyfriend back to the farm, whether she wanted to or not.

They found a shady spot along the Rio Grande near the San Juan Pueblo fishponds. For a picnic it was fine. But there were too many other visitors for a private, make-out session.

It wasn't until they were almost to the Artiga Reservoir that they found a suitable spot. A dirt road led to the top of a hill overlooking the lake. Juniper trees hid the truck from prying eyes. They chose a comfortable spot under a tree and began kissing in earnest.

Joy was satisfied with the heavy petting. Eric reached down to unfasten the top snap to her blue jeans. Joy pulled away.

"What do you think you're doing?"

"I want you, Joy. I want to be with you!"

"I want to be with you, too, Eric . . . But I'm not ready for us to have sex!"

"What are you talking about? I thought that's why we found a private spot . . . so we could be together!"

"Eric, this isn't up for debate. I'm not having sex with you or anyone else. When I'm ready to settle down with one person . . . and I hope that person is you . . . making love might be a part of the deal. But not now! I want to do other things in life besides having kids."

"I . . . I'm sorry." Gonzalez apologized. "I didn't realize that's how you felt."

"It is . . . If you want to have sex with someone, I can name a half-dozen girls from our class who would take care of you . . ."

"I know who you're talking about, and I wouldn't touch a single one of them. Joy, I want to be with you. If holding off having sex is important to you, it's fine with me. I can wait."

Neither teen had said out loud that they "loved" each other. But today, Eric had demonstrated something more important than saying he was in love. He showed her that he respected her. That thought gave her a peaceful, warm feeling inside.

As her eyes fluttered shut, the last thing Joy remembered seeing was Izel looking down at her from a dresser.

***

A firefly crawled out from the folds of the doll's dress. If Joy had been watching she would have seen the insect dissolve into a mist . . . a mist as large as a human that glowed with an inner light. The mist drifted silently across the room. The bedroom door opened, and the mist continued until it reached the outside yard.

The amorphous fog began to coalesce into a solid shape. It was the shape of a girl . . . a Mexican girl of sixteen. In the moonless night, she first appeared like a shadow. The shadow stretched and twisted as if it had been held in a confined space for a long time.

Fernanda loved her human form. She wanted to stay that way, assume the guise of an immigrant seeking a better life. She lifted her head and sniffed. Immediately she was drawn to the house across the road. It was a compulsion she had no power to resist. Taking a few steps, Fernanda stopped and turned her head. A nearer house enticed her even more.

She had fed well the previous three nights. Before that, she had gone nearly a month without a meal. She had come close to dying. Tina

Morales' blood sustained her . . . barely. It was the blood of children that gave her sustenance. Infant blood was like nectar to her.

It was that craving that drove her from Tetlapayac, the only home she had ever known. The children of the village were becoming sick. A baby had died. They all had bruises on their upper bodies . . . a sure sign they had been attacked by a *tlahuelpuchi*, a vampire.

Fernanda's father had protected her. For three years, ever since she reached puberty, they were able to keep the girl's curse a secret. Afraid he couldn't keep her safe much longer, Juan Huerta contacted a *brujo,* a male witch, from a neighboring village. A man vested in the dark arts might have a solution.

A neighbor recognized the *brujo* when he emerged from the Huerta shack. The villagers suspected they had discovered the reason for the illnesses and the infant's death. It was obvious the warlock was there to collude with Fernanda Huerta and her father. She had to be a vampire.

Accusations were passed in confidence. The *tlahuelpuchi* had to be destroyed.

Word got back to Huerta, and he knew the only way to protect his daughter was to send her away. He knew she lived under an evil curse, and what she did was an abomination. But she was still his daughter and he loved her. It was his love that enabled her to continue her atrocities.

Juan Huerta never let himself consider the harm his only daughter visited on the lives of others.

***

Fernanda turned toward the adobe house. The infant boy there would be her first target in this new village. She knew she could not allow the child to die. There would be many more children to meet her needs. She would be patient.

Chapter Forty-Two

If Lincoln Baca had to describe his first, deep meditative experience in one word, he would have said it felt like he was "floating." No longer restricted by physical laws, it was as if he was suspended in the heavens. There was no horizon because the Earth ceased to exist.

The universe was made of pinpoints of lights . . . stars . . . above him and below him. He knew if he concentrated on one light, he would be transported there.

He woke with a start. There was a disturbance in his universe.

The stars were a reality, but only above him. It was night. The blue flames danced in the stone circle. His body no longer drifted above the world. He felt the pull of gravity against him.

There were no night sounds. No crickets chirping, nor owls hooting. No coyotes howling in the distance. There was only Lincoln . . . and the fire . . . and a movement in the canyon beyond the flames.

Lincoln wanted to call out and demand who was there . . . but he knew he shouldn't. He needed to keep silent. Everything would be revealed.

The light from the flames danced against the canyon walls. A figure approached from beyond the glow of the fire. As the visitor grew closer, Lincoln couldn't tell if it walked or floated . . . the footsteps made no sound.

Lincoln could see the figure was a man. He was dressed in an ornate costume of radiant colors. Drawing closer to the fire, the colors of the figure's tunic became more distinct. There were bright blues and vibrant reds . . . splashes of white and yellow.

He was tall . . . majestic. A warrior. His height was accentuated by a fountain of feathers sprouting from his golden headdress/crown, making him seem two feet taller. In his right hand, he carried a staff, a spear-point at the bottom. The top was festooned with feathers that matched his headwear.

He wasn't just a warrior. He was a Warrior King.

The man's eyes were focused on Lincoln. They bored into him like a hot poker. The firefighter couldn't move. He was transfixed by fascination, not fear. Had Lincoln completed his quest? This man . . . this warrior, this warrior king . . . was he the Kachina the Puebloan was destined to find?

The silence was shattered by a rattle, the loudest sound the man had ever heard. The sound was amplified as it bounced off the canyon walls. Another time he would have leaped to his feet to find the source. That night, he realized this was part of the quest.

A creature appeared from behind the Warrior King . . . a snake, its head as big as a man's. Slithering into the light, it was the largest snake he had ever seen. The black eyes glistened in the flames as they fixated on Lincoln. As they did, the rattling stopped.

"Why are you here?"

The question came from the Warrior King. The words were in a language he'd never heard before . . . but he understood their meaning.

Lincoln racked his brain for an intelligent response. "I seek your wisdom . . . your guidance," he said out loud.

The Warrior King's stern look became even harsher. "You seek MY wisdom? You do not know who I am? Who are you to make such a request?"

While the snake's stare still bored into Lincoln's soul, the Warrior King turned to walk away. Looking from the snake to his master, a great revelation washed over him, as if the universe had spoken to him. Lincoln jumped to his feet and shouted, "I am no one! But You! You are Montezuma, King of the Aztecs, Emperor of Mexico!"

The Warrior King turned back to face the pueblo man. When he did, Lincoln dropped to one knee and bowed his head.

"Who told you where to find me?"

"I . . . No one," Lincoln sputtered, his eyes fixed on the ground. "I was told to go into the wilderness . . . on a quest. I didn't know who I sought. I found this fire . . ."

"My Fire!" the King corrected.

"Yes, yes. I found your fire. I knew this was where I had to be. I fasted. I purified my body. I cleared myself of all thoughts . . . I opened my mind . . . Then you came!"

Montezuma stood silent, holding the man in his gaze. For how long, Lincoln couldn't guess. Since entering the canyon, time ceased to exist. Lincoln could feel his thoughts being probed.

"You believe you suffer greatly," the Warrior King finally said.

"Yes, Lord Montezuma. I came to ask questions."

"I will consider your request."

"When will you return?"

"When you are ready."

Montezuma turned, then stopped. "When I appear, it will be here . . . at my sacred fire."

The Great Snake followed his master into the darkness. All Lincoln Baca could do was stare into the now empty canyon.

Chapter Forty-Three

"Mamma," Edie whimpered. "I wet the bed . . . I'm sorry!"

It was daybreak, and Dorothy Gonzalez had slept on the hard sofa/bed in her daughter's room. Just like any other mother, she slept lightly, in case she was needed.

"Oh, baby," Dorothy nearly jumped off the couch. "That's alright. You didn't do anything wrong." Gonzalez threw her arms around the four-year-old and almost squeezed her too hard.

"Let me push this," Gonzalez said, clicking the CALL NURSE button. "They'll send someone."

"Can I help you?" a voice asked over the intercom.

"Yes. My daughter's awake. Can you help us, please? She wet the bed."

"We'll notify your nurse . . . Someone will be right in."

"Why do I have this?" the child asked, holding up her arm with an IV line. "I don't like it!"

"Don't touch it, honey. You were sick . . . We couldn't wake you up. The nurses had to put that on your arm so they could make you well. Do you remember when we brought you here?"

"Huh-uh," Edie said, shaking her head. "Can I go home?"

"I hope so . . . The doctor needs to see you first. He has to make sure you're not sick anymore."

The door opened and Edie's nurse came in, followed by an orderly with a new hospital gown and clean linens. Both were female.

"How are you feeling, Sweetheart?" The nurse's nametag said SWEENY.

"I want to go home."

"We all want you to go home. We need to clean you up first."

The two women set about to quickly clean Edie, change her gown, and replace the sheets, even though she had slept on an absorbent pad for such accidents. Dorothy held her daughter while the bed was changed. The orderly stuffed the linens into the cloth hamper for soiled laundry and left.

"Is there anything else you need?"

"Do you know when the doctor will come in?"

"All I know is he'll do his rounds this morning. It'll probably be after breakfast. I'll be back in a little while to take her vitals."

Once mother and daughter were alone again, Edie knitted her eyebrows in concentration. "Who was that girl that came into my room?"

"Here in the hospital?"

"No. At home. She was in my room. She was nice. She kissed my head . . . then she lifted my shirt and kissed my body."

"Your body!"

When Edith was first examined in the ER, there were a half dozen bruises on her torso. Insect and spider bites were not ruled out. Holes were found in the center of the purple marks, but toxicology found nothing. When questioned, neither parent had an explanation. They needed to ask Edie what happened . . . when she awakened.

"Do you remember where she kissed you?"

Edie shook her head.

"Did she hurt you?"

"No," Edie whimpered. "Am I in trouble?"

"Of course not, baby." Dorothy thought for a moment. "This girl . . . what did she look like?"

"It was dark . . . but I think she was pretty."

"Didn't she say anything?"

"She just told me shh, cause she didn't want to wake up Mary or Donnie." Edie never could say Adonna as a toddler, so she settled on Donnie. The name stuck.

The worried mother couldn't help but think her daughter imagined this "girl" in her bedroom. But there were the bruises and small "bug-bite" holes. She decided when Edie was bitten, her mind conjured up a visitor to explain what she felt.

Chapter Forty-Four

It wasn't unusual for Cliff Lansing to work seven days a week. Showing up on a Saturday happened more often than not. He would have preferred taking the day off to help Oscar Vega. He was retrieving his new horse from the Wild Mustang Sanctuary at Loma Amarilla Ranch. Tina Morales volunteered to help, and Oscar gladly accepted.

With three murders to contend with . . . two hit-and-runs and a dead husband . . . the sheriff felt obligated to make progress on the investigations.

Karen Baker claimed her husband killed Victoria Sewell, the victim found near Navajo Lake. Lansing had his doubts. He also wanted to know if the Bakers had been near San Juan Reservation and if they had anything to do with the second hit-and-run.

If Baker denied any responsibility, Lansing wasn't about to manufacture evidence just to get a conviction. He wasn't an officer who simply closed cases. He was a lawman who solved crimes.

Lansing wanted to interrogate Karen Baker again, but he needed more information to prod her with. The autopsy report hadn't arrived yet, though he expected nothing new to be revealed.

In the dayroom, he had to start a new pot of coffee. Sidney Barnes, the weekend dispatcher, didn't drink coffee. Well, he didn't make coffee. He would drink it provided there was fresh coffee to be had. Otherwise, he satisfied himself with cokes.

While the coffee finished, he checked the duty board. Wilma Estrada had the weekend off. Marla Trumbull was on call for forensics work if needed. If he had to, he would request her to come in so he could have a female deputy present for another Baker interview.

Baker had been charged with a crime. She made it clear she would not say another word unless she had an attorney present. Lawyers, especially public defenders, were hard to come by on a weekend. It might be Monday before he could talk to her again.

William and Karen Baker were from Texas, so there was no one local who could provide background information about the couple. Lansing sat at his computer and searched for the number of the Abilene Police.

"Abilene Police Department, how can I help you?" a woman's voice asked.

"Yes, this is Sheriff Clifford Lansing, San Phillipe County, New Mexico. I'm looking for information on a married couple from your city."

"What kind of information, Sheriff?"

"I need to find out if your department has been called to their residence for domestic disturbances."

"I'm sorry, Sheriff. Today's Saturday. Our records department is closed. Is this important?"

"It is. I'm investigating a murder. The couple I'm asking about is involved."

"Our investigative services usually work Monday through Friday. If you leave me a number we can reach you at, I'll try to pass on your request. I'll also need the name and address of the people in your inquiry."

Lansing provided everything the operator requested. After a "thank you" and "goodbye," he wandered to the front office wondering if there was a new angle he could pursue.

"Something just came over the FAX, Sheriff," Sid Barnes said.

"Thanks," he replied, only half interested. He didn't want to be distracted from his current line of inquiry.

He was surprised to find the initial findings of William Baker's autopsy. He shouldn't have been. The Medical Investigator's office usually completed an examination in one to two hours. A detailed autopsy might take up to four. It was already mid-morning and the Albuquerque office worked Saturdays when work piled up.

Lansing took the three pages back to his office to read.

The cause of death was a shotgun blast to the chest. No surprise there. It was the other findings discussed that he found interesting. Baker's arms, particularly the forearms, were covered with bruises. The examiner suggested they were defensive wounds made by different, hard objects. The blows had been administered at different intervals, over weeks as opposed to hours. One side of the man's face had sustained first-and second-degree burns, probably from a hot liquid.

Toxicology results had not been completed by the lab. They would be included in the final report.

For Lansing, the pieces to a puzzle were beginning to fit together. There was indeed domestic abuse going on at the Baker trailer. The actual perpetrator of that abuse was not who he initially suspected.

Lansing had to consolidate all the information he had gathered and present it to the County Prosecutor. That wouldn't be until Monday. He hoped the Abilene Police could supply more fodder for his case. If they didn't, he was sure he had enough to take to a Grand Jury. At a minimum, he felt Karen Baker would face Second Degree Murder charges.

Chapter Forty-Five

Pauline and Joy Baca sat at the dining room table working on new pottery. Their technique was a thousand years old, handed down from generation to generation. A ball of clay was rolled on a flat surface to make a "rope." The rope was placed against an inverted mold. Building from the "top," down, the ropes were layered, pressed together, then smoothed flat each time a new rope was added.

This formed the outer walls of the vessel being made. It took days to prepare the clay before it could be worked. Once the basic pottery piece was built, it took hours to smooth the surface using watery clay and wooden tools. The process took longer if a motif was to be etched onto the surface. It took several days to completely dry the object before it could be fired in a kiln.

No Pueblo artisan would stoop to using clay from an art supply store. The making of pottery was a sacred act. Even though the works were sold, sometimes for thousands of dollars, the process of making each item was a spiritual endeavor.

Pauline hadn't remarked about her daughter's silence, but finally she had to ask, "What's bothering you?"

"Nothing," Joy said. She was being as honest as she could. "I just didn't sleep well."

"Something is bothering you. Are you worried about your brother?"

Joy shook her head. As a wildland firefighter, it wasn't unusual for Lincoln to be gone for days, even weeks at a time. He was off hiking somewhere. He knew how to handle himself. If anything, his absence was a convenience for her. She didn't have to beg to use his truck.

"Did you have an argument with Eric?"

'No, of course not."

She could have mentioned her boyfriend's attempt at having sex, but she didn't want to sour her parents' opinion of him. He backed off immediately when she demanded it. She admitted to herself her exposure to different men was very limited. She cared for Eric very much. However, she secretly hoped one day she would meet a man who would sweep her off her feet.

"Then why couldn't you sleep?"

"I kept waking up . . . I thought someone was in my room."

Pauline thought for a moment. "You didn't go outside last night, did you?"

"No. Why?"

"When your father got up this morning the front door was open."

"Mamma! Do you think someone broke into our house last night?"

"Good Lord, I hope not. You didn't see anyone in your room, did you?"

"No." Joy's voice quavered with worry. "It was just a feeling I had."

"We'll all have to be more careful," Pauline said. "I haven't heard of any break-ins around the Pueblo, but that doesn't mean it couldn't happen."

The two women continued to work on their pieces for another hour. Joy finally pushed herself away from the table.

Pauline looked up. "What's wrong?"

"I need to walk around for a while," she said, standing and stretching.

"Are you finished for the day?"

"No. I'll come back," she said, covering the mound of clay and her creation with a damp cloth.

It was cool when Joy stepped outside. The high for the day wouldn't reach 80°. A typically sunny, New Mexico morning, other neighbors stirred. Across the street, Mrs. Delgado was building a fire in her *horno*, the dried mud oven so few in the Pueblo still used. Further down, people worked in their family gardens.

Trying to decide whether or not to take a stroll, her thoughts were interrupted by the loud whistle of a bird. She looked up. On a branch, ten feet above her sat a bird gazing at her. It was large, at least 15 inches tall. Easily the size of a hawk, it had a hooked beak . . . just like a hawk.

What fascinated Joy was the bird was all grey. The head was light grey, the rest of the feathers darker. There were two distinctive horizontal white stripes on the tail. She had never seen such a bird before.

It was foreign to New Mexico, even to the United States. Called a Plumbeous Kite, it was common in Central America. It could range as far north as the Mexican states of Veracruz, Puebla, and Tlaxcala, but never further. The *tlahuelpuchi* had made a minor mistake by taking the form of a bird she was familiar with.

Fernanda Huerta hoped she never had to revert to the confining life of an insect again. As a bird, she had the freedom she needed. The tree next to the Baca house provided a home. The night would let her take her human shape, the only form that allowed her to feed.

Chapter Forty-Six

The Spanish conquest of New Mexico was sporadic, misguided, and bloody.

The first significant venture into the region was by Francisco Coronado in 1540. Only 19 years after Hernando Cortez defeated the Aztec Empire, Coronado was lured by the stories of the Seven Golden Cities of Cibola. He left New Spain with 350 Spanish soldiers, nearly 2,000 Mexican Indian allies, 559 horses, along with cattle and other livestock.

Coronado's first New Mexico conquest was Zuni Pueblo. The Zuni people were subjugated by force when they refused to accept the Spanish King's rule. Wintering on the Rio Grande near present-day Albuquerque, he came into conflict with the surrounding Tiwa Pueblos. The Tiguex War, as it was called, lasted for four months. By March 1541, every Tiwa speaking Pueblo except Sandia had been destroyed, the inhabitants either killed or scattered.

Coronado's forays reached as far north as the Grand Canyon and central Kansas. Ultimately defeated by the fact that his expedition found no riches, the explorer returned to New Spain in 1542 with his remaining 100 men.

New Mexico was essentially ignored for the next 50 years. English mischief in the New World prompted the Spanish Crown's renewed interest in exploiting the territory. It wasn't until 1598 that Don Juan Oñate launched an expedition to conquer the region. He had 129 soldiers, 83 wagons, 600 Spanish settlers, and 7,000 head of stock. There were also priests to convert the heathen and an untold number of Mexican Indians.

Proceeding north and encountering various Indian pueblos, Oñate took possession of the territory in the name of Spain through elaborate ceremonies. The natives were told they were now subjects of the Spanish king. Many of the new citizens surrendered only because of the threat of force. They were told how pointless it would be to resist the new over-lords.

To reinforce this notion of Spanish invincibility, they told the natives about how they vanquished the great king of the Aztecs, Montezuma. Thousands of Aztec warriors were destroyed by a handful of soldiers and their superior weapons. (The conquistadors conveniently left out the part where hundreds of Indian allies subjugated by the Aztecs joined in the fray.)

These stories about the defeated king had the opposite effect. Instead of instilling fear in the newly conquered, the legend of Montezuma spread among the Pueblo people. He was not viewed as a defeated enemy of the Spanish. A myth evolved that Montezuma was a great shaman who possessed mystical powers.

It was claimed he was born among the Rio Grande Indians where he became a great leader. He took a Zuni girl as his bride and queen, then flew south on a great eagle to build Tenochtitlán, the capital of his empire. By the time of the 1680 Revolt, Montezuma had been incorpo-rated entirely into the folklore of the Pueblo Indians.

Eventually, other tribes beyond the Rio Grande absorbed the Monte-zuma mythos as their own. He became a cultural hero for the Navajo, Apache, even the Pima. If it had not been for the treacherous Spaniards, it was claimed the Aztec king would have eventually ruled all the Indian tribes in the Americas.

A legend grew regarding the sacred fire Montezuma created before he flew to Mexico to build the Aztec Empire. If a person discovered it, some claimed they would be given eternal life. Others insisted the individual would be granted spiritual enlightenment.

Whatever the case, the Aztec leader was always accompanied by his *viborón*, a monster rattlesnake. Many claimed to have seen the mythical monster. Others had only seen its slithering tracks in the snow or sand. Praying to Montezuma, many shamans claimed the snake could be called upon to invoke justice where justice was needed.

Chapter Forty-Seven

The Turkey Vultures made wide circles in the sky. Often called buzzards, there were a dozen of them. Along with crows and ravens, they were the daytime scavengers. Coyotes, wild dogs, and occasionally skunks dined on the fallen prey at night.

For a long time, the airborne sanitation engineers had been plying their trade further south, clearing the aftermath of the Cerro Grande Fire. However, the fire had been out for well over a month, and the carrion eaters were searching in their old haunts again.

Sheriff Cliff Lansing had seen similar sights thousands of times in the cloudless, New Mexico skies. The vultures were a vital part of nature. Consuming the rotting flesh of dead animals, they prevented the spread of deadly diseases like anthrax, rabies, and cholera.

County Road 313 ran along the southern perimeter of the Lansing ranch. An anonymous caller reported seeing the vultures zeroing in on a meal a mile west of Highway 15.

Lansing assigned himself the task of checking on it. First off, it got him out of the office. Secondly, a part of him wanted to take a look at the carcass. He guessed the scavengers had spotted a dead deer, or possibly a steer. Deep inside, he wasn't sure if it was the rancher side of him whose interest was piqued or the lawman side.

Turning off Highway 15, the dirt road took him past a wooded hill. Heading west, the surroundings became flat, scrub desert, typical for that part of the county. The soil that supported stunted grasses and thick sage was only good for grazing. Barbed-wire fences lined the one-lane track.

A mile past the hill, the vultures circled above a clump of sage plants along the Lansing Ranch fence line. The sage was so thick it completely hid the fence. It also hid the vultures' target.

Lansing stopped his Jeep and got out for a closer look.

Pushing the brush aside as he walked the fence line, he finally found what he was looking for. However, it was not what he expected, not what he wanted to find. It was a human foot . . . a bare, human foot.

Pulling the sagebrush aside, he found the body the foot was attached to. It was a woman. By the sheriff's estimate, she wasn't much more than a girl in her late teens, or early twenties. The damage looked too familiar. At first glance, he was positive she was the victim of a hit-and-run.

"Dispatch," he said into the jeep's radio. "This is Patrol One."

"This is dispatch. Go ahead, Sheriff."

"Roger, Sid. I'm about a mile west of Highway Fifteen on County Road three-thirteen. I have a deceased female. It looks like another hit-and-run. I need Deputy Trumbull and her forensics kit out here. I'll also need an ambulance for transport. Copy?"

"Copied all, Sheriff."

***

Lansing hated doing nothing. He thought about pulling the sage away from the body. He knew that was a bad idea, though. Marla Trumbull needed to gather the evidence before anything should be removed.

He pulled out his cell phone, found the number he wanted, then hit dial.

After three rings, Jack Rivera answered. *"Hey, Cliff."*

"You're not busy, are you?"

"I was thinking about mowing the weeds before they got too deep. What's up?"

"I have a dead girl . . . Looks like another hit-and-run."

"*Damn! Where'd you find her?*"

"Along the fence line of my property. Some concerned citizen called it in."

"*They found the body?*"

"No. They were worried about circling vultures."

"*Do you need me there?*"

"Not really. I'm killing time till forensics gets here. That and an ambulance."

"*I don't mind. If I wait a week and don't water the lawn, those weeds will die. Then I won't have to worry about mowing.*"

"The more, the merrier. I'm on County Road three-thirteen, a mile off the highway."

"*See you in a bit.*"

Chapter Forty-Eight

Marla Trumbull took a series of photos of the surrounding area and the body before the sagebrush was removed. There was no apparent forensic evidence to collect. Lansing, Rivera, and Trumbull pulled the sage away from the victim for a better look.

"I think she's been dead for three or four days," Trumbull said, crinkling her nose. "The body is well past rigor mortis."

Rigor Mortis, or postmortem rigidity, usually begins to set in 2 hours after death. It starts with the facial muscles and progresses to the rest of the body. The process normally takes 6 to 8 hours. After that, the body can remain in rigor for another twelve hours. Twenty-four hours after death the process is complete, and the muscles relax again.

"But she hasn't been out in the open," Rivera observed. "There's hardly any animal activity."

"Somebody dumped her here recently." Lansing turned to his chief deputy. "It looks like her shirt has a logo. Do you recognize it?"

Rivera shook his head. "It's not familiar." He looked closer. "*Mike's Burger Barn.* Never heard of it."

"We need to find out where that is?"

The ambulance Lansing ordered was finally pulling up. The attendants, a man and a woman, removed a body bag from the back and approached. The ground was too rugged for the wheels of the stretcher, so it remained in the vehicle.

Lansing and his officers moved out of the way. As the workers positioned the victim in the body bag, the damage to the body became more apparent. The poor woman had been run over at least twice. Before closing the bag, Trumbull took the corpse's fingerprints. No one expected the prints would show up on any database. This was simply procedure.

Few words were spoken. Lansing signed the release form, allowing the body to be taken to Albuquerque for autopsy. One attendant wrote the case number on a piece of paper and handed it to the sheriff. From the arrival of the ambulance to its departure took less than ten minutes.

"I'll go to the office and download these photos," Deputy Trumbull said.

"Good," Lansing agreed. "Scan in those prints, as well."

"Will do. Anything else?"

"I'll follow you there. If I think of anything else, I'll let you know."

"Do you want me to come in?" Rivera asked as the other deputy pulled away.

The sheriff shook his head. "No. Go enjoy the rest of your week-end. Thanks for coming out and keeping me company."

"No problem."

After the others left, Lansing sat in his jeep mulling over the situation. It was obvious to him the anonymous caller knew what had attracted the buzzards. The caller put the body there. It followed that the caller was probably the killer, which immediately eliminated Karen Baker as a suspect.

If the Bakers weren't responsible for this death, they probably had nothing to do with the body found at San Juan Pueblo. Another killer was out there. He would need Deputy Barnes to see if he could trace the source of the anonymous call.

About to start his engine, his cell phone rang. He recognized the area code because he had dialed it earlier.

"Sheriff Lansing."

"*Yes, Sheriff. This is Lieutenant Harris, Abilene Police.*"

"Yes. Thank you for getting back to me."

"*What can I help you with?*"

"I have a woman in custody for shooting her husband. She's from your town . . ."

"*I saw the note from the call center. Karen Baker, right?*"

"That's her. I wanted to know if your department had any dealings with the couple."

"*The Battling Bakers . . .*" Harris chuckled. "*We're way too familiar with them. How badly was Billy hurt?*"

"Mr. Baker is extremely dead. Shotgun blast to the chest. I got the autopsy results this morning. The examiner said they found a lot of defensive wounds on the body, especially the arms. They weren't all recent, either. His face had been scalded with a hot liquid the morning he was shot."

"*You're holding Miss Karen for murder, then?*"

"She's claiming self-defense. I wanted to find out how valid that claim could be."

"*The Bakers never called the police or filed charges against each other. We only went to their place because of complaints from the neighbors. From my experience and from the reports I saw, the wife never had a scratch on her. Poor Billy is the one who caught all the grief. But there was never any gunplay. None that I heard of, anyway.*"

"So, Mrs. Baker's claim of self-defense is bogus."

"*Actually, Sheriff,*" the police lieutenant said, thoughtfully. "*It could be legitimate. Maybe Billy got tired of being a punching bag. He might have finally stood up for himself. If he did, that probably scared the crap out of Karen. She could have shot him because he was hitting back. It was the only way she could stop him . . . Have you charged her?*"

144

"Right now, I'm holding her on other charges. She won't see a judge until Monday. Plus, I still need to give the county prosecutor my evidence. He's the one who'll decide what charges to bring."

"Well, good luck, Sheriff. If there's anything you need from my department, don't hesitate to ask."

"I won't, Lieutenant. Thanks for calling on a Saturday."

Chapter Forty-Nine

"I've been wanting to ask you . . ." Peter Delgado stopped tapping on the drumhead to check the tautness. The drum was a cast-iron, potbellied kettle with three legs, half-filled with water. The buckskin head would produce a deep, resonant sound. "Why here?"

Jeremiah Black interrupted his own preparations for the evening. "Are you talking about this building? It's all I can afford."

"No, no. Why San Phillipe County? Why New Mexico?"

Black knew he had started his new church because of basic differences with the Oklahoma Native American Church elders. He knew the healing powers of the church services and the medicinal effect of peyote. He had seen lifelong alcoholics turn away from their addiction. He had seen domestic abusers face their cruelty and become more caring partners. He had known families to become closer and more loving.

The Native American Church considered the peyote cactus sacred and should only be used by church members. Jeremiah thought the healing process so protected by Native Americans should be available to all people. His beliefs were not welcome in his community.

"I'm trying to expand the reach of the church," the roadman said. It was a true statement, though incomplete. "I chose this place because of all the pueblos in the area. I hope others will follow my lead and strive to become priests in the church."

Delgado nodded, seemingly satisfied with the answer. Both he and the fireman, John Salazar, were from Ohkay Owingeh Pueblo. Delgado was an experienced drummer. He had participated in the Pueblo Dances and Ceremonies for twenty years, ever since he was a teen.

Jeremiah's church was less than a mile from the San Juan Pueblo Reservation. It made sense to look there first for willing participants.

Delgado was intrigued and managed to rope Salazar into attending with him. After their first night, they became dedicated converts.

Salazar was busy bringing dried cedarwood in from his truck. As the fireman, it was his duty to make sure the fire in the center of the gathering lasted through the ceremonies. The fire was contained in a metal pan. Participants sat in a circle around it. All the windows were open to keep the smoke, what little there was, from filling the room.

The church services Jeremiah Black attended in Oklahoma had been conducted in teepees. As many as twenty members could gather at one time. He hoped to eventually have his own traditional structure for future ceremonies. Even the Navajo, noted for their log and earthen dwellings called hogans, used teepees for their Native American Church services.

It was still a couple of hours before the first ceremony. Jeremiah knelt and rebuilt the foot-tall earthen altar. He would face west. The altar formed a crescent with the horns pointing east. The tips sloped gradually up to a flat space to cradle the peyote. A single groove was scratched through the middle of the crescent from one end to the other, symbolizing a soul's journey from birth to death.

He removed his paraphernalia from a cloth satchel: a fan of pheasant feathers, a beaded gourd rattle, an eagle bone whistle, a smoke stick, cigarette papers, and a pouch of cedar incense. Other sacred items were added: shredded tobacco, sage sticks, and peyote buttons.

All participants would sit in a circle. Delgado, the drummer, would be to the roadman's right, Salazar, the fireman, to his left.

The first ceremony involved prayers while making cigarettes. Jeremiah would begin, then pass the items to his right. Once everyone had made their cigarettes, the smoke stick would be passed around and the sacred tobacco would be smoked.

The incense blessing ceremony would come next. The roadman would remove his peyote buttons from the sack, then pass the bag to Delgado. Each member of the circle would be instructed to take only four buttons. For the inexperienced, four buttons would produce all the hallucinogenic effects they could handle without inducing psychosis. Nausea was not uncommon.

Before ingesting the cactus, the attendees needed to be sanctified. Jeremiah would crush a sprig of sage in his hand, inhale the aromatic essence, then rub his head, torso, arms, thighs, and legs with the herb. Each participant would copy his actions.

Once the incense blessing ceremony was complete, the members would consume the sacred peyote, spitting out the wooly centers. Throughout the entire experience, Delgado would maintain a steady cadence on the drum. It would become a beat not dissimilar to a throbbing heart.

A night of prayer, thanks, and contrite confessions would fill the night hours, not ending until dawn. It wasn't unusual for attendees to request special prayers to address a specific problem. Even as an experienced priest, however, Jeremiah Black was not completely prepared for the request he got that night.

Chapter Fifty

Tomas Hidalgo was a familiar face to Jeremiah. He was from Pojoaque Pueblo just south of Segovia. This would be his third time attending a ceremony. Behind him stood a man and a woman Black had never seen before.

"Tomas, I am glad to see you here tonight."

The roadman stood outside his building to greet attendees. The sun had already slipped below the Jemez mountains to the west and twilight wrapped itself around the countryside. Official sunset wasn't for another twenty minutes, five minutes before 8:00 . . . the time the ceremony would begin.

"Jeremiah," Hidalgo nodded. "I brought friends. Pedro and Alaina Sena."

"All are welcome here," Black said, addressing the couple. He noticed their solemn looks.

Hidalgo motioned for them to step closer. "The Senas are here with a special request."

"I see. What can I help you with?"

"Our granddaughter is dead," Pedro Sena said. "Someone killed her. We want to find out who did it."

"I'm sorry to hear that." Jeremiah frowned. "But isn't that something for the police?"

"We've talked to the Sheriff's office, the pueblo police, even the Segovia police department. They said they've found nothing."

"Where did she die?"

"No one knows," Tomas admitted. He pointed at the road. "Her body was dumped along there, a half-mile from here. Just inside the San Juan Reservation."

"That was your granddaughter?" Jeremiah asked. "A sheriff's deputy came by and asked if I had seen anything Tuesday. I told him I hadn't. I had been at work . . . but I don't understand what you want me to do. We can pray to the Great Spirit and seek his guidance. But isn't that something you could do at your own church?"

"No, no," Alaina said desperately. "Tomas says you have visions. You eat your dried cactus, and you see things. We want you to find who murdered our Regina."

"That's not how peyote works. It is a narcotic. It produces visual . . ." He hesitated to use the term. ". . . hallucinations. It expands your perception of the world around you. After you take it . . . and after several minutes . . . you'll start to see bright colors. They'll pulsate and dance around you. You'll smell things. You'll hear things. But I assure you, nothing will be real."

"Tomas said the first time he took the peyote he saw God," Pedro insisted. "Couldn't we take it to see who hurt our Regina? Couldn't you?"

The roadman was perturbed by the request. The peyote ceremony was a spiritual quest for enlightenment. The Senas wanted a magic act . . . someone with a crystal ball who claimed to be able to see all and know all.

"Mr. Sena, ma'am, you are welcome to attend our ceremonies. I would very much hope you will participate. We can ask the Great Spirit for help. I'm sure he already knows what you need. Other than that, I cannot promise you anything."

Black saw the pain and disappointment in their faces. The couple turned and walked a few paces away. Speaking in hushed tones, their debate lasted only a couple of minutes. Returning to Black and Hidalgo, the husband and wife nodded.

"We will participate in your ceremonies," Pedro said.

Chapter Fifty-One

Santa Clara Pueblo was dark at night. Only Key Street where the government offices were located had streetlights. There were higher priorities for the limited pueblo finances than running lights from dusk till dawn.

Most homes had lights near the front door. They were not porch lights. Most houses didn't have porches or coverings over the front door. In any case, no one left their lights on all night long.

When Joy stepped outside and closed the door behind her, only interior lights showed from the homes around her. With so little light pollution the stars glistened brightly. She looked up at the tree in the yard. The large, grey bird was gone. Out foraging, the teen guessed.

Little did she know how accurate that guess was.

Lost in her thoughts about Eric Gonzalez she didn't notice the shadow staring at her from the corner of her house. Even if she had seen it, there was nothing to fear. The *tlahuelpuchi* had no interest in her. Fernanda had designs on other poor souls . . . children too young to realize what was happening to them.

A shudder suddenly racked the pueblo girl's body. It was cool outside, but hardly enough, Joy thought, that she should shiver so violently. She immediately turned and went back inside, wishing she had worn a sweater.

Once she was in her bedroom, she stared at Izel, the doll she found in the Gonzalez yard the day before. When she first brought the porcelain beauty home, she appeared lifelike, almost animated. It was scary how human Izel seemed. Tonight, though, the doll was lifeless, dull. It was as if a spark had been extinguished. A wave of sadness washed over her. She felt like she had lost a friend.

Fernanda stretched, reveling in her human form. She waited patiently, watching as window lights darkened, one by one. It wouldn't be long before she could once more feed.

Chapter Fifty-Two

Lansing finished eating and pushed his plate away.

"You didn't eat much," Tina observed. She noted his brooding but didn't bring it up. When Cliff Lansing was ready to talk about what bothered him, he would.

"I ate enough."

She stood and picked up the dinner plates. "What did you think of Oscar's horse?"

"I don't know what he had to choose from, but I think he did alright." He stood as well. "Need help with the dishes?"

"I won't turn it down."

Tina washed and rinsed. Lansing dried.

Tina did all the talking, mostly about her visit to Loma Amarilla Ranch. There had been several improvements made, mostly with the fencing. With the mustang "gentling" program, the management could be selective on which horses would be kept in the herd. They could retain those horses with the most genetic markers for original Spanish bloodlines. With new additions and new foals, the herd stood at sixty horses now.

Lansing feigned interest with an occasional nod and an "Uh-huh," grunt.

Once the dishes were finished and the kitchen was clean, the two retired to the living room . . . Lansing on one end of the sofa with a whiskey, Tina at the other end with a glass of white wine.

After two sips of his bourbon, Lansing finally opened up. "I forgot to mention yesterday that we learned the name of the young lady we found at San Juan . . . Regina Sena. She was from Pojoaque Pueblo."

"How did she end up so far north?"

"Her body was dumped there. Just like the one I found along my property line." He paused and took another sip. "Both murders were done by the same person. The MO is identical. Right now, he's playing with us. He's the same guy who called my office to report the vultures. He knew there was a dead body there."

"Why do you say that?"

"He couldn't have seen any vultures from the highway. A hill blocks the view. He wanted us to find his victim."

"So, are you talking about a serial killer?"

"Not yet. We only have two murders. A third death will make these serial killings."

"That's because the hit-and-run near Navajo Lake was done by someone else?"

"Yup." He took another sip. "And we know who that is . . . well, we almost know who it is. According to Karen Baker, it was her husband, who is conveniently dead."

"You don't believe her?"

"To be honest, I don't believe anything that comes out of that woman's mouth. We had to bring her before a magistrate today. We charged her as an accessory to the hit-and-run. I'm hoping the county prosecutor upgrades the charges. We'll see."

The two sat silently, engrossed in their own thoughts, but still enjoying each other's company.

"Cliff, tell me the truth," Tina said, interrupting the quiet. "Are you worried about the primary?"

"No. Why should I be?"

"I don't know. You don't talk about it much."

"Nothing to talk about. I'm running for re-election. Some idiot councilman from Segovia is running against me. If I lose, I can retire to my ranch. Tapia is welcome to the job and all the headaches that come with it."

"You don't really mean that, do you?"

"No," he said, frowning. "My big concern is he will run off all my deputies and recruit a bunch of idiots like himself. San Phillipe may never recover. I won't be the only loser. Every person in this county will suffer under him."

"You're ahead in the polls. Do you think Tapia can beat you?"

"I hope not. It won't happen unless he pulls some dirty trick."

"Like what?"

The sheriff shrugged and finished his drink. "I have no idea, but I'm sure we'll recognize it when it happens." He got up from the sofa. "More wine?"

Chapter Fifty-Three

Lincoln Baca stared at the dancing flame. It was Saturday, midnight. He hadn't eaten since Thursday. The pangs of hunger and the thoughts of food had subsided.

He repeated his ritual at the spring earlier in the day. As he washed, he gingerly touched the gash above his eye. It was healing slowly. It was sticky, not having scabbed over completely. He couldn't help but wonder how bad it looked.

After he washed his body in the freezing water, he purified himself with smoke from his sage bundle. As he sat in the quiet canyon, he tried to remember how many times he had done the ritual. At least twice. Was it more? He couldn't remember.

Montezuma said he would return when Lincoln was ready.

That had been the night before . . . or had it been longer than that?

The more he fasted, the more acute his senses had become. There were smells he'd never noticed before. He swore he could hear an insect scurrying across the broken stones of the canyon. Only the concept of time seemed to elude him.

He had spent the day next to the stone circle. He hadn't completely recovered from his concussion. Waves of dizziness still washed over him. Closing his eyes and sitting quietly gave him relief. It gave him an added benefit. With his eyes closed his mind drifted off to places he'd never imagined. For minutes, maybe hours at a time, he escaped the real world.

The canyon became physical again when he heard the crunch of gravel behind him. But was it real, or an extension of his vision quest?

He remained completely still with his eyes closed.

Steps grew closer. Suddenly, he felt the hot breath against his neck. Then a sniff, followed by several more. A deep rumble came from the creature behind him.

At another time, in a different place, Lincoln Baca would have been frightened at this encounter. That day, though, he wasn't. He sensed the bear had no particular interest in him. It was only curious.

The visit was brief, and Baca listened to the footsteps fade as they continued out of the canyon. As Lincoln's mind drifted again, he couldn't tell if his experience had been real or imagined.

He only realized it was dark when he heard coyotes howling at each other. He opened his eyes to be greeted by Montezuma's fire. The brisk chill of the mountain air didn't bother him anymore.

He stood and stretched his legs. His thoughts were about the Aztec King. Would Montezuma return that night? He said he would return when Baca was ready.

Lincoln wasn't sure what that meant. The more he thought about it, he began having doubts that Montezuma visited him. The doctor's pamphlet listed hallucinations as a symptom of a brain tumor. He could have imagined it, just like he imagined the bear. He was feeling like a fool. He was wasting his time and energy on . . . what?

Baca's thoughts of self-ridicule were interrupted by the screech/scream of a mountain lion. It came from the far end of the canyon, beyond the fire.

The Puebloan turned slowly to face the sound.

Two eyes reflected the light of the fire. The animal repeated his threat.

Baca stood his ground. Again, fear failed to seize him. Whether the big cat was real or not didn't matter.

The lion approached, stopping short of the fire, eyeing the lone man in the canyon. The two stared at each other for a very long time. The animal finally let out what Baca could only describe as a loud "meow," turned, and disappeared into the darkness.

Once he was alone again, Lincoln wondered if he'd actually met a mountain lion in the canyon.

He took his seat in front of the fire again. An internal debate ensued. If his vision quest was to succeed, he had to embrace these encounters. The bear, the mountain lion, even Montezuma, had to be real, not products of his imagination. Accepting them as real could open his mind to even more possibilities.

Closing his eyes, he tried to clear his mind, but a small thought kept poking the back of his brain. "What else will I see while I wait for Montezuma's return?"

Chapter Fifty-Four

Lincoln slipped into his Dream State again. He didn't know if he was awake or asleep.

He felt himself floating. He opened his eyes and looked down. He saw himself sitting in front of Montezuma's Fire. There was no moon. The canopy of stars illuminated everything.

He closed his mind's eye and felt transported. When he opened it again, he was standing in front of his own home. It was still night. No lights shone from any house on the street.

From the corner of his eye, he saw movement. He turned his head to see the form of a young woman stepping from around the corner of the house. The shape glowed from a light within. He could see her face. She was the most beautiful creature he had ever seen in his life.

As she stepped/glided across the yard he tried to speak to her, but he had no voice. She didn't notice him, even though she passed close enough that he could touch her.

The woman continued across the yard, past Baca's truck, past his father's truck. Without hesitating, the fantom proceeded across the street to the closest house. Lincoln followed. When she reached the house, she opened the door quietly and glided inside.

The former firefighter stood outside the now-closed door. What was the woman doing? Why did she come to this house? He needed to know.

Willing himself forward, he found himself stepping through the solid door. He had been in this house hundreds of times. He had known the Chavarria family his entire life. Three generations lived there. Only six months earlier, a fourth-generation had joined the household.

What attracted the fantom beauty to this home?

The rooms were small and crowded. The large family room gave way to a short hallway and four bedrooms. The girl had disappeared. Even though he knew he could pass through solid walls, he respected the family's privacy. He listened for any sound that would betray the girl's location.

From a bedroom came the whimper of a child. The baby sounded uncomfortable . . . maybe annoyed . . . as if someone had disturbed it.

Lincoln found the door open. The mysterious young woman was bent over the crib. The parents, not much older than the fireman, lay asleep just a few feet away. They were oblivious to their baby's discomfort.

Lincoln moved closer to see what was happening.

Somehow, his fantom beauty sensed another presence. She turned and looked in his direction. She still could not see him. But he could see her. He could see her face. She was no longer the beautiful vision he had seen outside his house. She looked like a demon. Her face was a mask of terror. He could see the tiny drop of blood at the corner of her mouth.

He jumped back in horror, falling backward onto the canyon floor.

He was in front of Montezuma's Fire again, confused.

What had he just witnessed? Was this an omen? A premonition about what might happen? Or had he watched the incident in real-time?

The cold mountain air enveloped him. He began to shiver. Moving closer to the fire he tried to warm himself. There were no more thoughts about closing his eyes and attempting to dream again. He wasn't sure if he wanted to ever sleep again.

He wanted daylight. More than that, though, he needed to meet Montezuma once more. Lincoln had slipped into a world he didn't understand. A world that scared the hell out of him. He had to know what it meant.

Chapter Fifty-Five

Jeremiah Black stood outside his church, alone, finishing his third cup of coffee. The blue, cloudless sky and the bright sun warmed his soul. Peter Delgado and John Salazar had remained after all the other congregants had left to help clean, but they were gone now.

**

Black's service began at 8:00 the previous evening and lasted until 6:00 that morning. A total of twelve people attended, eight men, and four women. Pedro and Alaina Sena were the only new members. The rituals were probably strange to them, Black guessed. But they watched the others and participated completely.

There was never any need to rush the activities. The making of the cigarettes, the passing of the lighting stick, and the purification ritual all took time. Each action prompted a prayer of thanks. The invocations were spoken in the English, Spanish, and Tewa languages, whatever the individual found most comfortable.

Peter Delgado's drumbeat gave life to the otherwise seemingly slow rituals. The greatest pause in the activities came when the participants ate their peyote buttons, spitting out the wooly centers. Nausea quite often followed once the peyote was ingested. Alaina Sena and another woman had to throw up. Plastic buckets had been strategically placed to accommodate such needs. For the rest of the night, prayers were said, songs were sung, supported by the rhythms of the drum and gourd rattle.

Each participant experienced similar effects of the mescaline narcotic. They passed through stages. At first, there was a wave of euphoria... a feeling of vitality and rebirth. Slowly each person was consumed with overwhelming sadness, even a sense of impending death. The depth of the depression depended on how much hopelessness they carried with them in their daily life. As the narcotic took effect the misery and despair faded to a numbing pain in the head.

The fire at the center of their circle became a focal point. The dancing flames fractured into shards of bright colors . . . reds and yellows, greens and blues. In the distance they heard Salazar's drum and Black's rattle, pounding rhythmically to the beats of their own hearts.

Each member of the circle took four buttons of the dried cactus. It was enough for them to reach a mild level of hallucination. During a normal service, Black himself usually consumed six to eight buttons to gain the same effect. That night, because of the Sena's request, he felt compelled to ingest twice his usual amount. He had taken as many as sixteen buttons before and knew he could handle that amount.

Black guided the prayers and songs. He began the process by professing his own thanks.

"Great Spirit . . . Creator of all things . . . Thank you for this night. Thank you for this gathering of souls . . . Souls who humbly implore your guidance, who seek your help. Allow each one of us to express our deepest fears and our greatest needs. Open our hearts and minds to receive your counsel."

He nodded to Salazar, who expressed what he was grateful for while keeping a steady beat on his drum. Once he finished, the next person in the circle offered their prayer of thanks. The invocations continued, each individual accepting the opportunity when it came to their turn.

Alaina Sena's voice quavered when she spoke. "I cannot give thanks because my heart is heavy. My granddaughter was taken from us. She was murdered. I ask one thing. That You reveal the man who killed her. Let there be justice in this life, so we can give thanks to You."

The roadman listened to each person's words, though the voices seemed distant. His visual hallucinations pulsated with the beat of the drum. He kept cadence with the gourd rattle, unconscious of the fact that he was doing it. His psychedelic journey came to an abrupt end when the suffering woman began speaking. Her voice was clear and close by.

His vision shrunk to a single point of light. He wanted a vision. He wanted to see what happened to Regina Sena. He hoped the saturation of mescaline would transport him back to the night the girl was murdered.

The point of light exploded into a kaleidoscope of colors. They danced and pulsated to the drumbeat, as they had before. No matter how hard he tried, Black could not summon an out-of-body experience. There was no hallucinogenic vision. Only the drug-induced distortion of reality.

***

As dawn broke, the effects of the mescaline/peyote dissipated. A wave of relief, even joy, washed over the participants. The Senas joined the others in smiles. They didn't know if their prayers were answered, but they knew their psyches had been touched. The grief they brought to the meeting, though not gone completely, was less debilitating.

A thirty-cup electric coffee maker finished brewing and Salazar brought in a basket of sweet rolls his wife had prepared the day before. The attendees enjoyed the modest breakfast. There were suggestions that they all go to the Segovia Denny's for a full meal. A few agreed to meet there. Jeremiah Black and his assistants declined. They had work to do.

Before Pedro and Alaina Sena left, they approached Black.

"We both thank you for allowing us to attend your service," Pedro said.

"You are welcome any time. I hope you found what you were looking for."

Black could see the questioning looks on the couple's faces. "Had he seen anything?" A part of him wanted to say he did have a vision, but he still couldn't tell them who killed their granddaughter. That would have been a giant lie. Instead, he simply shook his head. He could feel their pain as they left, disappointed.

***

As Black closed the door to his church, a familiar lowrider pulled off the asphalt road. Kicking up dust as it approached, it slowed to a stop in front of Black. Chaparro was accompanied by three friends.

"Hey, preacher man, when do the services start?"

"About twelve hours ago." Jeremiah Black turned and headed for his trailer for a long nap, leaving the lowriders more than a little confused.

Chapter Fifty-Six

Father Roberto stood outside the church, saying goodbye to his parishioners. He smiled broadly when Lansing and Tina Morales approached.

"I'm so glad to see you both here again," he said, extending his hand. He grasped Tina's first, then the sheriff's.

"We agreed there was something missing in our lives," Tina admitted. "That was a wonderful sermon."

Lansing nodded, without saying anything.

"I'm glad you enjoyed it." He looked directly at Lansing. "I hope you make attendance a regular thing again."

Again, the sheriff only nodded.

Father Roberto was used to Lansing saying little. He guessed the nod was as close a commitment as he'd get from the man. He made the sign of the cross and said, "*Vaya con Dios.*"

***

"You didn't say much back there," Tina observed as they drove back to the ranch.

" 'Silence is golden.' Isn't it?"

"Sometimes you can be too silent." She studied her partner for a moment. "Are you still angry with Father Roberto?"

"Anger's an empty emotion. It just wastes energy. I'll admit it did feel good to go to mass today. But as far as the father goes, I can take him or leave him. I could care less about what he thinks of our relationship."

"Good." She reached over and squeezed his hand.

"So, you still want to take the horses out his afternoon?"

"You're not going to your office today?"

"I'm entitled to a day off once in a while. Besides, Jack Rivera's on duty today. He can handle any calls."

"Are we inviting Oscar?"

"Absolutely. I want to see how 'gentle' his new mustang really is."

"I'll pack sandwiches. We can have a picnic of sorts."

"Sounds like a plan."

Chapter Fifty-Seven

"Where did you go last night?" Pauline Baca asked. She was in the kitchen, washing the breakfast dishes.

"What do you mean?" Joy was still at the dining room table. "I didn't go anywhere." She gave her mother a funny look.

"One of the neighbors said they saw you last night."

"I went outside for just a moment, but it was chilly. I came right back in. You saw me."

"I know about that. I'm talking about later . . . after midnight."

"I was in bed." Joy came into the kitchen. "Who said I was out after midnight? Wait. Let me guess. Emily Diaz. That old woman loves to spy on everyone."

If the people of Santa Clara Pueblo had one common sin, it was gossip. Ethnographers noted in the 1930s that neighbors in the pueblo loved to talk about each other behind their backs. Not all the gossip was necessarily friendly, either. Though the habit had been eradicated through most of the population, there were some who still hung onto the old ways.

"What did Emily tell you?"

Pauline didn't try to deny the source. "She said you were in the yard with some sort of flashlight. She said it wasn't very bright, but it was enough to see you. She said you went across the street and went inside the Chavarria's house."

"Why would I do that?"

"That's what I was going to ask you," her mother admitted. "Why did you go over there?"

"I didn't!" Joy snapped. "I don't know what or who that old hag saw, but it wasn't me!"

She started for the front door.

"Where are you going? You're not going to bother Emily Diaz, are you?"

"No. I'm going to talk to the Chavarrias. If someone went into their house last night, I want to make sure they know it wasn't me."

***

Despite being Sunday, the men of the Chavarria Clan had left to work in the fields. In the kitchen, Rosaland and her mother hovered over Jenny and her baby, Mateo. Joy couldn't help but notice the worried looks on their faces.

"What's wrong?"

"It's the baby," Rosalind said, almost in anguish. "Something bit him last night. He's sick this morning."

"Can I see?" Joy stepped closer.

Jenny looked up, tears in her eyes, and nodded. She gently un-wrapped the cotton blanket, revealing Mateo's naked, upper body. There was a large, swollen welt on the child's shoulder and neck. The redness told Joy there might be an infection. The baby had indeed been bitten.

Mateo barely squirmed. If anything, he was lethargic, lifeless.

"My God!" Joy exclaimed. "How long has he been like this?"

"I just got him up," the child's mother admitted. "It was time for his bottle. This is the way I found him."

"He needs to see a doctor!"

"We don't have a car!" Rosalind whimpered.

"I have my brother's truck. Rosaland, you and Jenny meet me across the street," Joy ordered. "I need to get the keys. It's only three miles to the hospital. We'll go straight to the emergency room."

***

"I can't figure out what's going on," Dr. Sam Baxter said.

Rajiv Garnapudi, the chief emergency room physician, looked up from the chart he was studying. "What are you talking about?"

"I've had two young children in the past three days with acute anemia."

"I heard about the four-year-old who came in Friday. There was another one?"

"This morning . . . a six-month-old boy. As soon as we got his blood type, we started an infusion. So far, he's responding well."

"That's the same treatment we used on the girl, isn't it?"

"It is. We admitted her for observation. I don't know if she's been released or not."

"What do you think is the common denominator?"

"That's just it. I haven't found anything, yet. The four-year-old girl is from a farming community up in the mountains. The baby boy who came in today is from Santa Clara Pueblo. They both had marks on their necks and shoulders . . ."

"Marks?"

"They looked like scratches. There was also some bruising. The boy's mother thought it was a bug bite."

"A bug bite won't cause anemia."

"I know that. I'm still waiting for a toxicology report on the girl. She might have been exposed to pesticides."

Garnapudi nodded. "Yes, something like that could cause anemia. What about the boy?"

"We need to get him stabilized . . . then we can start looking closer."

"You're admitting him, aren't you?"

"Absolutely."

"Good. Keep me informed."

Chapter Fifty-Eight

The sun was making its annual trek toward the southern hemisphere. The Autumnal Equinox was over a month away. The result was, even at noon, the sun was not exactly overhead. Shadows bathed many canyons all day.

The canyon where Lorenzo Spring was located ran from the southwest to the northeast. The bottom of the canyon enjoyed sunlight most of the day. When Lincoln Baca did his cleansing ritual, he enjoyed the sun's warmth. He sat for a long time next to the spring, eyes closed, thinking of nothing.

He didn't concern himself with the lack of food. When he started his fast, he reminded himself about the Rule of Threes. An individual could go without air for three minutes. They could survive three days without water and three weeks without food.

When he first started meditating it was a struggle to clear his mind of any thoughts. After three full days of fasting, he felt like he had complete control of his mind and body. At least, that was the lie he told himself. He could free his mind for short periods, but now he was plagued by the nightmare/vision from the night before.

He wasn't sure how long he sat in the sunlight. He was in no hurry to move back toward the fire. His canyon was already deep in shadow. He only stood when he realized he needed to complete his cleansing ritual with the sage smoke. Filling his two water bottles, he started back to his canyon and Montezuma's Fire.

Accustomed to being alone, he paid little attention to his surroundings. He only snapped back to reality when he approached the stone circle he had built. A rattlesnake, coiled and ready to strike, had positioned itself where he normally sat. It was warning him to stay away.

Lincoln studied the snake for a long moment, trying to decide what he should do. Finally, he crouched near the reptile and spoke to it softly. "My brother, I have no quarrel with you. If I may have this small space, I forfeit all claims to the rest of the canyon. It is yours."

The snake studied this intruder. Its tongue darted in and out of its mouth, smelling the air. The furious rattling of its tail stopped as the creature made a decision. It uncoiled itself and began to slither away, not giving the man a second look.

Lincoln watched the snake slither up the canyon, and disappear into the rubble of the canyon floor. Taking his seat next to the stone circle, he pondered his experiences of the past few days: meeting Montezuma and his *viborón*; his encounters with the bear, the mountain lion, and now, the rattlesnake; the vision of the demon at the pueblo.

He refused to believe he suffered from hallucinations. These events were real. The tumor was not affecting him.

Montezuma would return when Lincoln was ready. In his heart, the Puebloan believed he was. Montezuma would return that night.

Chapter Fifty-Nine

Jeremiah Black woke with a start. His alarm clock displayed 4:00 pm. Rubbing his eyes, he knew he had to get up. If he didn't, he'd never sleep that night. There were still four hours until sunset, plenty of time to finish cleaning his church.

Slipping on a T-shirt and blue jeans, he stepped out of his trailer. The sun was still bright. Halfway to the adobe building, he stopped to yawn. He couldn't fight off the pangs of frustration. He never promised the Senas that he could find the person who killed their granddaughter. All he said was he would try. When nothing happened, he could only apologize.

A truck sped along the county road, heading toward San Juan Pueblo. He thought about the events of the previous week. A deputy had come by to ask if he had seen anything unusual Tuesday. It had to do with the dead girl they had found a quarter mile away . . . Regina Sena. Had he seen something that might have caught his attention? He said he hadn't. He'd been at work.

Monday, though, he suddenly realized he had seen something . . . a red SUV creeping along the road. He dismissed the sight, guessing the driver was looking for something. It now occurred to him what exactly the driver was looking for . . . a place to dump a body.

He turned around and headed back to his trailer. The deputy had left a business card.

"*San Phillipe Sheriff's Office, Deputy Barnes speaking. How can I help you?*"

"Yes, deputy. My name's Jeremiah Black. I'm calling about that dead girl they found last week. I might have seen something . . ."

***

"You couldn't see the driver?" Jack Rivera asked, making notes on a small pad of paper.

Black shook his head. "It was early evening. The only thing I know for sure is that it was a Chevy Trailblazer . . . red."

He had planned on running into Segovia for something to eat. Dinner had to wait until he was finished with the sheriff's office. He was pleasantly surprised at how quickly the deputy showed up.

"You sure about the model?"

"I'm an auto mechanic. I may not know much, but I do know cars."

"Okay," the chief deputy conceded. "This red . . . was it a bright red?"

"No. It was a dark, dark red. I think it's called Brandywine."

"You never saw him stop, though?"

Again, Black shook his head. "And I really didn't think about that car until today."

"Why today? What happened?"

The mechanic-turned-preacher could have gone into a long explanation about his services and meeting Pedro and Alaina Sena. None of that information seemed relevant.

"Nothing happened. The other deputy left his card and said to call your office if I remembered anything. That's what I did . . . Do you think it will help?"

Rivera shrugged. "Maybe. There are a lot of SUVs running around these days. We do appreciate you contacting us, though." The deputy extended his hand.

"Sure." Black shook Rivera's hand. "I appreciate you coming all the way out here to interview me."

"Just doing my job. Take care, Mr. Black. Call us if you think of anything else."

Chapter Sixty

In her bird form, Fernanda watched the fevered activity from her perch in the tree. The young woman . . . the one who now possessed Izel . . . had gone into the same house Fernanda had visited the night before. Her stay was brief. She came running out of the house and back to her own.

Two women emerged from the first house. One carried a bundle. They hurried across the street and stopped at a truck not far from the tree.

Fernanda's knowledge of English was limited. She heard two words she did understand, "baby" and "doctor." A baby was ill. It had to be the same child the *tlahuelpuchi* had fed on the night before. It was most likely the bundle the younger woman carried.

The woman who had gone into the house emerged with a pocketbook in one hand and keys in the other. She joined the two women at the truck. They climbed inside, then sped away.

Fernanda could not stamp down her curiosity. Launching from her branch, she leisurely followed the truck. After a short drive, it turned off the highway, toward a large, two-story building. Big, red letters read "Hospital." The word was the same in Spanish and English.

Parking toward the back of the building, all three women hurried through a door announcing an "Emergency Room." Emergency and *emergencia* were close enough in spelling for Fernanda to translate the word for herself.

Landing on a low building across the street from the Emergency Room, the grey kite tried to remain innocuous. The *tlahuelpuchi* cursed herself. She was driven from her home because she lost control. She made too many children ill. She killed too many children. Fernanda had promised herself, in this new land, she would not draw attention to her nightly forays. She would no longer gorge herself. She would be moderate when she took blood, especially from young children.

If this baby in the hospital survived, she would no longer visit it. Fernanda knew there were ample other opportunities in this new town. She would be more selective. She would be more careful. She would consume only what she needed to survive.

After a good while, the woman who drove the truck emerged from the building. The other two women with the baby were nowhere to be seen. The kite could only assume doctors were attending to the child.

With her curiosity satisfied, Fernanda took to wing and followed the truck back to the pueblo. She hoped the baby would recover, though she didn't give a whit about the child's life. She only wanted to keep her presence a secret.

***

The *tlahuelpuchi* never thought of herself as evil. She simply was what she was.

When Fernanda turned thirteen, she lost all interest in food. As the poor girl grew weaker, Maria, her mother, sat with her day and night. On the fourth day, as Maria wiped her face with a damp cloth, the teenager grabbed her mother's hand and bit it, drawing blood.

Maria recoiled in horror as her once beautiful daughter transformed into a crazed demon.

"*Mas! Mas!*" Fernanda demanded. She needed more blood.

Tears rolled down Maria's face. Hesitating at first, she finally extended her hand to her suffering daughter so she could feed. It was at that moment Maria knew her beloved daughter was cursed and would forever be an outcast. She was now a creature of the devil. As a *tlahuelpuchi*, Fernanda would only cause others to suffer.

Once the girl fell asleep, Juan and Maria Huerta sat up the entire night, debating on what they should do. Neither had the strength nor inclination to kill their only daughter. But Fernanda had to be fed.

Maria Huerta made the sacrifice. When Fernanda needed nourishment, her mother became her source. For three long months, as the girl learned and tested her newfound powers, Maria continued her duties as a devout parent. It was a duty that couldn't last forever.

Fernanda never noticed her loving mother fading away. Like many teenagers, the girl was consumed with her own wants and desires. Like a drug addict, her whole life revolved around feeding her needs. She didn't see she was draining the lifeblood from the woman who had nurtured her from birth.

When Maria passed away, Fernanda wanted to feel remorse. Instead, she felt nothing. There was no guilt that she destroyed her own mother. The only thing that drove her was her need for human blood. It was a curse . . . an all-consuming curse and nothing else mattered.

Chapter Sixty-One

"How is little Mateo?" Pauline Baca asked as soon as Joy walked through the door. After her daughter left that morning, Pauline attended mass and lit a candle for the child.

When Joy grabbed the truck keys earlier, all she told her mother was the Chavarria baby was ill. She was driving Mateo, his mother, and his grandmother to the hospital. She would be home as soon as possible.

Joy shrugged. "I don't think he's doing well. He's so tiny and frail. To me, it looked like he was bitten by something."

"An insect?"

"I don't know. I couldn't go to the exam room, so I don't know what the doctor said. Martina came to the waiting room while Susan stayed with her baby. She was told they wanted to keep Mateo in the hospital. She thanked me for the ride and told me to go home."

"How will they get back?"

"The men will go up there when they're finished in the fields."

"Since you were at the hospital, did you ask about Eric's sister?"

"Crud! I forgot all about Edie." Joy plopped down at the dining room table across from her mother. "I should go back up there." She thought for a moment. "No, I should call Eric." She absent-mindedly looked around. "Where's dad?"

"He went over to your uncle's house. They're watching a baseball game on TV." Pauline looked up from the clay bowl she was working. "Did Martina say if someone went in their house last night?"

"No. We were all so worried about Mateo I forgot to ask." Joy thought hard for a moment. "Do you think someone snuck into their house and did something to the baby?"

"He sleeps in his parent's room, doesn't he?"

"I think so."

"Then how could someone hurt that little baby without the parents knowing? That doesn't make sense."

"I guess you're right." Joy nodded, mostly to herself. "I need to finish that bowl I was working on." She stood. "No, I need to call Eric!"

She walked over and picked up the phone. Before she dialed, she stopped, then returned the receiver to the cradle. "No. I'm going to drive up there."

"Call him first," Pauline said, calmly. "You're sounding a bit frantic. I don't think you need to be driving at the moment."

Joy took a deep breath after considering her mother's suggestion. She picked up the phone again. "You're right. I'll call Eric first . . . then I'll drive up to the farm."

Chapter Sixty-Two

As his eyes fluttered open, Lincoln sat up and tried to remember what day it was. He left home on Thursday. He counted on his fingers, one, two, three, four. This would be his fourth morning in the canyon. Monday morning. It would begin his fifth day of fasting. During Lincoln Baca's last physical as a firefighter, the doctor estimated the fat content of his body was 3%. Even though he had gained some excess weight while convalescing with a broken arm, it wasn't much.

He could tell his fat reserves were gone. His body was feeding off his muscles now for energy. He reminded himself he still had to hike out of the mountains.

"How much longer," he thought, "do I need to pursue this quest? And why am I even doing it?"

The evening before, he had prepared himself for Montezuma's return. He had questions. He knew in his heart he was ready to face the great king again . . . but he never appeared.

Lincoln felt himself drowning in a sea of self-doubt.

Had he really encountered Montezuma and his giant snake? Or did he hallucinate?

The bear, the mountain lion, the rattlesnake . . . were these just delusions?

No. They couldn't be. They were all too real. As was the demon . . .

***

For the second night in a row, immersed in a dream state, he found himself transported again to the front of his home. The beautiful demon-maiden stepped from the corner of his house. Dimly glowing, she again walked/glided across the yard. He followed.

This is the same dream as I had before, he thought. But it wasn't.

Instead of continuing to the Chavarria house, she proceeded down the street. She stopped occasionally and lifted her head as if listening for a sound. Three houses down, she turned her attention to a new target . . . the Tafoya home. Like so many Santa Clara Pueblo homes, multiple generations lived there.

Again, she walked up to the front door and opened it. Again, Lincoln followed, passing through the solid door as he had the night before. He stayed close to the demon to watch what she did.

Without hesitation, she stepped through a bedroom door. A double bed filled most of the room. Two figures slept beneath the covers. The demon-maiden approached the smaller figure. She gently pulled back the covers to reveal a young girl.

If Lincoln remembered right, it was three-year-old Emma Tafoya.

The demon lovingly caressed the child's long, black hair. Emma stirred slightly, responding to the touch. The demon carefully lifted the child closer to her.

Lincoln knew what the creature wanted . . . blood . . . the little girl's blood.

He tried to call out, but he could only be a frustrated observer. He reached for the demon, only to realize his form had no substance. Even so, the bloodsucker stopped and turned to look in Lincoln's direction. The demon had the same hideous face he had seen the night before. This time he didn't recoil in horror. He knew what to expect.

The demon sensed his presence, but without form, he couldn't be seen. It immediately returned to its task of assaulting the child.

Lincoln had no idea how long he watched the scene. When the demon had its fill, it covered the child with her covers, then turned to leave. Again, it could tell the man was there, standing between her and the doorway. She raised her hand and clawed at him with razor-sharp nails.

Suddenly, he found himself back in the canyon, sitting in front of his stone circle and Montezuma's Fire.

***

Morning found him lying on his side. He couldn't remember falling asleep. What sleep he did have was filled with the same nightmare playing over and over. He followed the demon-maiden into the Tafoya house and watched her attack the little girl. When she was finished, she turned and attacked him. When the dream restarted, he was following the demon again.

He sat for a long time, debating with himself about what he should do.

If he was not simply having nightmares . . . If he was really observing a demon attacking the children of the pueblo . . . Where did it come from? How could he stop it? Could he even stop it?

What about Montezuma? Was this Great Spirit ever going to appear again? And if he did, would he know what needed to be done?

Why, Lincoln thought, was he wasting his time?

He stood defiantly and looked to the top of the canyon cliffs and shouted.

"Great Montezuma, I seek your help . . . not for me, but for my people! Evil has come to my village. I have to stop it. You said you would return when I was ready. I have spent the past two nights waiting for you. I AM ready. But I will wait for you no longer . . . unless you give me a sign! Do you hear me? I need to know you will give me your help!"

Lincoln stood still and listened, wondering what kind of sign to expect . . . or if there would even be a sign.

Only the slightest breeze brushed his face. From the corner of his eye, he saw something flitter from the top of the cliff. At first, he thought it was a leaf. As it drifted down, it grew larger. It was a feather, an iridescent, turquoise blue feather, nearly two feet long.

Lincoln ran to it as it settled gently on the canyon floor. When he picked it up, he recognized it as one of the plumes from Montezuma's headdress.

Montezuma would return that night . . . and he needed to prepare himself.

Chapter Sixty-Three

Lansing stared at his computer screen. He wanted to know if other counties had hit-and-run victims like the two in San Phillippe County. The Department of Public Safety kept raw numbers. The summaries covered the sex and age of the victims. There was no discussion regarding how the bodies were found or if they had been moved.

Most of the pedestrian accidents occurred in urban areas like Albuquerque and Santa Fe. Male victims outnumbered females by three-to-one. The totals didn't specify if the pedestrian fatalities were hit-and-runs.

San Phillippe County averaged four pedestrian deaths a year. Lansing already had three on his hands and they were all hit-and-runs. One had been solved. From all indications, the other two were done by the same person. That individual was taunting him. The man called in reporting vultures circling over a dead carcass. The carcass turned out to be the body of a young woman. The caller could have only known the location if he was involved in placing it there . . . along the sheriff's ranch property line.

Deputy Marla Trumbull spent her Sunday tracking down the identity of the newest victim. The woman's work shirt had a logo for *Mike's Burger Barn.* It turned out to be a fast-food restaurant in Taos. One of their workers, Mandy Gomez, hadn't been seen since leaving work Tuesday night.

Mandy's invalid mother provided a photo of the twenty-year-old. Fingerprints and DNA samples were gathered for positive ID, but the deputy was confident she already knew who the victim was.

The autopsy results hadn't arrived from Albuquerque yet. Lansing expected no surprises. Mandy died from a catastrophic impact by a moving vehicle. She was probably run over a second time. Bruising from blood pooling will show the body had been moved after death.

The woman had been dead for four days. However, she had not been exposed to the elements. Lansing guessed the perpetrator had stashed the body in a safe place until they were ready to dump it.

He looked up when there was a knock at his door.

"Hey, Jack. Come on in." He glanced at his wall clock. "You're a little late this morning."

Chief Deputy Rivera stepped inside with a cup. "It's never too late for coffee." He sat at the chair in front of the desk. "And I'm not late. I was chasing cattle off the highway before seven this morning."

He opened his notepad. "We got a call yesterday from a Jeremiah Black. He lives about a quarter-mile from where we found Regina Sena's body. Danny Cortez asked him last week if he saw anything unusual Tuesday.

"Originally, he said he'd been at work. Yesterday, he remembered something. He didn't see anything Tuesday, but Monday evening he saw a red Trailblazer driving slowly along the road next to his place. He thinks the driver might have been looking for a place to dump a body."

"He's sure about the make and model?"

"He said he's a mechanic and knows his cars."

"Could he identify the driver if he saw him again?"

"No. He didn't get a good look."

"Okay," Lansing nodded. "That's something to add to our file . . . which is still pretty thin. We know Miss Sena was from Pojoaque and was probably killed down there. She went missing Saturday, but the body wasn't found for three days. Your mechanic is probably right. The driver could have been looking for a dumpsite."

The sheriff's desk phone rang. "Lansing."

"*Yeah, boss,*" Desk Sergeant Montoya said. "*I have a couple of agents from the State Bureau of Investigation up here. They want to talk to you.*"

"Talk to me? About what?"

"*They didn't say.*"

Lansing thought for a moment. "Send them back."

Rivera raised an eyebrow. "What's going on?"

"God only knows. . ."

The deputy stood. "Do you want me to leave?"

"Oh, no. I don't know what's going on, but I want a witness present."

Chapter Sixty-Four

When the two agents from the State Bureau of Investigation entered, Jack Rivera moved aside and took a position near the window. Lansing stood. One of the agents looked familiar, but he couldn't remember the man's name.

The man stepped forward and extended his hand.

"Special Agent Adam Dale."

Lansing took his proffered hand. "Cliff Lansing."

"We met last year," Dale said. "The Chaco Canyon missing person incident."

"That's right," Lansing nodded.

"This is Special Agent Kevin Ramos."

The two men shook hands.

"This is Chief Deputy Jack Rivera." Lansing nodded in his deputy's direction. He then indicated the two chairs in front of his desk. "Please sit. What brings you to Las Palmas?"

"It's been brought to the Bureau's attention that San Phillippe has a serial killer on its hands."

"What are you referring to?" Lansing's distrust of the SBI started when he was still a deputy. The Bureau had done little to change his mind over the intervening years. The result was he shared the bare minimum of information. He also needed them to reveal their intent first so he couldn't be blindsided.

"The hit-and-run incidents. We understand you have three unsolved crimes."

"Where did you get your information?"

"Our switchboard got a call Saturday."

"Some anonymous caller I take it."

"No," Ramos interjected. "It was actually a person with government ties."

"Oh, really?" Lansing's curiosity was aroused. "Who was that?"

"I don't think that's relevant," Dale continued. "What concerns our office is that the most recent victim was found on your property. We need to know if you can explain how that happened."

Lansing felt his anger building. If this was an accusation, it wasn't the first time the SBI tried to pin a crime on him. He kept calm.

"You don't waste much time, do you? Our office got a call Saturday. Someone reported circling vultures. I went to investigate."

"Oh, so you found the body!" Ramos said. "That must have been convenient."

"Now wait a minute . . ." Rivera interrupted.

Lansing held up his hand, indicating his deputy needed to be quiet.

"Let's get some facts straight," he said, keeping his composure. "Right now, we have two unsolved deaths. We're holding a person of interest for the first hit-and-run. The body I found Saturday had been dumped along the fence line of my property . . . on a county road."

"How do you know it was dumped there?" Dale asked.

"We haven't received the autopsy yet. The body was probably moved from the crime scene. The victim was from Taos. She went missing Tuesday evening after leaving work. There was no reason for her to be in San Phillippe County."

"Did you know the victim?" Ramos asked.

The accusation was blatant. Lansing stared at the special agent for a tense moment, before saying in a soft voice. "I never had the pleasure."

The room filled with an icy quiet.

"That does clear up a few issues," Dale finally said, clearing his throat and trying to get control of the situation. "Our office knows your manpower situation. We're just here to help."

Jack Rivera let out a snort. Lansing shot the deputy a look that said shut up.

"Our resources are at your disposal," the agent continued. "It would help if you could fill us in on your two unsolved fatalities."

"I have two young women who were killed by persons unknown. They were from different towns and their bodies were dumped in my county. That's all I have."

"Do you think they were killed by the same person?"

"That's one idea we're pursuing."

"What about the autopsies? We'd like to see those."

Lansing shrugged. "Sure. They're public records. Check with my desk sergeant on your way out. He'll give you the Medical Investigator's case numbers."

"You're not very cooperative," Ramos snapped. "We'd like to see your files."

"Oh, we haven't started any files, have we Jack?" Lansing tried not to sound sarcastic. "It's a manpower issue. You understand. I'm afraid you made that long drive today for no reason at all."

Ramos scowled but said nothing. Special Agent Dale stood and produced a business card from his suit jacket. "If you need anything at all, don't hesitate to call me."

Lansing stood as well, taking the offered card. "Let's hope it doesn't come to that."

The two agents headed for the door, not bothering to acknowledge Rivera.

"Don't forget to get those case numbers from my sergeant," Lansing added as they left the room.

"What the hell was that all about?" Rivera asked once they were alone.

Lansing sat back down, staring at Dale's card. "I'm not sure, but I have my suspicions."

"Do you think they were really trying to pin those hit-and-runs on you?"

"No. That was a fishing expedition. All they have is a phone call with a flimsy accusation."

"And what about this caller? Someone with 'government ties,' " Rivera growled. "What does that even mean?"

"That means someone is trying to discredit me."

"Who?"

"Like I said, I have my suspicions."

Chapter Sixty-Five

Joy visited with Eric and his family for most of the afternoon. Mrs. Gonzalez insisted she stay for supper. It was a sort of celebration. Edie had been released from the hospital.

The conversation at the table centered around little Edith. How she was medically treated by the doctors. How she felt now. The hospital staff could only guess it was a virus that made her so sick.

Joy asked questions but didn't mention her trip to the hospital with the neighbors. To her, it seemed improbable that Mateo Chavarria and Edie Gonzalez suffered from the same affliction.

But then Mrs. Gonzalez said Edie talked about a woman who came into her bedroom. She had visited two nights in a row. All the child could remember was that the woman was beautiful, and she glowed with an inner light. She said the woman came close to her neck and kissed her. At least, she thought it was a kiss. Then she fell asleep.

Joy immediately thought about the woman her neighbor, Emily Diaz, claimed she saw the night before. Just as quickly, she pushed the thought out of her mind. The Chavarrias said no one came into their house. And even if someone had gone in, it couldn't be the same person Edie allegedly saw.

Eric and Joy helped with the dishes. Afterward, they snuck off for some alone time, but Joy broke off their necking session early. The sun was sinking behind the mountains. Half of the six miles to state road was gravel and not very straight. She didn't want to make the drive to Highway 296 in the dark.

The drive from the Gonzalez farm was tediously slow. Joy concentrated on the road, grateful there was no car in front of her kicking up dust. County Road 194 paralleled *Cañones Creek* all the way to High-way 296.

Once she reached the village of Polvadera, the road was paved. That helped a little. The asphalt portion was still narrow with no shoulders and no guardrails for the sheer drop-offs into the valley. Joy didn't dare drive faster.

From the farm, it took eighteen minutes for her to reach the state highway. Already 7:30, the sun had dipped well below the western mountains, even though the official sunset was still twenty minutes away.

As Joy turned onto the highway, the engine began a horrendous knocking sound. The steering wheel shook. Her first impulse was to pull onto the shoulder, but there was no shoulder, only a guardrail.

Then came a final bang. The engine stopped running. The head-lights dimmed and the power steering failed. Joy struggled to keep the truck from running into the railing. Ahead, she could see the bridge that crossed *Cañones Creek*. The guardrail ended at the far side. She hoped and prayed she could coast until then.

After crossing the bridge, her brother's truck had just enough mo-mentum for her to exit onto a gravel road. It took all her strength to turn the front wheels. When she came to a stop, the truck had cleared the blacktop of the highway, though just barely.

Joy's first thought was what the hell did she do to Lincoln's truck? That was quickly followed by the realization her brother was going to kill her. She had ruined his pride and joy.

She calmed herself by taking several deep breaths. One problem at a time. She had to figure out how to get the truck back to the pueblo.

No! She had to figure out how she was getting back to the pueblo.

She got out of the truck, then looked up and down the highway. There was no traffic. The nearest farm was a mile-and-a-half back the way she came. Walking up the shoulder less road in the dark scared the hell out of her. The little town of Lobo was ten miles west. Highway 15 was four miles east, across the Artiga Dam. From there she guessed she could catch a ride to Artiga, just a few miles further south. She could call her father from the Phillips 66 gas station.

As she retrieved her purse and the keys from the cab, she heard the crunch of gravel behind her. She turned to see a red, Chevy Trailblazer rolling to a stop.

The driver rolled down his window. "Miss, could you use some help?"

"Yes!" she exclaimed. "Could you give me a ride to Artiga? I need to call my dad."

"Hop in!"

Chapter Sixty-Six

"My name's John," the driver said, smiling.

"I'm Joy." The rider smiled back. "Joy Baca."

"You're lucky I came by. Not a lot of traffic down this road on a Sunday night."

Joy nodded but said nothing. She was lost in her thoughts, trying to figure out how long it would take for her father to show up. She paid little attention when they turned onto Highway 15. It was only after the Trailblazer made an abrupt turn onto a dark, gravel road, that Joy became aware something might be wrong.

"What are you doing?" she blurted, looking at the driver.

"Just relax Joy Baca. We're making a little detour."

"I want out!" she shouted, fumbling with her seatbelt.

"You're not going anywhere!"

It was at that moment, that the teen noticed the man had a gun pointed at her.

"This won't take long."

"You're going to rape me!" she screamed.

"No," he replied calmly. "I am not going to rape you."

The SUV proceeded along the road for only a short distance before coming to a stop. John turned off the engine and the headlights. He flipped on the dome light.

"Open the glove box," he ordered.

Joy did as she was told.

"Take out one of those zip ties," he commanded. "Make a loop . . . put it around your wrists . . . and pull it tight with your teeth."

The pueblo girl followed John's instructions. She kept her eyes fixed on the gun, as if, somehow, that would prevent her from being shot.

Once she finished her task, John turned off the dome light and got out of the car. He walked around to the rider's side and opened the door. Without saying a word, he unbuckled her seatbelt, then pulled her around so her feet dangled out the door. He pulled off her shoes and socks, throwing them to the side of the road.

"Come on," he said, roughly pulling her from her seat.

"Where are we going?" Joy squeaked.

"Shut up!"

The pleasant man who stopped to pick her up had disappeared. He half-dragged, half-carried the girl down the gravel road. Joy stepped carefully. Her feet were tender. It had been years since she had gone barefoot outside.

John stopped in the middle of the road, ten yards from his Trailblazer. He forced Joy to kneel.

"Wait right here," he barked. He then turned and headed back to his SUV. A moment later he was in the driver's seat and had the engine running. Turning on the headlights, he stopped short of putting the vehicle in gear. His quarry was gone.

"Son-of-a-bitch!" he swore. He reached across to the glove compartment and pulled out a flashlight. Grabbing his gun from the side pocket of the door, he jumped out leaving the engine and headlights on.

He ran to the spot he had left the girl and flipped the flashlight switch on. Nothing happened. He banged the light against his palm. It produced a meager flicker. He banged it again, this time getting a bright beam.

He pointed it first down the road. It was empty. Shining it to his left and then to the right, he saw the girl running away. He didn't bother yelling. He simply pointed the gun at her and fired.

She dropped immediately.

***

Once John's back was turned and he was walking away, Joy scrambled to her feet. She wasn't going to wait to find out what he had planned for her. Little was visible in the moonless night as she moved from the road into the rugged desert.

Unable to see where she was going, she tried to step silently, ignoring the pain. Twenty feet in she tripped, letting out an involuntary "Oof." With her wrists bound, she had to break her fall with her forearms. Scrambling back to her feet, she heard the SUV engine starting up.

She attempted to pick up her pace. As her eyes adjusted to the meager starlight, she could make out shapes: larger rocks and juniper bushes. She counted herself fortunate that she managed to stop short of a yawning arroyo. The drop-off looked steep, and she couldn't see the dark bottom.

Standing on the arroyo's rim, something slammed into her right shoulder, pitching her forward. A millisecond later she heard the report of a gun as she tumbled down the slope. She rolled head-over-heels for twenty feet, finally crashing onto the dry creek bed.

Joy laid, stunned, but for only a moment. She was running for her life, and she knew she couldn't stop. She stood, unsteady but determined. Stumbling down the arroyo like a drunk, the sides were too steep for her to climb out. On top of everything else, she could tell the front of her shirt was becoming wet.

She fought through the fog of pain, trying to figure out what had happened to her. From the sound of the gunshot, she knew she must have been struck by a bullet. But it hit her from the back. Why was the front of her shirt becoming soaked in blood?

The bullet . . . it went all the way through. She was bleeding from the exit wound.

That realization was no consolation. If anything, it made her dizzy. She needed to stop. She needed to sit.

To her left was a clump of juniper bushes. She fell to her knees and began to crawl. With her wrists still bound by a zip tie, she struggled to wriggle forward. Eventually, though, she managed to completely squirm her way under the low branches.

Exhausted, she dropped onto her side and closed her eyes. The pain dissipated as she was engulfed in blessed oblivion, slipping into a deep, dreamless sleep.

***

The driver's attempt to track his victim was thwarted by his flashlight. It failed completely by the time he reached the arroyo. With only starlight, he couldn't tell how steep the walls were or how deep the gully went.

He listened for any sound coming from the darkness below. He heard nothing.

Joy Baca had obviously fallen into the arroyo. John was positive his shot had found its target. He debated if he should try to find the body. He didn't want to climb down only to discover he couldn't climb back out. Also, it would be a waste of his efforts if he found that Joy Baca was dead. He had no intention of dragging her out of the desert. He would leave her for the coyotes.

If Joy Baca was still alive, he didn't think it would be for long. With no shoes, her hands bound, and her fall into the arroyo, there was little chance she was in any shape to find her way back to civilization. Besides, if his bullet had found its mark, she would probably bleed to death before morning.

Satisfied he had nothing to fear, John was soon back in his Trailblazer, heading down Highway 15 toward Segovia.

Chapter Sixty-Seven

After the confrontation with the SBI agents, Lansing needed a break from the office. It was too early for lunch, so he opted for a cruise in his jeep. It was the middle of August, so tourist season was in full swing. He had a full complement of deputies on duty, so he wasn't especially needed on patrol.

Highway 15 north of Las Palmas was crowded with campgrounds and lodges. To avoid the congestion, he chose to take a leisurely drive south toward Segovia. There were a couple of good burger places he could stop at.

Lansing expected plenty of traffic in that direction as well. There were popular attractions like O'Keeffe Ranch and a few miles further south Artiga Reservoir with its camping and boating.

Thirty minutes after leaving his office the sheriff reached the turn to Highway 296 and Artiga dam. A mile later he passed a dirt road that led into the Carson National Forest. The highway made a lazy turn to the right. A guardrail along the northeastern side protected cars from a steep drop-off.

A car was stopped at the end of the metal railing, facing in his direction. Lansing spotted a man and a woman several yards from the car, kneeling over something on the ground. With plenty of time on his hands, he decided the scene warranted his attention.

Once he passed the car, he pulled onto the shoulder. After waiting for traffic to pass, he made a U-turn and parked behind the other car . . . a late model Subaru station wagon with Illinois plates.

The man noticed Lansing approaching and stood, a worried look on his face.

"Thank God you're here, Sheriff," he said. "We were getting ready to call for an ambulance."

The woman looked up. Next to her was a young woman with long, black hair. Her pale-green blouse was soaked in blood. Lansing knelt and placed two fingers against the artery on her neck.

"She's still breathing," the kneeling woman said. She gestured toward a nearby dried creek. "We saw her stumbling out of that gully."

"Do you have any water?" Lansing asked.

"We have some in a cooler," the man said, starting toward his car.

"Grab one," Lansing requested, pulling his cell phone from his pocket and dialing 9-1-1. "Yes, this is Sheriff Lansing. I need a medevac helicopter, ASAP. I have a gunshot victim. She's lost a lot of blood. I'm five miles west of Artiga on Highway 15."

He listened for a moment. "No, he won't need to land on the road. We're in an open area on the north side of the highway." He listened again. "Late teens, early twenties. Hispanic, maybe Indian . . . Alright we'll be watching for it."

He hung up his phone, then dialed a second number. "Yes, Marilyn. Sheriff Lansing. I need a deputy for directing traffic. As soon as they can get here." He gave his location.

"When we first found her, her wrists were tied together with this." The woman picked up a white zip tie from the ground next to her. "Pat cut it off with his penknife."

Lansing nodded, taking the plastic tie and stuffing it into his pocket.

The tourist from Illinois returned with a bottle of water, opening it before handing it to the sheriff. Lansing carefully lifted the girl's head and tipped the bottle toward her lips.

The girl's eyes fluttered open, and she parted her lips to receive the liquid. She started to choke after taking too big a gulp.

"Take it easy there," Lansing said.

The girl had to squint in the bright sunlight. "Sheriff Lansing?"

"We know each other?" He was surprised she recognized him.

"I'm . . ." Her voice trailed off as she passed out.

He brushed the hair from her face. She did seem familiar, but the sallow expression and ashen look made identification impossible.

The helicopter arrived ten minutes later. Deputy Jake Redwine showed up at the same time and immediately began directing rubbernecking drivers to keep moving along.

The paramedics rushed to the victim with a stretcher. After getting as much information from Lansing and the tourists as they could, the emergency crew secured the girl in the helicopter. The Presbyterian Hospital in Segovia had a good, Level-III emergency room. That was where they would go. Although a trauma Level-I ER was preferable, the paramedics weren't sure the victim would last all the way to Albuquerque.

"Do you think she'll be okay?" The man's name was Pat Wilson. He and his wife, Connie, were halfway through a two-week vacation. It was their first trip to New Mexico.

"I don't know, Mr. Wilson," Lansing admitted. "But her chances are a lot better since you took the time to stop and help." After thanking them, he gave them a business card. They could check-in in a few days if they wanted to see how the girl was doing.

It wasn't long before Lansing and Redwine were the only ones at the scene.

"Jake, I have no idea who that girl was," the sheriff said. "She knew who I was, though."

"What should we do?"

"You can get back on patrol . . . Thanks for the help."

"Are you heading for the hospital?"

"Not yet." He nodded toward the arroyo. "The Wilsons said they saw her coming from that creek. I'm going to take a walk and see if I can figure out what happened."

Chapter Sixty-Eight

From where the victim fell to the arroyo was one hundred feet. The creek bed, Lansing found, was mostly hard-packed sand. Still, the girl had left faint tracks the sheriff could follow.

Over eons, the summer rains had cut a channel from north to south. All the runoff dumped into the Rio Cohino. Where Lansing entered the arroyo, the bank was nonexistent. As he moved north the walls of the mini canyon became higher and steeper.

He kept his eyes fixed on the ground. Sometimes, the tracks disappeared only to resume several feet further on. More than once Lansing found a spot where the girl had fallen. He guessed he had walked half a mile when he found where she had crawled under a clump of juniper bushes. The sand was disturbed where she had scooted under the branches. There were also splotches of dried blood.

It was obvious this was not where she was shot.

Lansing continued further up the arroyo. Two hundred feet further on he found where she had tumbled into the gully. She had left a large splotch of blood where she landed.

He looked up. The wall of the ditch was twenty feet high and steep. It took him a few minutes to find a convenient way up. When he reached the top, he went to the spot the girl fell from. Fifty feet away was a dirt road. Lansing guessed it was the same forestry road he had passed on the highway. That had to be the road the girl's assailant used to bring her there.

He began a zigzag search from the arroyo's lip to the road, not quite sure what he was looking for. It wasn't until he reached the dirt track that he found something . . . a 9mm cartridge. Looking around, he found a small stick. He used it to pick up the brass casing, then carefully dropped it in his shirt pocket. He hoped it had a partial fingerprint they could use.

Thirty feet up the road, he found a pair of woman's tennis shoes and socks. He guessed they were the victim's. He picked them up to return to the owner.

***

"Dispatch, this is Patrol One," Lansing said into the mic once he was back at his jeep.

"Patrol One, go ahead."

"Roger, Marilyn. I'm heading for the Presbyterian Hospital. No one's called in about the girl's status, have they?"

"No, Sheriff."

"Anything going on I need to know about?"

"Deputy Redwine reported a broken-down truck a mile from Artiga Dam."

Lansing wasn't a fan of coincidences. An abandoned truck just a few miles from where a girl was assaulted seemed too convenient.

"Did he check the registration?"

"Let me ask Sergeant Montoya." The dispatcher was offline for a long moment. Finally, she said, "It's registered to a Lincoln Baca, Santa Clara Pueblo."

"Damn," Lansing swore. He had met Baca only a few months earlier during the Cerro Grande Fire. He had also met his sister, Joy, that same night . . . while they huddled around a campfire, trying to keep warm.

"Is anything wrong?"

"The girl who was shot . . . I know who she is. I'm heading for Segovia. I'll check in later. If I'm needed, I'll have my cell phone with me. Patrol One, out."

Chapter Sixty-Nine

"How bad is she?" Lansing asked the attending physician. The two men stood outside the ER room where Joy Baca was being treated.

"She lost a lot of blood. We had to close the entry and exit wounds before starting the transfusion. I'm confident she'll make a full recovery," Dr. Baxter said. "Physically, she was in great shape. That's probably how she survived. She was fortunate the bullet passed completely through her. Somehow it missed the scapula and ribs. The lungs and arteries are fine. All we need to do is get the hemoglobin levels up."

"Has she been able to speak?"

"No, not yet," Dr. Baldwin said. "We've started her on the second unit of whole blood. Once she's stabilized, we'll move her to ICU."

"I'm pretty sure I know who she is," Lansing said. "Her name is Joy Baca. She's from Santa Clara."

"One of the nurses saw her yesterday. She brought in one of her neighbors, but we didn't know her name. Do you know how to contact the family?"

"I'll drive down to the Pueblo and talk to the tribal office. They'll know who to contact."

Before leaving the Emergency Room, Lansing left his business card with the Nurse Supervisor. He asked that his office be notified when Joy woke up. He needed to find out who attacked her.

***

It was a short, three-mile drive from the hospital to the Pueblo.

The Santa Clara Government Offices were in a long, single-story, adobe-style building adjacent to the Senior Citizen Center. Labeled the

Neighborhood Facility, the building accommodated the Office for Economic Development, the police department, and even the governor's office.

Lansing found a parking spot near the double doors leading to the interior offices. He quickly located the office he wanted. Police Chief Marco Padilla was at his desk. He stood when Lansing entered.

"Sheriff, what brings you here?" The two men shook hands.

"Chief, unfortunately, it's not good news. One of your pueblo members was found shot near Highway fifteen."

"Who?" Padilla was shocked and concerned with the news.

"Joy Baca."

"How badly is she hurt?"

"She lost a lot of blood, but the doctor said she'll be alright."

"You're sure it's Joy?"

"Yes. Her brother's truck was abandoned a few miles away. I didn't recognize her at first. When the truck was found, I put two and two together."

"Have you contacted the family?"

"That's why I'm here. Do you know where they live?"

"I can look it up." Padilla pulled out a small tribal directory and thumbed through the first few pages. "The Bacas live a half-mile from here on Cloud Road. I can contact them if you want."

"I'd like to tell them in person. Could you take me there?"

"Absolutely. Your car or mine?"

"I'll drive."

***

Pauline Baca took the horrible news the same as any mother would. "How badly is she hurt?"

"The doctor said he was sure she'd recover," Lansing said soothing-ly.

"I need to be with her." Pauline began searching for her purse. "We knew something was wrong when she didn't come home last night. The Gonzalezes said she left their farm before dark. Simon went looking for her. All he found was Lincoln's broken-down truck."

"Simon?" Lansing asked.

"Her husband," Padilla explained.

"Why didn't you contact my office?" Lansing pressed.

"I don't have time for questions."

"Do you want someone to take you?" Padilla asked.

"No, no. I have our truck."

"Shouldn't someone go with you?"

Pauline nodded. "I'll call my neighbor, Martina. She'll come with me."

"I can follow you to the hospital, if you'd like," Lansing offered.

"I can handle this . . . but Marco," she said to Padilla. "Find my husband and tell him what's happened. His crew is doing roadwork near Puye."

"I'll be glad to, Pauline."

"And, Sheriff," Pauline said stiffly. "I apologize for snapping. I do thank you for coming here and telling me about my daughter."

Chapter Seventy

When Matthew Franco opened his first *Magnifico Burgers and Burritos* in the early seventies, it was the only restaurant on North Riverside Drive. Since then, a dozen other taco, burger, and family-style diners had popped up along the busy boulevard. He had wisely purchased several acres behind his food outlet. As his empire grew, he could afford a separate office building behind his flagship store.

As District Manager for Northern New Mexico, John Tapia had a plush, comfortable office. It reflected his state's rich, Spanish heritage. The normal elegance, though, had been covered by campaign posters. Any visitor knew instantly of Tapia's intent to become the next San Phillipe Sheriff.

A spare office in the building was his campaign headquarters. Employees were conveniently recruited to make phone calls to potential voters, hang posters, and hand out fliers.

Any donations to Tapia's campaign could be saved for future elections.

The city councilman was sitting at his office desk when his secretary buzzed him.

"Yes, Cheryl?"

"I have a Mr. Paul Trevino out here. He says you're expecting him."

It had been nearly a week since the cousins got together. Trevino had expressed his intent to help get Tapia elected. But the councilman had not heard a thing in six days. There were only three weeks until the primary and he couldn't conceive of anything Trevino could do to aid the effort.

"Send him in," Tapia said reluctantly.

Trevino walked in, all smiles. Tapia didn't bother to stand and greet him.

"What do you want, Paul?"

Trevino took a seat in front of his cousin's desk, his smile not as sharp as it was when he entered the office. "You don't sound happy to see me."

"I'm a busy man."

"Well, you're going to be even busier. You remember our talk last week?"

"Vaguely."

"I told you your campaign needed an October Surprise in August."

"Yeah. So?"

"I've pulled some strings and put the wheels in motion. All you have to do is capitalize on them."

"What are you talking about?"

Trevino pulled a folded sheet of paper from his suit jacket and handed it across the table. "This press release is going out today. You need to cut a new commercial this afternoon. Make sure every voter in the county knows what's going on."

Tapia opened the folded sheet and read its contents. He gave Trevino a doubtful look. "Is this true?"

"True enough."

"I don't suppose you know who this anonymous state official is?"

Trevino held up his hands to indicate his innocence. "It wasn't me. As I said, I pulled some strings. No one can trace the statement back to your campaign."

Tapia read the press release a second time. "And you're sure this is going out this afternoon."

"It's scheduled for a three o'clock release."

The candidate thought about what his next move should be.

"If you were smart," Trevino urged, "You'd have a new commercial on the radio for drive time today."

"You're probably right," Tapia nodded, standing. "You want to come down to my campaign HQ? You and my campaign manager can put a commercial together. I'll record it this afternoon."

"I'll pass," Trevino said, standing as well. "I want to keep a low profile. I enjoy this behind-the-scenes intrigue."

"I'll bet you do." Tapia held up the sheet of paper. "Thanks for the heads-up. I think you just won me the primary."

Chapter Seventy-One

Radio Campaign ad.

Announcer: *There have been three hit-and-run deaths in San Phil-lipe County in the last two weeks. No one has been brought to justice for these deaths. Santa Fe announced today the State Bureau of Investigation has launched an investigation into Sheriff Cliff Lansing's handling of these murders. Two SBI special investigators were dispatched today to Las Palmas to make inquiries. Not only is there concern for a cover-up. There is speculation regarding the sheriff's personal involvement since one body was found on his property.*

John Tapia: *My fellow voters, this is Councilman John Tapia. For too long San Phillipe has suffered from Sheriff Lansing's incompetence. Today we learned of his possible connection to the murders of three young women. If Lansing is reelected, how much longer do you think he will be allowed to serve? How much longer will we have to support a suspected murderer?*

You can make a change. I am asking that on September fifth, in the Democratic Primary, you vote for that change. Vote for me, John Tapia, for sheriff.

Announcer: *Paid for by the committee to elect John Tapia for Sheriff, San Phillipe County.*

***

"Is any of that ad true?" Norman Salerno asked, frowning.

"Pieces of it," Lansing admitted, calmly. "Not all."

"What pieces are true?"

"Two SBI agents did stop in. They did make an inquiry about the three hit-and-runs. Other than that, nothing else in that campaign ad is true.

"I explained we had a suspect in custody for one of the deaths. Two are still unsolved. But no dead woman was found on my property. The body was dumped next to my fence line.

"I am not a suspect in these deaths. There is no active investigation regarding me or my office. Tapia and his people are telling lies."

"I called around," Norman Salerno growled. "The SBI only made that press release an hour ago. How in the hell did Tapia know about it?"

"Connections in the State Capital," Lansing said, refusing to be flustered. "Someone in Santa Fe misinformed the SBI about our hit-and-runs. That's why they showed up. I'd bet a year's salary whoever called my office Saturday is the same person who talked to the SBI."

"Who was that?"

"I wish I knew. I also believe it's the hit-and-run driver. He's killed two women, at least. A third one got away."

"You're kidding! Can she identify this guy?"

"Let's hope. She's in the hospital being treated for a gunshot wound. She lost a lot of blood. I'll talk to her when she wakes up."

"Well, we need to put a new ad together immediately. Some people believe everything they hear on the radio. I'm sure the TV stations in Albuquerque will have something in their evening broadcast."

Lansing nodded. "This is one time I'm not going to fight you about doing an ad."

"Your office and the campaign are going to be flooded with requests for a statement. We need to put one together."

Lansing pulled out a sheet of paper from his top drawer. "I worked on this earlier."

"What?" Salerno said, taking the paper. "You knew Tapia's ad was coming?"

"No. I knew someone would get wind that the SBI came for a visit. I wanted to be ready if anyone started asking questions."

The lawyer read over the paper. "Not bad. Do you mind if I tweak it a little? We can use most of it for your new ad."

"Do whatever you think needs to be done. I'm driving down to Segovia in an hour. I need to visit the Presbyterian Hospital. Can we get studio time for the new ad?"

"That shouldn't be a problem. I'll make a call."

The phone on Lansing's desk rang. "Lansing," he said when he picked up. He listened for a moment. "Tell them we'll release a statement soon." He listened again.

"Clem," he said to the desk sergeant, "I already know. It has to do with a press release about the SBI visit. Don't worry about it. I've got it under control."

After hanging up, he looked at his campaign manager. "Norm, you need to start tweaking that statement. The calls have begun."

Salerno started for the door. "It won't take long."

"And let me know when we can record the new ad."

Chapter Seventy-Two

"I'm sorry, Sheriff," the nurse supervisor said. "Only immediate family is allowed to visit ICU patients."

"Ma'am, you don't seem to understand," Lansing said. "This is a murder investigation. I need to find out who shot her . . ."

"No, sir. You're the one who doesn't understand. Miss Baca arrived at the hospital in critical condition. She was on the verge of death just a few hours ago. We are monitoring her closely since she's not out of danger yet. We'll move her to a regular room if she's better tomorrow. If that happens you can speak to her then."

"Now, wait a minute . . ." the sheriff began but was cut short.

"That's enough, Cliff," Tina said, touching his arm. "You need to let the poor girl rest."

Lansing looked at her, frowning, then nodded. He glanced back at the nurse. "I'll call in the morning to see how the girl's doing."

***

"You know that nurse could have called security if you kept pushing," Tina said, once they were in Lansing's jeep.

"She wouldn't dare," Lansing huffed. "I'm the sheriff."

"You aren't in uniform."

"I have my ID."

Tina ignored his protest. "Have you decided where we're going to eat?"

"We have a little time before we have to be at the radio station. How does *Marisco's* sound?"

"Sounds good. I could go for a *Filete Marinero*."

"*Marisco's* it is."

The drive was short. There was no place in Segovia more than 15 minutes from any other place. When they arrived, the parking lot was nearly full . . . unusual for a Monday evening. Even worse, there was a twenty-minute wait to be seated.

Tina suggested dining somewhere else, but her partner insisted there was plenty of time.

***

"Sorry, Norm," Lansing said when they walked into the recording studio. "Dinner took longer than I expected."

"Hi, Tina." The lawyer gave her a short wave of his hand. "I hope you realize we only booked the sound engineer for half an hour," he snapped at Lansing. "We have ten minutes left."

Lansing scowled at his campaign manager. He wasn't used to being scolded.

Salerno ignored the nasty look as he handed his candidate the radio script. "Read over this. Let's see if we can get the ad in one take."

Lansing read over the sheet of paper, then nodded. "This isn't exactly the press release I gave you, but I like it."

"Good," Salerno said. He looked at the sound engineer. "Bill, are you ready?"

The engineer nodded.

Lansing cleared his throat before starting.

Friends, this is Cliff Lansing. I have been in public service my entire adult life. For the last eight years, I have been your elected Sheriff. As a public official, nothing is more important than being honest with the people who entrusted you with that responsibility. So, I will be honest with you now.

214

Recently my office was visited by two special agents from the State Bureau of Investigation. They asked about three recent hit-and-run deaths in San Phillipe County. They were told a person of interest was in custody for the first death. The other two are being actively investigated.

Despite claims to the contrary, no one in my office is under suspicion for those two deaths, including myself. There is no active investigation being conducted out of Santa Fe.

Assertions made against me and my office are, at the least, fantasies. At their worst, they are blatant lies. I have already provided a public statement addressing the press release from Santa Fe. It says the same thing I just said to you.

I know you expect honesty and integrity from the people you elect . . . and you should. Since first being elected sheriff, I have kept those values foremost in my thoughts and actions.

If you chose to re-elect me, I promise you I will continue to serve the good people of San Phillipe County with the same high principles you expect from your sheriff.

Thank you for listening.

"How was that?" Lansing asked.

He was greeted with big smiles from Tina and Salerno, plus a thumbs up from the sound engineer.

"That was great!" Tina stood on her toes to give him a congratulatory kiss.

"I have to admit, you work well under pressure," Salerno nodded. "I'll put a campaign tag at the end, and we'll get it on the air first thing in the morning."

"Okay," Lansing said. "Do you need anything else from me tonight?"

"That's it. I'll see you tomorrow."

Chapter Seventy-Three

Lincoln Baca's ability to concentrate was being tested. Ever since he witnessed the feather floating from the clifftop, he was consumed with anticipation. He went through his daily preparations . . . washing at the spring and purifying his body with the sage smoke. But closing his eyes and drifting into a dream state seemed beyond him.

Frustrated, he walked to the far end of the small canyon, then back to the stone circle twice. The little bit of exercise was more taxing than he expected. After completing the second trip, he found his legs wobbly. Sitting at the nearly invisible fire, he wondered if he would have the stamina to climb out of the canyons and make his way home. He reassured himself that after the Aztec king's visit, his vision quest was complete. He could eat again to rebuild his strength.

The walk had served its purpose. Assuming the pose he had used for four days, he found he could free his thoughts again. Closing his eyes and being aware of nothing but his own breathing, he was wrapped once more in the twilight cloak of consciousness. He drifted between aware-ness and sleep.

He had no idea how long his dream state lasted. When he opened his eyes, the fire danced in front of him. The rest of the canyon was dark.

He fought the impulse to stand and stretch. The anticipation he fought earlier in the day was creeping back into his thoughts. Without realizing what he was doing, his hand began a rhythmic beat against his leg. In Tewa, a language he truly didn't know, he began chanting the Eagle Dance.

The words he struggled to remember a few days earlier now flowed effortlessly. He was immersed in his ancient culture as joy washed over him. There was a pride he'd never experienced before. He never wanted the feeling to end. It was the Aztec king's voice that ended his chant.

"You are ready!"

Lincoln opened his eyes to see Montezuma and the *viborón,* his snake. The king was again festooned in his great feather robe and magnificent headdress.

"Why am I ready?" he asked out loud, honestly wondering what had changed.

"You faced the bear, the mountain lion, even the snake, and did not waiver from your quest. More importantly, though, you rediscovered your real purpose.

"You remembered this world is not about you. Your duty is to care for others . . . to care for the people of your village. You knew that when you fought fires. When that was taken, you forgot your purpose. You cared only about yourself. You allowed self-pity to consume you."

Lincoln moved to a kneeling position. "Great King, you don't understand . . . I may be dying."

"Do you fear death?"

"No!" Lincoln was adamant.

"Then treat each day as if you knew it was your last. Your visions showed you that you need to become a protector. That is your destiny."

"You know about my visions? Are they real?"

"They are."

"These things I saw . . . Were they premonitions?"

"No, they are about now. An evil has descended on your pueblo . . . an evil you saw."

"What was that 'thing?' "

"It is a *tlahuelpuchi* . . . a tormented soul that drinks the blood of others. It seeks the blood of children."

"Where did it come from?"

"It is from the mountains east of Teotihuacan . . . my capital city. It is a creature of the Nahua, a people the Aztec conquered."

"It looked like a ghost, but it glowed."

"In Nahuatl, the name means 'a haze lit from within.' "

"I followed it. I watched it feed on a baby. It turned into a demon."

"Its true form."

"How did it get to my pueblo?"

"I do not know."

"Can I stop it?"

"Yes. You can kill it, but only when it is in human form. Otherwise, its powers are beyond your abilities."

"Can you help me?"

"I cannot . . . but if you must, you can summon the *viborón,* my great snake. He is an instrument capable of facing this evil in all its manifestations."

"How? How do I summon him?"

"On the flat stone in front of you, there is a bone . . . an Eagle's bone."

Lincoln looked from Montezuma to the stone circle. There was a bone, just as he was told. He picked it up for a closer inspection. The hollow bone was open at both ends.

"It is a way to call my *viborón.* Blow through it. It produces a whistle only he can hear. He will know what you need . . . Your quest has ended . . . It is time for you to return home."

"Will we meet again?" Baca asked desperately.

The great king gave his head only a small shake. "No. I have served my purpose . . . You must forge your own fate."

"But what if I return to your fire?"

"After tonight, you will never find your way to my fire again."

"Why not?"

Baca never received an answer. The great king along with his snake turned and disappeared into the darkness.

He was alone again. There was only himself and Montezuma's Fire.

Chapter Seventy-Four

Tina Morales turned off her cell phone when Lansing recorded his campaign ad. Something she never did. Accustomed to leaving it powered continuously, she forgot to turn it back on that evening. She didn't realize her mistake until after she finished breakfast.

She turned it on as she gathered her materials for the last day of "in-service" preparation for the new school year. The small screen flashed brightly and registered missed calls. Curious, Tina selected the "Calls" screen, then the "Missed Calls."

The first two numbers on the calls were 52, Mexico's country code. The rest of the numbers she readily recognized. It was her grandmother's home phone. She had called three times.

Alarmed, Tina immediately punched a sequence of fifteen numbers. It took a few moments before the phone rang. Juan Sanchez picked up after four rings.

"Hola?"

"Grandfather," Tina said in Spanish, "this is Tina. You called three times last night. What's wrong?"

"Ah, little one, that was your grandmother. You must speak with her. I will put her on."

Naomi Sanchez's voice came over the receiver. "Tina? This is your grandmother."

"Hi, Grandma, I'm worried about you. Why did you call?"

"It is about that doll, Izel."

Tina rolled her eyes. "Grandma, I know you don't like it. I told you. I don't have it anymore. I gave it away."

"I know you did. To a little girl. You must find that child and save her."

"I don't understand. It's just a doll."

"Yes, it is just a doll. But a creature of darkness attached itself to that doll. That's what I sensed when you bought it."

"What are you talking about?"

"That doll harbors a *Vampira*. It is also a *cambiaformas*, a shapeshifter. It hid in the folds of the dress."

Tina was quiet for a few seconds. "Grandmother, where are you getting this wild tale?"

"Your cousin, Luis. He told me."

"Grandma, I really need to go to work," Tina said impatiently.

"No, no, no!" Naomi pleaded. "You must listen to what I've been told."

"What does Luis know about vampires and shapeshifters? He makes saddles."

"But he knows people. He talked to them."

"I'll tell you what, Grandma. I'll call you after work. You can tell me everything Luis said then. Okay?"

"This cannot wait! That child is in danger . . ."

"If anything had happened, I'm sure I would have heard about it. Now let me get to work. I'll call you back later. I promise. Love you, Grandma."

Tina quickly hung up before Naomi Sanchez could mount another protest. She was already running late. As much as she revered her grandmother, the poor dear's thoughts meandered aimlessly more and more as she grew older. Vampires and shapeshifters were topics Naomi had never pursued before. Tina suspected these were just a reflection of declining mental capacity.

A tear trickled down Tina's cheek as she turned onto the highway, toward Las Palmas. She had gone to Nogales to learn as much from her grandmother as she could before Naomi Sanchez's health failed her.

Now she feared the old woman's mind would desert her first. The very thought made the high school teacher sad . . . very sad.

Chapter Seventy-Five

Jeremiah Black was not overly concerned after Chaparro's visit on Sunday. The man and his friends had made a point to follow him home a few days earlier. He suspected they were interested in his stash of peyote. He was positive they would return while he was at work.

"Forewarned is forearmed," was the saying he remembered. On Monday when he went to work, he took his rifle, pistol, and remaining peyote buttons. If his trailer was broken into, there would be nothing worth stealing.

Black went about his job at the repair shop, nearly forgetting about his precautions. After work, he picked up a bucket of fried chicken for dinner. What he didn't finish that night would be lunch on Tuesday.

Pulling to a stop in front of his trailer, the door stood wide open. He wasn't surprised. When he inspected the interior, he found his belongings tossed around and the cabinet doors almost ripped off. It was evident that every possible hiding place had been thoroughly investigated.

Black was angry that he needed to repair the damage and replace the lock on his exterior door. He had to make clear to Chaparro and his friends that such destruction would not be tolerated.

Tuesday morning, he visited the repair shop's office. Thumbing through the files he found the invoice he wanted and quickly wrote down a phone number. Taking his break around ten, he called the number.

A woman with a heavy Hispanic accent answered. "Hola?"

"Yeah," Black said. "I need to speak to Chaparro."

"No. He's not here."

"This is his number, right?"

"Si."

"I want you to give him a message. This is the 'preacher man.' Tell that sawed-off runt if he or his buddies come near me or my property again, I'll shoot their ass. Do you understand?"

"Oh, si. You're going to shoot their asses."

"Only if they come near me," he said for clarification. "Okay?"

"Okay, si. If they come to you, you'll shoot their asses."

"Close enough."

Hanging up the phone, Black hoped Chaparro got the correct translation. Whether he did or not, didn't matter. The mechanic knew from there on out he needed to watch his back.

Chapter Seventy-Six

Lansing found Pauline Baca in the hospital room with her daughter. Joy didn't look like the same woman he saw just the day before. She was alert, color had returned to her face, and she had been bathed. She even smiled at Lansing when he came in.

"Hi, Sheriff!" Her voice wasn't strong.

"Hi, Joy." He nodded toward her mother. "Mrs. Baca." He handed her a paper bag he was carrying.

"What's this?" she asked, looking inside.

"I'm pretty sure they belong to your daughter." He looked at the patient. "Your shoes and socks. So, Joy, do you mind if I ask you a few questions?"

"This won't take long, will it?" Pauline asked. "She's still weak."

"That's alright, Momma," Joy said. "Go ahead, Sheriff."

Pauline sat in the room's only chair, so Lansing simply stepped closer to the bed. Removing a notepad and pen from his uniform shirt pocket, he began. "Do you remember what happened Sunday night?"

Joy nodded. "I was driving home from Eric Garcia's farm. He's my boyfriend."

Lansing smiled. "I remember."

"Anyway, I wanted to start home before it got dark. But my brother's truck broke down as soon as I turned onto Highway two-ninety-six. I had to pull over. I wasn't there long before a man stopped and asked if I needed a ride."

"This is the man who shot you?"

"Yes."

"What was he driving?"

"It was an SUV . . . a Trailblazer, I think."

"The color?"

"Red. A real dark red."

"Okay," he said, jotting down the details. "So, you got into his car?"

Joy nodded again. "I asked him if he could drop me off in Artiga so I could call my dad. He seemed like a nice man."

"What did he look like?"

"He was Hispanic. Probably in his thirties, I guess."

"Any distinguishing features. Mustache, balding, glasses?"

"No. Nothing like that. He just looked like a regular guy."

"What was he wearing?"

"A western-style shirt . . . long-sleeved. Blue jeans and boots."

"Then what happened?"

"We turned onto highway fifteen. I wasn't paying much attention, but we hadn't gone far before he turned off onto a dirt road." Tears started welling up in her eyes and her voice cracked. "I thought he was going to rape me. I even asked him if that was what he was going to do."

Lansing held up his hand. "That's alright, Joy. Let's take a break. Mrs. Baca, maybe she could use a drink of water."

The sheriff stepped aside and let Pauline care for her daughter. After a few minutes, Joy regained her composure and nodded to Lansing that she was ready to resume.

"I don't suppose he gave you his name."

"He said it was John."

"That's it? Just John?"

The girl nodded.

"Okay, please continue."

Joy recounted the gun being pointed at her, the zip tie on her wrists, and John removing her shoes and socks.

"Why do you think he took your shoes?"

"So I wouldn't run away. He dragged me to a spot twenty or thirty feet down the road, then made me get on my knees."

"Is that where he shot you?"

"No. I don't think that was his plan. He told me to stay where I was. He went back to his car and I'm pretty sure he wanted to run me over. As soon as he got to his car, I jumped up and started running."

"That must have been hard with your wrists tied and bare feet."

"I fell down at least once. My eyes adjusted to the darkness enough that I could see stuff. I stopped when I got to the edge of the arroyo. Otherwise, I would have fallen in."

"I thought you did fall in. I found the spot where you landed."

"Well . . . yes. I did fall in, but not until that man shot me."

"Oh, my God," Pauline whispered, taking her daughter's hand in hers. "Baby, I'm so sorry you went through all that!"

"So, you fell into the arroyo," Lansing pressed. "Did John chase you?"

"I don't know. I thought he would. I got up and started running down the creek bed. I kept tripping and falling. Finally, I had to stop. I was bleeding. I was hurting. I just couldn't go anymore. I crawled under some bushes and just crashed. I didn't wake up till the next morning."

"That's when you started walking for the highway?"

"I guess. I don't remember anything after I woke up. The next thing I knew I was in the ICU." She looked up at the sheriff. "Is that alright? Did I do okay?"

"You did great, young lady. All you need to do now is get some rest. Thank you for your help."

Lansing headed for the door. Pauline followed and stopped him in the hallway.

"Sheriff, this man who hurt my girl . . . He's not going to try again, is he?"

"I don't think so. This John person probably thinks he left her for dead. As far as I know, only a few of us know the truth. I intend to catch this guy before he learns she's still alive."

"I sincerely hope you do."

"So do I." *If he kept this to himself.*

Chapter Seventy-Seven

Alone in the canyon and with his quest complete, Lincoln decided he had earned the right to eat again. He relished the taste of the jerky as he tore pieces from the dried strips of meat. He knew better than to eat his fill. His stomach had held nothing but water for five days. He wanted to preempt an attack of indigestion. His ploy didn't work.

An hour after he ate, the digestive acids felt like they were dissolving his stomach lining along with the jerky. He had learned a trick from his firefighting brothers. Swallowing small bits of charcoal from burnt wood could settle an upset stomach by absorbing excess acid.

His immediate problem was that the mystical fire in front of him was not fed by wood. He had to scrounge in the dark until he found a piece of wood to burn. He didn't hesitate to desecrate Montezuma's Fire this time. His personal comfort seemed more important.

The impromptu remedy eventually worked. He managed to get a few dreamless hours of sleep before dawn.

***

Lincoln made one last visit to San Lorenzo Spring to fill his two water bottles. He chewed a few more shreds of jerky. Just in case, he had kept pieces of charred wood in his pocket. Fortunately, he didn't need them. The more he ate, the stronger he began to feel.

His confidence building, he began looking for a path out of the canyon. Different animals obviously visited the spring. They must have used an easier trail than the one he tried to blaze a few days earlier.

It took half an hour to work his way to the canyon rim. There was still more climbing to go. State Road 565 ran along the crest of an even higher ridge. It was almost midday when he reached the road. Already exhausted, he sat on the edge of the track, sipping water and eating another strip of dried meat. He reassured himself his trip would be mostly downhill from there.

From his perch on the ridge, he could see for miles. He guessed Santa Clara Creek was 2 miles due south. The Puye Cliff dwellings were 3 miles from where he would intercept the creek.

He wasn't too proud now to accept a ride the rest of the way. If someone didn't pick him up along Canyon Road, he knew he could hitch a ride from the Puye Cliffs Visitor's Center.

Looking again for the same 4-wheeler track that brought him to the ridge-top, he became more and more concerned about getting home. His thoughts shifted to the evil he needed to confront. Would he recognize it? Would he know what to do when he did?

This was all strange, new territory for him. He wasn't sure anyone would believe him. Who in their right mind thought vampires existed?

He knew he was alone. Even Uncle Eluterio wouldn't have the slightest idea of what to do.

Chapter Seventy-Eight

The drive from Segovia to Las Palmas took an hour. That gave Lansing lots of thinking time. He wanted to set the priorities for his office. He knew Karen Baker wasn't a problem . . . not in the short term, anyway.

The woman had been involved in two deaths. She shot her husband and might have been the driver during a hit-and-run. She claimed her husband's death was self-defense. After talking to the Abilene police, Lansing was convinced Karen Baker was the aggressor. She had a history of assaulting her husband. Plus, the autopsy showed Bill Baker was struck repeatedly and scalded with hot liquid just prior to his death.

Lansing didn't care much for James Lujan, the county prosecutor. If there was a chance he might lose a case, he wouldn't pursue it. After Lansing made an arrest, he was never sure if Lujan's office would press charges. The Karen Baker situation was becoming typical. Lujan said statements from Texas authorities were only hearsay and weren't admissible. Of course, the autopsy results would be considered during the coroner's inquest. However, Karen Baker was considered innocent until proven otherwise.

Lujan refused to press charges for the hit-and-run. Despite discrepancies in Baker's statements about the evidence found in her truck, Lansing had no proof her husband wasn't the driver. The state couldn't even prove she helped move the body. Unless Lansing had an eyewitness, there was nothing they could legally charge her with.

Despite Lansing's protests, Karen Baker was released. Even though Abilene was 500 miles away, she was allowed to return home so she could work. She promised to be available for the inquest.

Inquests were conducted in Albuquerque. It might be a few weeks or even a few months before the coroner was ready for his findings. Lansing sincerely wondered if he would ever see her again. He might not be sheriff by the time the inquest was held.

He knew Norm Salerno would insist Lansing's highest priority should be the election. With the primary three weeks away, and his newest campaign ad just released, he felt there was nothing more he needed to do. It was up to the voters now.

Lansing decided his highest priority was finding the serial killer in his county. There were two deaths with the same MO. A third had almost happened. It was only by the grace of God and Joy Baca's stubborn refusal to die that he didn't have that third fatality. Whoever the killer was, Lansing was sure Regina Sena was not his first victim.

Joy Baca might have been a target of opportunity, but it was obvious the killer was actively hunting victims. He also enjoyed taunting the police. He intentionally dumped Sena's body in a place to cause confusion, maybe conflict, between his office and the San Juan Pueblo police. It was no coincidence that he dumped Mandy Gomez's body next to his property.

He told the sheriff's office about the body and somehow that information got to the SBI. The intent was to trigger an investigation.

"Yeah," Lansing admitted out loud. "An investigation just before the primary. How convenient."

His suspicions about who was behind these machinations were beginning to solidify. He wanted to bounce his ideas off someone else before making any accusations. Tina Morales was always his first choice. She was at work and probably busy. His oldest friend in the department, Jack Rivera was an easy second choice.

***

232

"So, you're saying John Tapia contacted the State Bureau of Investigation?"

"It had to be him," Lansing said from behind his desk. "That Agent, Dale, said they got their information from a government official. Tapia also knew about the state press release before it came out. How else could he have a campaign ad on the air an hour later?" Almost as an afterthought, he asked, "What kind of car does Tapia drive?"

Rivera shrugged. "I don't know. Why?"

"I keep tripping over coincidences. The mechanic you interviewed said he saw a red Trailblazer the day before Regina Sena's body was found. Joy Baca told me this morning the man who shot her drove the same kind of car."

"What does that have to do with Tapia?"

"Baca said the man's name was John."

Rivera frowned at his boss. "There are a lot of Johns out there. I think you're reaching, Cliff."

"I know I am. Find out what Tapia drives, anyway. I need to find out if they pulled a print off that shell casing I found yesterday?"

"Who are 'they?' "

"Segovia Police forensics."

Jack Rivera stood. "If you don't have anything else, I'll check on Tapia's car."

"No, that's all I needed to talk about. Thanks, Jack."

Once Rivera left, Lansing picked up his phone and dialed the number of the Segovia police.

"Chief Solano, please."

"Who can I say is calling?"

"This is Sheriff Lansing."

A moment later, *"Solano."*

"Yeah, Ernie. This is Cliff. I need to ask a favor."

Chapter Seventy-Nine

"Who shot her?" Lincoln demanded.

It was 3:00 when Lincoln Baca spotted his father's road crew. They were doing general maintenance on the gravel road that led from the visitor's center to the ruins atop Puye Mesa.

Puye, Tewa for *the place where rabbits meet* and the ancestral home of the Santa Clara people, had been first occupied by 1250 AD. There were two sets of ruins. The summer homes were located on the top of the mesa. The winter homes were caves dug into the volcanic tuff. They were the back rooms of adobe and stone homes built on the cliff face, none of which still existed. Facing south, they retained the heat of the sun during the cold months. Visitors followed a mile-long dirt road from the valley floor to the upper ruins.

Santa Clara Reservation had 100 miles of roads to manage. Only 25 miles were paved. The road crews fell behind their planned maintenance schedule because of the Cerro Grande Fire. That, coupled with the recent monsoon rains, kept Simon Baca and his coworkers busy playing catch-up.

Simon was surprised to see his son waving at him. Lincoln had been gone for nearly a week. Their recent arguments were forgotten. The father was thankful his son was safe . . . especially after Joy was nearly killed. As his son grew closer, Simon climbed down the road grader.

Lincoln was shocked when his father embraced him in a bear hug.

"What in God's name happened to you?" Simon asked.

"What are you talking about?"

"That scab on your face . . ."

"Oh, that," Lincoln said, lightly touching his wound. He'd forgotten about it. "I fell the first day out." He didn't elaborate. "Does it look bad?"

"Yes." Simon parted his son's hair to see how far up the scab went. "You should have gotten stitches."

"There weren't any doctors where I went." After his father's reaction, Lincoln was in no hurry to examine his injury.

"We don't know who shot her," Simon admitted. "The sheriff is investigating."

"Where is she?"

"She's still in the hospital. Probably will be for a couple more days."

"I need to see her. Could you drive me to the house? I'll take my truck to the hospital."

"That won't happen."

"I know you're busy, Papa. Could one of the other guys drive me?"

"It's not that. Your truck broke down."

"What?"

Simon shrugged. "I don't know. It quit running when Joy was driving home. A man picked her up along the highway . . . he's the one who shot her."

"What about your truck?"

"Your mother has it. I'm sure she's at the hospital."

"I can't believe this . . ." Lincoln was going to finish with an expletive but stopped himself. "What am I supposed to do now?"

"Let me radio the pueblo police. They won't mind running you up to the hospital."

Simon made his call. Police Chief Padilla said he'd be there in 15 minutes.

"How was your camping trip?" Simon asked as he climbed up to the machine's seat.

"What?" Lincoln hadn't thoroughly explained his reason for visiting the wilderness. The term "camping trip" confused him.

"Your hike up to the mountains . . . how was it?"

"Oh, that." When he left the canyon that morning, he was burning with resolve. He had to confront the *tlahuelpuchi* tormenting the pueblo. He had to destroy it.

Nearly eight hours of strenuous hiking, though, had worn him down. His strength still waned from his five-day fast. The double gut-punch of Joy being shot and his truck breaking down stamped on his mood even further. The demon he had seen in his dreams seemed less important now.

"It was alright, I guess."

"What's wrong, Linc?" Simon noticed the sudden depression.

"I'm just worried about Joy," he lied. A thousand things bothered him, and he didn't think his father would understand. There was only one person he could talk to . . . Uncle Eluterio.

Chapter Eighty

Preparation for the new school year was completed. Somehow Tina found she wasn't nearly as excited as she had been in the past. Especially today. Her thoughts kept drifting back to the conversation she had with her abuela. She felt guilty over cutting the conversation short. The more she thought about it, the more she realized Naomi Sanchez would not have called unless she was truly concerned.

The principal, Chester de la Cruz, treated his staff like professionals. He didn't micromanage. If the teachers had done their prep, he didn't require them to stay any longer than needed. He knew they had lives beyond the school walls.

Tina headed back to the ranch at 2:00. She was dialing her grandparent's number twenty minutes later.

"Hola," Naomi said.

"*Mi Abuela*," Tina apologized, "I am so sorry I had to hang up this morning. I had to get to school."

"I know, I know . . ."

"We can talk now for as long as you want."

"Bueno . . ."

Naomi began. She worried about the doll Tina purchased during her visit. She sensed there was something wrong with it. The thing had an evil aura, but Naomi couldn't pick out exactly what it was from. Then, when the doll told Tina they shouldn't be together, she knew she needed to know more.

Naomi asked Tina's cousin, Luis Sanchez, to go to the *mercado* and find out as much as he could. The owners said their cousin, Miguel Santos, brought it from his village of Tetlapayac in the State of Tlaxcala. That's all they knew about the doll, other than its name, Izel.

The grandmother needed to know more, but Luis said the town was too far away. It would take him over a week to drive there and back. He couldn't miss that much work. He had friends in Mexico City, though. This town, Tetlapayac, was an hour away. He would ask if they could find this Miguel Santos and ask him about the doll.

Luis came by the night before. He reported everything he had learned.

His friend found Miguel. The man was not as reluctant to talk as he would have imagined. Miguel Santos was a troubled man . . . a very troubled man . . . over what he had done.

Miguel told his story, then took the man to Juan Huerta, the man behind the whole matter. Initially, Huerta was slow to open up. He had to be prodded. Miguel insisted they were both guilty of turning an evil loose on the world. Huerta finally spoke.

The inhabitants of Tetlapayac were Nahua, a very ancient people. They had been in their lands as long as the Maya had lived in the Yucatan, over 2,000 years. Only their brujos and shaman held onto the old religion. What they retained was powerful magic, handed down from long-forgotten primordial spirits.

Huerta's daughter, Fernanda, had been damned before birth. Someone with a deep hatred for Huerta or his wife hired a brujo to curse the innocent child. It was the kind of curse that couldn't be lifted. It was the kind of curse that took years to unfold.

When Fernanda turned thirteen, the parents discovered she could only survive on human blood. She had become a *tlahuelpuchi,* a vampire. Huerta spent every penny he earned hiring a brujo to teach Fernanda skills she would need to survive. She learned how to become a shapeshifter. Her poor mother died keeping her alive.

For three years, Huerta was able to keep his daughter's curse a secret. But Fernanda couldn't stop her cravings. Very young children were her victims of choice. As Fernanda grew older, her desire for blood increased. Too many children in Tetlapayac were becoming ill. Some were dying.

The villagers suspected Fernanda was the cause. She was a recluse, seldom leaving the house. She had to be the *tlahuelpuchi* inflicting so much pain in the town. She would have to be destroyed.

Huerta would keep her safe by sending her away. Miguel Santos reluctantly agreed to help. Miguel and Fernanda traveled by bus with Izel wrapped in the girl's arms. It took five days to reach Nogales.

Before arriving at the *mercado*, Fernanda transformed into a firefly and hid in the folds of Izel's dress. The hope was that some tourist from the United States would purchase Izel and take her across the border.

Miguel was told the doll was sold within a week. Who bought her or where she was now, neither man knew.

"But dear heart," Naomi said. "We do know who bought her and we do know where she is, don't we?"

Tina had listened quietly to Naomi's story. Her grandmother insisted she repeated Luis' exact words. Luis thought the story was unbelievable, but his friend claimed the two men he talked to were sincere. The looks on their faces told him they were not lying.

"I don't understand," Tina finally said. "If this Fernanda is such a monster, why did her father turn her loose on the world?"

"He loved her . . . more than anything else. He didn't want to watch her die."

Tina wasn't completely convinced. Still, she had seen a firefly in her room the first night home . . . a coincidence, she hoped. She rubbed the inside of her wrist where a bruise mysteriously appeared. She always bruised when she got a shot. Could Fernanda have sucked blood from her?

"Well, if any of this is true," Tina attempted to sound reassuring. "I'm sure we would have heard something."

"You already know things," Naomi observed. "You said the doll didn't want to be with you. You told me the first little girl you gave the doll to was afraid of it after only one night. What happened to the second child who received it?"

"I don't know." Tina's response was slow and thoughtful. "I'll have to ask Cliff."

"Call me back when you learn anything."

"I will, Grandma. I will."

Chapter Eighty-One

After his kiss on her forehead, Joy looked up at her big brother, fighting back the tears. "Linc, I need to tell you something."

"If it's about the truck, I know already." He saw Joy's questioning look. "Dad told me. I ran into his road crew at Puye."

"I'm so sorry."

"It's just a truck. I can get another one . . ." He smiled. "Sisters are a little harder to come by."

Joy and her mother glanced at each other. They had been shocked at the gash on Lincoln's face. He had seen the damage for the first time that day and claimed it wasn't as bad as he expected. But something else was different. This wasn't the same brooding Lincoln Baca they remembered from the week before.

"Speaking of your father," Pauline said. "I need to go home and fix his supper. Lincoln, do you want to come with me or are you going to stay for a while?"

"I'll stay."

Pauline started for the door. "Your father and I will be back as soon as he eats. Will you be hungry when you get home?"

Worried about his sister, Lincoln had forgotten his hunger pains. He blurted out his answer, "Yes!"

Lincoln sat in the now empty chair. "What happened?"

"With the truck? I don't know . . ."

"No," he grimaced. "What happened to you?"

Joy gave an abbreviated version of her story. From the look on her brother's face, she could see his anger building. "Linc, there's nothing we can do. I trust the sheriff. He'll find out who did this to me."

Lincoln took a deep breath. He knew she was right.

"You know, mom and dad were upset that you took off like that."

"I told mom I'd be gone for a few days."

"Yeah, but no one knew where you went."

"I needed to get away," Lincoln shrugged. "Besides, I can take care of myself."

"Sure, you can . . . Just look at your face." She ignored his scowl. "So, where did you go?"

"Up in the mountains . . . somewhere . . . I don't know if I could find the place again."

"What place?"

"The canyon I stayed in."

"Wasn't it cold?"

"I brought a jacket, so that helped." He hesitated before his next statement. "Plus, I had a fire every night."

Since leaving the canyon that morning, the events of the last five days felt more and more distant. They also seemed less real. Did he actually encounter the great Aztec King, Montezuma? Did he truly have visions of a demon attacking the children of the pueblo?

Or were these hallucinations, courtesy of his tumor?

Still, he sat next to a mysterious fire every night . . . a fire he hadn't built or didn't need wood for fuel. That experience was real. He was sure of it. He wanted to tell Joy about his visit to the mountains, but how could he if he had his own doubts.

Lincoln felt exhaustion taking hold. It had been a long day. Physically, he was worn out. The emotional stress of Joy's injury pulled at him. The idea of a full stomach and stretching out in his own, soft bed, bubbled to the surface. Suddenly, it was all-consuming.

"When do you think mom and dad will get here?"

Joy glanced at the wall clock. "Pretty soon, I guess. Why?"

"Now that I know you'll be okay, I just want to go home, eat, and sleep."

"They'll be bringing my dinner tray soon. You're welcome to have it."

"Is hospital food as bad as they say?"

Joy laughed. "It might be worse."

"I can wait until I get home."

Chapter Eighty-Two

When Lansing pulled up to the ranch house, Tina was waiting for him on the porch. He had called to tell her he was knocking off work early. As he walked up, she gave him a kiss, then handed him a cold bottle of beer. He gave her a questioning look.

"You sounded like you needed one."

He gave her one of his half-smiles, then took a sip. "You know me too well."

"Bad day?"

"Not bad . . . Just typical."

She led him into the house. "I haven't started dinner yet."

"I'm in no hurry. Let me change out of my uniform."

Getting into his civilian clothes was part of Lansing's ritual for de-compressing. That was always followed by a visit with the horses. Tina joined him on the walk to the corral.

"So, what made your day so typical?"

"Lujan, the county prosecutor, turned Karen Baker loose today."

"She's the one who shot her husband?"

"Yeah."

"Why was she let go?"

"Insufficient evidence . . . Lujan's go-to excuse when he's not sure he'll get a guilty verdict. He'd rather see a killer go loose than ruin his perfect record for convictions. He did order her to be available for the inquest."

"When's that?"

"Who knows? She's on her way back to Abilene."

"What about her husband's body?"

"She'll make arrangements to have it shipped home when the Medical Investigator's finished."

They reached the corral's wooden fencing. Lansing's three horses, Cement Head, Little Orphan Annie, and Paladin, trotted over to greet them. Oscar Vega's little pinto, Chico, kept his distance. Each animal took their turn nuzzling its human friends.

"Don't worry. You'll get fed. Oscar will be home soon," Lansing promised. His ranch foreman was usually back from his horse-gentling job by 6:00.

Once again in the ranch house, Lansing opened a second beer. He sat at the kitchen table while Tina sliced ham for sandwiches.

"I talked to Joy Baca today . . . the girl who was shot. We know for sure now we're looking for a dark red Trailblazer. She even gave us a first name . . . John."

"That's the name he told her?"

"Yes."

"How do you know he wasn't lying?"

"I guess we don't, but why would he lie?"

"Why tell her the truth?"

Lansing shook his head. "You're getting cynical in your old age."

"Comes from hanging around a cop."

"I didn't realize I was such a bad influence."

"Oh, you're not always bad."

"That's good to know." He paused and stared out the window. "I asked Ernie Solano, the police chief in Segovia, to see if his folks could pull a partial print off the shell casing I found."

"Did they?"

"Nothing usable. If they had, I'd have it checked against John Tapia's fingerprint card."

"Why would they have his fingerprints?"

"He used to be on the force."

"Ah . . ." She gave Lansing a doubtful glance. "I guess that's one way to win an election."

"What do you mean?"

"Charge your opponent with a crime. Even if it doesn't stick, you've damaged his image."

"You think I would stoop that low?"

"Do you really think Tapia is your hit-and-run driver?"

"No," he admitted. "I couldn't link him to a Trailblazer, either."

"The campaign is getting to you, isn't it?"

"Maybe a little," he snorted. "But as far as Tapia goes, I was doing my job. I eliminated him as a suspect."

"Un-huh," Tina grunted as she began slicing a tomato. "I talked to my Grandmother Naomi today." Her tone was casual.

"Anything wrong?"

She shook her head. "No, of course not."

As much as she loved Naomi, she had a hard time buying into her grandmother's tale about Mexican vampires. It didn't hurt to probe a little, though.

"That little girl you gave Izel to . . . does she like it?"

The sheriff shrugged. "I suppose so. I haven't heard anything. Why?"

"Just curious. My grandmother mentioned her. I had told her that Deedee Rivera was afraid of the doll. She asked if anyone else had a problem with her. I told her I would ask."

"Does your abuela think something's wrong with the doll?"

"Oh, no . . . Not at all!"

Tina answered almost too quickly . . . and the denial didn't ring true to Lansing. "I can check with the family tomorrow, if you want. Make sure everything is okay with the doll."

"You wouldn't mind?" Tina sounded relieved.

"It won't be a problem."

Chapter Eighty-Three

John Tapia sat at his office desk brooding. He was surprised at how quickly Cliff Lansing countered his accusatory campaign ad. Even though his campaign manager told him not to worry, he did. He had hoped they could get a big bounce in the polls before Lansing could respond. Now, he wasn't so sure.

The buzzer on his intercom went off.

"What?" he snapped.

"There is an Abigale Fontana here to see you."

"What?" This time he choked on the word.

"Abigale Fontana . . . from Santa Fe. She said you two have business together."

"Yes-yes," he sputtered. This was not good. He didn't need Abbie Fontana in his life now. Not ever again. He thought he had given her the brush-off. After regaining his composure, he told his secretary, "Send her in."

The secretary opened the door and ushered the visitor in. Tapia stood and walked to the front of his desk.

Abbie was dressed in an expensive-looking business suit. Her hair was professionally styled, her makeup perfect. She beamed with a smile that exuded confidence.

"Thank you, Ann," he told the secretary. Once the door was closed, he scowled at his lover, not sure what to say.

"What do you think?" She slowly turned, modeling herself.

"What the hell are you doing?" Tapia asked through gritted teeth.

"I wanted to surprise you." Her smile faded a little.

"I don't need any surprises. Not today. What's this all about?"

"Last Friday, after we were together, I found out I passed my real estate exams. Don't look so surprised. You've known for years I've wanted my real estate license. I have my application already prepared to submit to the state board. Aren't you happy for me?"

"Why are you here? Now?"

"I wanted to tell you, in person. I'm relocating to San Phillipe County. I'm going to be a real estate agent and we'll be able to be close together." She noticed Tapia's scowl deepen. "What's wrong, Johnny? I thought you'd be excited. I mean, you told me I was an important part of your life."

"Yeah, right. Of course." He tried to force a smile. "It's this campaign. It's got me bogged down. And I wasn't ready for such . . . good news."

"That's okay, Sweetie. I understand."

She stepped closer, threw her arms around him, and gave him a big kiss on the lips. Tapia pulled away. Moving around his desk, he opened a drawer and pulled out tissues to wipe the lipstick off.

"What's wrong, Johnny?"

"Right now is not a good time."

"Don't worry. I am driving up to Las Palmas anyway. I want to see what housing is like up there." She thought for a moment. "I might have to spend the night. Are there any motels?"

He shrugged. "Sure."

"I don't suppose you could tear yourself away from your campaign for a little while, could you?"

Tapia was not ready for any distractions, especially from an ex-lover who was now a major nuisance. He had to think fast.

"Abbie, you know I want to be with you."

"I want to be with you too, Johnny."

"We have to be careful."

"I understand."

"I can't afford for you to call me directly." He wrote a number on a sticky note. "This is a friend of mine. If you do get a room for the night, call and tell him where you're staying. He'll pass it on to me." He noticed her concerned look. "Don't worry. I'll tell him to expect your call."

"Okay if you say so."

She started around the desk to plant another kiss, but he held up his hand to stop her.

"Not now, Abbie. We'll have plenty of time later."

"You promise?" she pouted.

"I promise."

"Okay. I'll see you tonight, Sweetie." She stopped at the door and blew him a kiss.

Tapia mouthed the words "I love you."

Once he was alone, Tapia picked up the phone and dialed the same number he had given Abbie.

"Hello."

"This is John. I have a problem."

Chapter Eighty-Four

Lansing stopped at the door to the day room. Deputies Cortez and Trumbull were filling their coffee cups. "Danny, Marla, I need for you to come to the front office for a moment."

"What's up, Sheriff?" Cortez asked, but his boss was already gone.

When the two deputies reached the front office/reception area, the sheriff had positioned himself in front of the county wall map. Two other deputies were at desks. The dispatcher, Marilyn Bea, and Desk Sergeant Montoya listened from their stations.

"I passed this on to the day patrol before they took off this morning. And I want the rest of you to listen up. The San Phillipe Sheriff's Department is not pursuing an active investigation against City Councilman John Tapia.

"Queries from our office yesterday regarding Mr. Tapia simply followed legitimate leads. As of this moment, he is no longer considered a suspect in our hit-and-run investigation . . . or any other investigation."

Lansing had a hard time getting to sleep the night before. Both Jack Rivera and Tina Morales had questioned his motive behind trying to tie Tapia to the hit-and-run deaths. If the two people closest to him doubted his intentions, he realized he had to look at those intentions as well. He kept telling himself he had sincere concerns. But he also admitted his probe approached pettiness. Was he really looking for a killer or trying to eliminate a rival for his office?

"I accept complete responsibility for any confusion. I apologize for any misunderstanding I may have caused during our fact-finding efforts. Are there any questions?"

Deputy Cortez raised his hand.

"Danny?"

"Do you think you're going to lose the election?"

"No."

"Is there a chance though?"

"I refer you back to my last answer." He looked around at the rest of his audience. "Are there any serious questions?"

A chuckle wafted through the group, relieving the tension.

"Okay, good. Let's get back to work."

Back in his office, Lansing frowned at the stack of reports piled on his desk. He knew half of them weren't worth looking at. He wished there was room in the budget for an administrative assistant. They could toss out the chaff and leave him with the important papers to look at. He thought it was more important, though, to have an extra deputy on the road than a glorified file clerk.

As he dug through the stack of papers, there was a short knock at his door. Lansing looked up.

"What are you doing here, Jack? It's your day off."

"Susan's at work. Deedee's in school. I finished my 'honey-do' list," Rivera said. "Thought I'd sign out one of the ARs and head down to the State Police firing range."

"That's right. You have your annual recertification next month."

"I do, indeed." The Chief Deputy hesitated. "Listen, Cliff. I talked to Clem Montoya a minute ago. He told me about your little speech this morning."

"Okay," Lansing said, knowing Rivera wasn't finished. "And?"

"You made the right decision. I think any Tapia investigation would come across as an election spoiler. Also, taking responsibility for the whole thing was a nice touch."

"Thanks, but that was the 'no-brainer' part. Admitting my real motives to myself . . . that was the struggle."

"For what it's worth . . ." He gave his boss a thumbs-up before stepping away from the door.

Lansing simply nodded in appreciation, then turned back to his task.

Chapter Eighty-Five

When he walked from his house to the Senior Citizen Center, Lincoln Baca was surprised by how much his legs hurt. Climbing up and down the ridges and hiking over ten miles as he had the day before never bothered him like this. He suspected sitting cross-legged for five days and nights had something to do with it. It was just another reminder of how out of shape he'd become.

He stood outside the Center until the shuttle arrived with Uncle Eluterio and four other elderly visitors. Lincoln dutifully stood near the shuttle's door so he could assist those who needed help stepping down.

Eluterio beamed when he saw his grandnephew. "Ah, Lincoln, my boy. Where have you been?"

It was obvious the old man had forgotten about Lincoln's vision quest.

"I'll tell you all about it when we get inside."

He took his uncle by his arm and guided him to the Center's door. They followed the rest of the small procession into the building. A dozen other seniors were already in the activities room when they got there. A female attendant was trying to drum up interest in a rousing game of bingo.

Not wanting any hurt feelings, Lincoln explained he and his uncle needed to discuss family business. The attendant reluctantly agreed once she had most of the others willing to play.

Lincoln moved two chairs next to Eluterio's favorite window.

"How about a cup of coffee?"

Eluterio nodded. "No sugar."

Lincoln retrieved two paper cups of coffee from the 30-cup maker along one wall. While the bingo game droned on behind them, the two men talked in low tones.

"Uncle, do you remember telling me last week I should go on a vision quest?"

Eluterio thought hard. "Vision quest?" He nodded slowly. "You haven't been to see me because you went on a quest."

"Yes. Exactly."

"You were depressed . . . You wanted guidance . . . Guidance I couldn't give you."

"Right! You said I should look to a higher power through fasting and prayer."

"I do remember telling you that!" He studied his nephew. "You went away from the pueblo?"

Lincoln nodded. "I went into the wilderness . . . up in the mountains . . ."

"You saw something, didn't you?"

The younger man hesitated. As time and distance grew, he doubted his experience more and more. When he woke that morning, Lincoln wasn't sure he had even gone on his quest. He looked for reassurance that he had been gone for nearly a week . . . reassurance his mother provided at breakfast. Yes, he had been gone for five days. Why would he ask such a strange question? "I was just curious," was the best response he could muster.

"I saw . . ." Lincoln looked for the right words. "This is what I think I saw . . ."

He told his uncle about everything . . . from the first moment he stumbled upon the fire in the canyon to the emergence of Montezuma and his giant snake. He went into great detail about how he purified himself each day . . . washing in the spring, then wafting himself with the sage smoke. He described his deep meditation, and how he was physically transported back to the pueblo twice.

The old man constantly interrupted his nephew's story, asking for clarification on some things, and more details on others. He became uncomfortable when Lincoln described his encounter with the *tlahuelpuchi,* the vampire/demon. He listened but asked no questions . . . not even how the young man learned the name of the creature.

Lunch was served at 12:15. Lincoln had talked for two hours and still had more story to tell. Eluterio peppered him with questions as they ate the squash soup and corn cakes.

The Center closed at 2:00, so Lincoln found himself hurrying to finish telling his uncle everything. When he reached the end, Eluterio asked, "When you started, you said you were going to tell me 'what you think you saw.' It took you four hours to tell me what happened. You had far too many details for your story to be a figment of your imagination."

Lincoln hadn't told his uncle about the tumor. He had hoped to bring the grand feather Montezuma dropped into the canyon as his pledge to reappear. It was nowhere to be found when he left for home. The single, most important item of proof that he met the Aztec king was gone. Others would doubt his encounter. Now, he did as well.

"You believe that I had that experience?"

"I remember the old legends about Montezuma . . . Montezuma and his *vibóron.* There were tales about his sacred fire and the great wisdom the Aztec king would reveal. Did you hear those stories when you were younger?"

Lincoln shook his head. "I don't think I knew anything about him before this past week."

"How, then, could your imagination conjure up what you experienced?" The old man shook his head. "I don't think it could."

He grew very serious. "I am most bothered about the demon-girl from your dreams. You said the Aztec believed she was real. He could even tell you what she was and where she was from."

"Yes, Uncle."

The attendant had finished collecting the lunch bowls. She announced it was time for the seniors to start moving outside to board the shuttles.

Eluterio was never bothered by much. The attendant's announcement annoyed him.

"Witch," he muttered. "Lincoln, can you visit me tonight?"

"If my dad doesn't need the truck, sure."

"Call first. Make sure I'm home."

"Where are you going?"

"There are wise men I must talk to . . . men much wiser than me. When you come tonight, I will tell you what they say."

"I'll be there."

Chapter Eighty-Six

On weekdays, Lansing always kept one deputy on office duty. After sorting through the papers on his desk, Lansing gave Jake Redwine the shorter stack for filing. Back in his office, Lansing glanced at his clock. He fully expected Tina to call him during her lunch. When she did, she was going to ask if he . . . did what?

"Damn, that's right!" he mumbled. "I was supposed to call the Gonzalez farm and ask about that stupid doll."

It took him a few minutes to locate the phone number.

"Hello?" Dorothy Gonzalez said.

"Hi, Mrs. Gonzalez, this is Sheriff Lansing."

"Oh, hi, Sheriff. What can I do for you?"

"This may sound like a silly question, but my friend, Tina Morales . . . she's the one who bought that doll I gave your daughter . . . Tina was curious how the two were getting along."

"I wish I had never seen that . . . thing. I wish you had never brought it here!"

"I . . . I'm sorry," he stammered, shocked at her response. "What happened?"

Dorothy detailed their experiences the week before. They had the doll in the house for two days. After the first night, Edie woke up feeling ill. The second morning she was so sick, they had to take her to the hospital. Esteban, her husband, immediately blamed the doll.

Edie kept talking about a woman who came to visit her both nights. She said she was pretty and always kissed her. I thought she only imagined the visits, but her older sister backed up her story . . . but Adonna said the woman scared her.

"How is Edie now?"

"Much better . . . They gave her a blood transfusion because of her low blood count. The doctors suspect she had been exposed to an insecticide. That was their diagnosis. But I'm not so sure. None of the other kids got sick.

"I think Esteban was right. Since we got rid of that doll, Edie's gotten well, and that woman hasn't been back."

"This woman . . . you're saying she broke into your house and made Edie sick?"

"I don't know . . ." the worried mother confessed. "All I can tell you is once the doll was gone, Edie got better."

"Where's the doll now?"

"Esteban threw it in the yard. Eric, our oldest, said his girlfriend found it and took it home."

"That's Joy Baca, right?"

"Yes, the poor girl. Eric visited her yesterday at the hospital. He said she may be released today. Have you found who shot her?"

"We're looking. It's our top priority," the sheriff admitted. "I guess I need to talk to her about the doll." He hesitated. "Listen, Mrs. Gonzalez, I can't tell you how sorry I am about your daughter. I truly hope that doll had nothing to do with her illness."

"I don't think there's anything you can say that will change my opinion."

"I understand." He didn't believe he really understood how she felt. It seemed like the right thing to say. "If there's anything you need, please, let our office know."

"I will, Sheriff. Thanks."

After the call ended, Lansing stared at the phone. What the hell was going on? He wanted to call Tina and ask what she knew. That wasn't possible. She was teaching. He suspected she knew something, though.

Why else would she want him to call the Gonzalez farm and ask about the doll?

Tina had talked to her grandmother the previous afternoon. What did Naomi Sanchez know about the doll? What did she tell Tina?

He needed to talk to the teacher . . . and Joy Baca.

Chapter Eighty-Seven

Izel was not sitting on the dresser where she had left her!

That was the first thing Joy noticed when she walked into her bedroom. She had been in the hospital for two days. It seemed a lot longer. Her doctor agreed to let her go home with the stipulation that she take things easy for at least a week.

She didn't argue with the order. She was unsteady on her feet when she climbed into the family truck from the wheelchair. Her mother stayed close on the short walk from the truck into the house. Joy, stubborn like everyone else in her family, wanted to manage on her own. She was surprised at how tired she was when she got inside. Pauline offered to fix a place for her on the sofa, but Joy wanted the comfort of her own bed.

"Where's Izel?"

Her mother had no idea who she was referring to. "Who's Izel?"

"My doll . . ." She nodded toward her dresser. "The one I brought from Eric's place."

Pauline shrugged. "I have no idea what you're talking about."

"Don't you remember? That porcelain doll . . . I showed it to you."

"Oh, yes. The Mexican doll." She glanced at the dresser. "It's missing?"

"Yes, she was right there." Joy pointed at the empty spot in front of the dresser mirror. "Did Linc come in here and take it?"

"Why would he do something like that?"

"Where is he?"

"He said he was going to visit Uncle Eluterio at the Senior Citizens Center. He'll be back later."

Too tired to argue, Joy accepted the fact that she would need to solve the missing doll mystery later. Her mother helped her get into a night-gown. Even though she had been in bed for almost two days, Joy had no problem falling asleep.

***

It was late afternoon when Joy stumbled into the dining room. Paul-ine and Lincoln were seated at the table, talking.

"What are you doing out of bed?" Pauline scolded.

"I'm hungry," Joy said, yawning.

"Well, sit down before you fall down," Pauline said, jumping up to help her daughter. "Supper's on the stove."

"What are you fixing?"

"Green Chile Casserole."

"O-o-o, that sounds good." Joy sat in the chair her brother pulled out for her. "How long before we eat?"

"Not till your father gets home. You know that. Would you like some salsa and chips, or a sandwich?"

"Chips and salsa would be great."

When her mother stepped into the kitchen, Joy turned to her brother. "Did you go in my room and take the doll from my dresser?"

"I never go in your room." Lincoln was indignant at the accusation. "Aren't you a little too old for dolls?"

"This one was special. I got it at Eric's house. It was a beautiful, porcelain doll."

"What was so special about it?"

"I don't know . . . It just was. Eric said the sheriff gave it to his little sister, Edie. He said it came from Mexico . . ."

"From Mexico!" Lincoln suddenly became very interested in Joy's missing doll. "Where in Mexico?"

Joy was surprised at her brother's response. "I don't know. Does it matter?"

"It might. Why did the little girl give you her doll?"

"She didn't. Their father didn't like it for some reason. He threw it in their yard. That's where I found her. Eric said I could have her, so, I brought her home."

"When was that?"

"Saturday?" She thought hard for a moment. "Yeah, it was Saturday. I got shot Sunday night."

Lincoln did a quick review of his days and nights in the canyon. Saturday night was when he had his first dream about the demon. "Did anything happen here at the Pueblo Saturday night?"

"Like what?"

"Like did anyone see a stranger wandering the streets? Someone they'd never seen before. Or was any house broken into?"

Joy almost said no, but then she remembered what sent her to the neighbor's house Sunday morning. "Old Emily Diaz told mom she saw me go into the Chavarria house Saturday night."

"Why did she think it was you?"

"I guess she saw some girl with a flashlight walk from our house to the neighbor's. I went over there and asked if anyone broke into their house. They said they didn't see anyone."

"So, nothing happened?"

"Their six-month-old baby, Mateo, was sick. I drove them to the hospital."

"What was wrong with him?"

"The doctors weren't sure. His blood count was low, so they gave him a transfusion. One of the nurses mentioned malnutrition, but I don't

261

think anything came of that. His mom showed me where he was bitten by bugs. I think that's what made him sick."

Yeah, he was bitten, alright, Lincoln thought. But not by any bug.

"How is Mateo doing now?"

"Oh, I don't know." Joy cracked a half-smile. "I've been a little out of touch recently."

Lincoln wanted to say something about his dream and the encounter with the demon/vampire. Uncle Eluterio made it clear. He shouldn't say anything until Eluterio talked to others. They didn't want a panic.

The home phone rang, and Pauline answered on the kitchen extension.

"Joy," she said from the doorway. "Sheriff Lansing wants to talk to you."

Chapter Eighty-Eight

"Hey, Preacher Man!"

Black looked up from the engine he was working on. Chaparro stood inside the open bay door. Behind him were two friends, both much taller. All three wore sunglasses.

"This area is for employees only," the mechanic growled. "Get out!"

"You told *mi abuela* you would 'shoot my ass' if I came near you. What kind of talk is that?"

"I said, Get out!"

"Then you come outside. That car won't go nowhere." Chaparro and his friends stepped out of the shadows of the garage bay and into the sunlight.

Black grabbed a rag to wipe his hands as he followed. He stopped a few feet short of his visitors, just out of reach. Three Lowrider cars sat in the lot behind the three men. "I'm busy. What do you want?"

"Why did you say those things to *mi abuela*?"

"What's an abuela?"

"That's a grandmother, you stupid . . ." one of Chaparro's friends started to say.

Their short leader held up his hand to silence the man. "Like Lupe says . . . abuela means grandmother. So, why did you tell her you were going to shoot me?"

"I said, if you come near my property, I'd shoot your ass."

"Why would you say that? What did I ever do to you?"

"You tore up my trailer. It took me two hours to fix everything!" He could have mentioned the money he spent, but Black wanted to keep their conversation short.

"Man, why do you think I would do that?"

"Call it a hunch."

Chaparro shook his head. "I thought you and I were friends, Preacher Man."

"Why did you think that?"

"You invited me to your church."

"No, I didn't. Only Native Americans can attend."

"When me and my compadres showed up Sunday, you said we were too late for your service."

"Even if you had shown up on time, I wouldn't have let you in."

"Man, what do you have against me?" The lowrider became animated, gesturing toward Black, then his friends. "What's wrong with me and my friends?"

"I'm sure you're all nice guys . . . I just don't need any new friends right now. This job and my church keep me busy enough."

"So, even though I didn't do nothing, you're still going to shoot me and my friends if we visit you?"

"I guess we'll never know. There's no reason you need to step onto my property, so there'll be no reason for me to shoot you."

With that Black turned and headed back to the car he was working on. As he walked away, one of Chaparro's friends called him a *"pendejo,"* whatever the hell that was. He didn't bother to look back.

After he finished the project he was working on, he walked to the shop's office. Glancing at the lot, the Lowriders were gone. When he reached the phone, he dug a piece of paper from his wallet, then dialed the number written on it.

"This is Peter," the man said when he answered.

"Yeah, Peter, this is Jeremiah. I was wondering if you were working tonight."

Peter Delgado was the drummer for Black's ceremonies. He worked maintenance at the *Ohkay Hotel Casino. "No, not tonight."*

"I need your help." Black told him about Chaparro and his visits. The lowrider was a persistent cuss, and the preacher was sure he'd get a visit that night. Did Delgado have any weapons, and could he help?

"*Do you think going to war with a Mexican gang is such a good idea?*"

"I don't know if it's a gang, but what am I supposed to do? Back down? Let them run all over me? Isn't that something Indians have had enough of?"

"*When you put it like that . . .*" Delgado was quiet for a moment. "*I have a twelve-gauge, pump.*"

"What's the capacity?"

"*Five plus one in the chamber . . . but I need to pick up a box of shells.*"

"I'd grab two boxes . . . just in case."

"*Damn, Jeremiah, how many lowriders are you expecting?*"

"How many are there in Segovia?"

"*More than we could ever handle.*" The drummer sounded worried.

After a long pause, Black said, "I was going to ask you to show up before dark but never mind. Maybe this wasn't such a good idea."

"*I'll be there if you need me.*"

"No, forget about it. I need to come up with a better idea than having a shootout. I don't want to kill anyone and I'm not looking to be killed."

Chapter Eighty-Nine

Tina's conversation with Lansing at lunch was short. As a cafeteria monitor that day, she didn't have time to explain what her abuela said about the doll. He asked if she could stop by his office before going to the ranch.

Even though it was the first day of the new school year, the science teacher had a hard time concentrating on the lesson plans. Her thoughts kept drifting back to what Lansing said. "I think there's something wrong with that doll of yours. We need to discuss what Abuela Naomi told you."

"You go first," Tina said, taking a seat in front of Lansing's desk. "What did the Gonzalezes' say?"

Lansing repeated everything Dorothy Gonzalez told him. The doll was a curse and she wished she'd never seen it before. Over two nights, Edie got progressively sicker, and Esteban blamed the doll. The mother was genuinely upset that Edie talked about a woman coming to her bed at night and kissing her. At first, Dorothy thought the little girl imagined the woman or that this was a manifestation of her illness. But another daughter saw the same woman both nights.

"What happened to Izel?"

"The husband threw it away. Joy Baca found it on the ground and took it home."

"Isn't that the same girl that got shot?"

"Yes."

"Can we talk to her? I mean, is she in any condition to be bothered?"

"I think she'll be fine. Before I talk to anyone, though, I want to know what your grandmother told you."

Tina's doubt over what Naomi Sanchez told her had disappeared. Deedee Rivera's fear of Izel, the mystery woman in Edie Gonzalez's bedroom seen by two children, Edie's illness, and the revelation she needed a blood transfusion . . . These facts were like tumblers falling into place to unlock a safe. The teacher had no problem with admitting what she'd been told.

Lansing listened intently for thirty minutes as Tina recounted the discussion with her grandmother. When she was finished, he sat quietly thinking about the teacher's story. Finally, he said, "I think your grandmother believes everything she told you. But how much can we believe?"

"What do you mean?"

"The two men in the village . . . the supposed father and the man who took the doll to Nogales . . . they told a story to your cousin's friend. The friend tells the story to your cousin. Your cousin repeats the story to your grandmother. She tells you. You tell me. How much of the original story did I hear?"

"All of it!" Tina snapped.

"You don't know that. It went through three filters before it reached you . . . the friend, your cousin, and Naomi. We all have selective hearing. We think we remember what we were told. You and I both know that doesn't happen."

"You don't believe what my grandmother told me?"

"I said your grandmother probably believes the tale she told. That's what I believe."

"You don't think there could be a vampire roaming the countryside?"

"I know anything is possible."

"What about what Mrs. Gonzalez said? Do you believe her?"

"So far, yes."

"Isn't it possible the woman the two girls saw in the bedroom was the vampire? I mean, Edie needed blood when she went to the hospital . . . and her mother didn't think it was from exposure to pesticides. Maybe she needed blood because it was drained from her."

Lansing mulled over Tina's assertion for a long moment. "You're saying this vampire girl transforms into an insect, hides in the folds of a Mexican doll's dress, so she can move around undetected."

"How else did she get into the bedroom?"

"If that's the case, then your vampire is now at the Santa Clara Pueblo."

"It's time to call the Baca girl, don't you think?"

Lansing nodded. Without saying a word, he reached for the phone and called the hospital. He was connected to the nurse's station where he was informed Joy Baca had gone home that morning.

The Baca phone number was on a note. Lansing had looked it up earlier. When he called, Pauline Baca answered.

"Hi, Mrs. Baca. This is Sheriff Lansing. I understand Joy was released from the hospital today. How is she doing?"

"Much better, Sheriff. Thank you for asking."

"If she's available, could I talk to her?"

"Certainly."

A few muffled words were spoken before Joy picked up the receiver.

"Hi, Sheriff. Can I help you?"

Chapter Ninety

Lansing used the speakerphone so Tina could be part of the conversation. Joy was confused over the teacher's interest in Izel. Tina was forced to give a brief recap of what her grandmother told her. Then Lansing summarized his conversation with Dorothy Gonzalez. Joy already knew what happened to Edie, though the revelation of the woman in the bedroom was new to her.

Tina confided her fear that Joy brought this vampire to the pueblo.

Joy shared her experiences. One of Joy's elderly neighbors had possibly seen the vampire Saturday night. Sunday, she took a mother and her baby to the hospital. The baby had to have a blood transfusion as well. Like Edie, little Mateo survived.

Lincoln listened to Joy's half of the conversation. He wanted desperately to contribute what he knew. However, he stuck to his promise to Eluterio that he would say nothing about his visions until his uncle spoke to "wiser men" than himself.

Lansing and Tina both were shocked to learn Izel had been removed from Joy's bedroom while she was absent. The pueblo teen admitted she hadn't mounted a search yet, but she was still regaining her strength. Her alarm over the missing doll increased tenfold after her conversation with the sheriff and teacher. She would enlist her mother and Lincoln in looking for Izel.

"What should I do when I find her?"

Tina didn't hesitate to answer. "Destroy her . . . anyway you can."

"Will that stop this vampire thing?"

"That would eliminate her hiding place," Lansing observed.

"At least one of them," Tina agreed.

"I'll let you know what happens," Joy said before hanging up.

The partners stared at each other after the call.

"What do we do now?"

Lansing shook his head. "There's nothing we can do. I have no jurisdiction in Santa Clara. Even if I did, how would I arrest a vampire? What would I charge her with?"

"Shouldn't you call the Pueblo Police . . . tell them what's going on?"

"I can call Chief Padilla and ask him nicely to talk to Joy Baca. She can fill him in on what we think is going on. It would be better that he hears it from a pueblo member rather than an outsider."

"I'm frustrated we can't do more," Tina said, fighting back tears. "It's my fault . . . all of it. If I had just listened to my abuela and left the doll at that store . . . She said there was something wrong with it!"

Lansing stood and walked around his desk. Tina stood as he approached. The sheriff kissed her on the forehead, then wrapped her in his arms. He could feel her shake from crying.

"You did nothing wrong, Sweetheart." His voice was calm and soothing. "You had no idea any of this would happen."

"But if I . . ."

"No," he said firmly. "That's enough."

He held her for nearly five minutes. Her weeping gradually subsided. Finally, he said, "When you're ready, I'll walk you out to the car."

She nodded, separating from him to search for a tissue.

"I'm ready," she said after drying her eyes. She removed sunglasses from her purse to hide the redness.

As Lansing walked her out, Tina waved at Marilyn but said nothing. She slipped into her driver's seat and looked up at Lansing. "Thank you, Cliff."

"For what?"

"For being you."

"Thanks." Never good at getting compliments, Lansing was embarrassed. "I won't be late."

He stood in the parking lot and watched her drive away, grateful she was part of his life. For a moment he forgot about the election, the hit-and-run murderer, and the alleged vampire terrorizing Santa Clara Pueblo.

Chapter Ninety-One

Uncle Eluterio sat alone in his bedroom, lit only by a floor lamp over his shoulder. He stared straight ahead, his elbows resting on the arms of his wooden rocker. When Lincoln opened the door, the old man remained as still as a statue.

"Uncle Eluterio," the younger man said softly. "I'm here."

Eluterio didn't respond until Lincoln spoke his name a second time. He blinked his eyes as if emerging from a trance, then turned his head to look at the visitor.

"Lincoln?" The old man's voice was gravelly and hoarse.

"Yes, uncle. You told me earlier today to come over this evening . . ."

"I remember," Eluterio snapped. "I haven't lost my mind!"

Lincoln was shocked at his angry response. He'd never seen his uncle in such a foul mood. "What's wrong, uncle?"

"Sit, so we can talk," he commanded.

The sparse bedroom had only one chair and a bed. Lincoln sat on the mattress edge, a few feet from his uncle. Afraid to say anything, he let Uncle Eluterio speak when he was ready.

The old man stared straight ahead again, his eyes fixed on the floor.

"We met in the kiva." Most Pueblo people had abandoned the circular holy place dug into the earth. A single, large room now filled the purpose. "Both the Summer Moiety and the Winter Moiety Chiefs came. Six other elders . . . men who once held important offices . . . attended.

"I told them first about your vision quest . . . how you discovered Montezuma's Fire and how you were visited by the great king the second night. I explained how you fasted and purified yourself every day. I told them about how you meditated."

Eluterio continued. Everything he described was a repeat of what Lincoln told him earlier in the day. He included Lincoln's experience with the vampire/demon.

"I told them . . . Montezuma chose you, Lincoln." Eluterio shifted his gaze from the floor to his nephew. As he spoke, he got angrier. "You have been selected to be a protector of our people. That's why you were shown the evil that has descended on our village. I told them we must all rise up and defeat this threat and that you would lead us!"

"What did they say?"

"They laughed at me!" The old man slammed his fist on the arm of his chair. "Cisneros, the Winter Chief, said, 'Is this the nephew who saw a family of atosle during the Great Fire? No one believed him then. And now he claims he met Montezuma!' He called me an old fool and you a liar!

"They claimed they knew about the baby, Mateo. He had been bitten by insects. No more children had gone to the hospital. They said your demon was no more real than this Aztec king you invented. The others nodded and chuckled.

"I didn't wait for more insults. I left before I said something wrong."

"Calm down, uncle," Lincoln said as quietly and soothingly as he could. He moved closer and gently touched the old man's arm. "It doesn't matter what those old turtles say. You and I . . . we know the truth."

There was a time when the Pueblo elders' ridicule would have angered Lincoln. Old men were set in their ways. Their personal experiences defined their realities. Anything beyond what they believed was automatically rejected. The former firefighter knew this and was fine with it. A new serenity had taken hold of him.

"I appreciate that you went to the elders on my behalf," he said. "It's not your fault they have rocks for brains."

273

Eluterio patted Lincoln's hand, his way of saying thanks.

"Will you be alright?"

"Yes, my boy. I will."

Lincoln stood.

"Are you leaving so soon?"

"I have to. There is still a demon preying on this Pueblo. She must be stopped . . . no matter what those old fools think."

"I should come with you!" Eluterio tried to stand.

"No, uncle. This has been a long day for you. You need to rest."

"How are you going to stop this . . . evil?"

"I'll figure out something. Tomorrow, I'll tell you what happened."

Back in the family truck, Lincoln shuddered at the thought of confronting the vampire/demon in the flesh. Even worse . . . he had no idea how he would destroy it.

Chapter Ninety-Two

Jeremiah Black looked around the interior of his trailer. He wanted to make sure nothing was left behind. He had moved his living accommodations into the adobe church. His plan was to keep the trailer lit at night. When Chaparro and his crew arrived, he wanted their focus away from where he would make his stand. If bullets did fly, the solid walls of his new parsonage were better protection than a thin, aluminum shell.

Stepping outside, the sun was setting. Shadows, stretching like long fingers, grabbed at the land. The cool of the high desert washed over him. Oklahoma had nothing like this. In the summer, the nights were hot and sultry. Growing up with no air conditioning, his family would drag their metal-framed beds outside, onto the lawn. There was a chance they could catch a hint of a breeze, just enough to lull them asleep.

Black hoped he wouldn't need to abandon his new home. He liked the weather. He liked the people he met . . . for the most part.

His attention was drawn to traffic on the county road. A pick-up truck had come from the direction of San Juan Pueblo. It slowed, then turned onto Black's property. As it drew closer, he realized it belonged to Peter Delgado.

The drummer stopped his truck next to Black's. As Delgado climbed out, another man the preacher didn't recognize emerged from the opposite side.

"I told you I didn't need your help, Peter."

The Pueblo man shrugged and pointed a thumb at his companion. "This is my cousin, Raphael."

Raphael nodded at Black. "Hello."

Black gave a small wave and nodded back. "Are you two sure you want to be here?"

"It's Wednesday night," Delgado said. "Nothing else going on."

"I appreciate your boredom. I hope things stay boring."

"How sure are you these lowrider friends of yours will show up to-night?"

"Pretty sure."

"I don't know." The drummer shook his head. "A cautious man would wait a week, maybe two. Lull you into thinking they won't show up. Then surprise you."

"You haven't met Chaparro. He is not what you would call cautious. I left him a message yesterday, and he showed up at the shop today, wanting to fight. He's not going to bide his time."

"What did you say in your message?"

Black told him.

Delgado nodded. "Yeah, that would put a burr under my saddle."

As they talked, another vehicle turned off the county road. This time it was a car. It parked behind Delgado's truck and John Salazar stepped out. The fireman waved at the gathering as he walked around to his trunk. A moment later he approached cradling a hunting rifle.

"I see you didn't want to miss the fun," Delgado called.

"Hope I'm not late. Dinner took a little longer than usual."

"Didn't miss a thing. John, this is my cousin, Raphael."

The two men shook hands.

Black was becoming concerned. He had spent the afternoon trying to figure out a way to defuse the situation with Chaparro. He was worried displaying a show of force on his part would escalate things.

"Listen, gentlemen. I really don't want any shooting if I can help it."

"You gotta understand, Jeremiah. This is our church too," Salazar protested. "My whole life I've wanted to go to a worship service that meant something to me. This place . . . this holy place . . . I spend all week looking forward to Saturday night. I want to be here. I want to be here with people I know and trust. If we have to protect what we have, we will do it no matter what it takes."

"There's something else, roadman," Delgado added. "I have never had friends beyond the reservation boundary. You and John . . . you are my friends. I too want to protect this place."

Black felt his throat tighten. He knew what his church meant to him. He hadn't realized that after just a few weeks, his followers felt the same. He cleared his throat.

"We need to move our trucks to the other side of the trailer. That way they won't be seen from the road. I've cleaned out my trailer. Moved my gear into the building. Come inside and I'll show you the set-up."

Chapter Ninety-Three

Tina found Lansing in the stables, brushing Cement Head.

***

When he got to the ranch after work, she asked him when he wanted to eat. Wednesday was their traditional mid-weeknight to eat out, at least when school was in session. They both forgot the routine that week, so Tina had quickly thrown something together.

"I didn't leave the office once today!" The sheriff's mood was sour. It was a stark contrast to when Tina saw him a few hours earlier. "I'm taking Cement Head out for a ride."

"So, you want to eat when you get back?"

"I don't know." He said absently. "Maybe . . . probably." He headed for the bedroom to change into civilian clothes.

Lansing had gotten Tina through a tough moment when she stopped by his office earlier. She wanted to return the favor. She waited until he was changed. As he headed for the front door, she intercepted him, pleased to see him wearing his new vest.

"That leather sure looks good on you!"

"Thanks," he mumbled.

"Would you like company?"

He stopped, giving her only a cursory glance. He tried not to sound gruff. "No . . . if you don't mind."

"I understand, Cliff." She really did understand. Occasionally her man needed his alone time. "I can warm up your supper when you get back."

***

The sun was setting when he returned. Only the open stable door told Tina he had finished his ride.

"How was it?"

Lansing was startled. "I didn't hear you come in!" He continued brushing his horse. "You mean the ride? It was good!"

Tina could tell he was in a better mood. "Are you hungry?"

He nodded. "I could eat. Let me finish up with my old buddy here and I'll be in shortly."

***

It wasn't until Lansing had eaten dinner that Tina asked him why he came home in a foul mood.

"Remember Monday when I told you I got a visit from the State Bureau of investigation?"

"Yes."

"I got a call from Santa Fe this afternoon. The agents I talked to didn't like my answers when I was questioned. Their higher-ups think the SBI should put a task force together to find the San Phillipe Hit-and-Run Murderer. They said I have a potential serial killer and my office is not equipped to handle something that big."

"When is that going to happen?"

"They're sending the Mobile Crime Lab up here tomorrow."

"Can they do that . . . just take over your case?"

"The state can investigate anything they want. But they won't be taking over the case. My office will keep working on it . . . a parallel investigation. This is still my county."

"I can see why you're mad."

"I was." He stood and picked up his plate.

"I'll get that!"

Lansing waved her off as he walked to the sink. "I had a long talk with that horse of mine. I honestly think he's getting smarter."

"Oh, really?" She said, smiling.

Lansing began scrubbing the plate. "He made me realize I wasn't pissed at the State. I was mad at the Tapia campaign. They'll try to convince the voters the state stepped in because I'm incompetent. I'm still convinced it was Tapia who contacted the SBI, to begin with."

"What are you going to do?"

He set the plate in the dish rack, turned, and smiled. "Absolutely nothing."

"Nothing? That's not the Cliff Lansing I know."

"That is the Cliff Lansing you know," he said, still smiling. "It's my job to serve and protect the people of San Phillipe County. If the State wants to help, who am I to stop them? If their involvement gets a murderer off the streets, great! The sooner that happens, the better."

"You got all that from Cement Head?"

"More or less."

"What are you going to do now?"

"Sit down, have a whiskey, and start reading the new Dan Baldwin western you got me."

"Don't stay up too late." Tina tried to sound seductive.

"I won't, Sweetheart. I won't."

Chapter Ninety-Four

The Baca family sat at the dining room table. Lincoln had finished an abbreviated account of his hike into the mountains. He emphasized the visions he had over two nights . . . the phantom vampire and her visits to adjacent homes.

His parents' initial reaction was silence. Lincoln couldn't tell if they believed him. They seemed uncomfortable with their son's story. The revelation about the vampire wasn't new. However, his encounter with the Aztec king was. The account pushed the limits of credibility.

Joy was the first to speak. "Why didn't you tell us this earlier when the sheriff called?"

"Uncle Eluterio asked that I not tell anyone until he spoke to the Pueblo elders."

"And he spoke to them?" Simon Baca asked, breaking his silence.

"Earlier this afternoon."

"What did they say about all of this?"

Lincoln cleared his throat. He refused to be intimidated by the old men of the village. "They called Eluterio an old fool. They called me a liar."

Simon sat quietly considering what he was told. The other three at the table could see the patriarch getting angrier. Finally, he exploded, slapping the tabletop with his open palm. "My son is not a liar!" He turned to Lincoln. "I believe you, Linc, but why are you telling us this?"

Lincoln looked outside. It was already dark. "I have to stop it . . . kill it, if I can."

"Can it be killed?" Pauline asked.

No one knew the answer. Joy finally spoke up. "Her father sent her away so the other people in their town wouldn't kill her . . . So, yes, she can be killed."

"How?" her mother pressed.

"He can use my hunting rifle," her husband offered.

Lincoln shook his head. "I don't want stray bullets flying around. Besides, I'm not that good a shot."

"But I am," Simon said. "I can come with you. I will shoot this thing!"

Lincoln almost turned him down. But the whole purpose of alerting the elders was to get help to stop the demon. "Thanks, Dad. That would be great."

Pauline looked worried. "Do you know where to look for this thing?"

Lincoln's two encounters with the vampire started in front of their house. "I think we should wait here for her."

"Why did she start from here?" Simon asked.

"It was because of Izel," Joy suggested. "The vampire is tied to the doll, somehow. She needs to be close to it." She fell silent for a moment, then, "But there's a problem."

"What?" her father asked.

"Izel is missing, and I don't know where she is."

Chapter Ninety-Five

Chaparro turned his Chevy Impala off the county road, onto Jeremiah Black's property. He was followed by two other Lowriders, both as decked out as their leader's car. It was hard to tell, though. It was already dark.

Chaparro drove past the unlit, adobe church and continued toward Black's trailer. The preacher sat on the steps in front of the open door, his rifle resting on his lap. Coming to a stop a dozen yards from the trailer, he left his car running when he stepped out. His passenger got out, as well. His two companions parked their Lowriders on either side of the Impala. The bright headlights were blinding, and Black had to shield his eyes.

"I'm here, preacher man," the Hispanic man shouted. "You gonna do something about it? You gonna shoot my ass, maybe?"

"I don't want to shoot anyone," Black responded.

"So, what does that mean, Indian?" Chaparro tried to make the last word sound like an insult.

"I made a mistake. Someone trashed my trailer, and I was angry. I assumed it was you. I lashed out. I apologize."

"You hear that, *mi compadres*?" Chaparro addressed the other drivers who now stood next to their cars. "The preacher man apologizes. I need to tell you something, Mister Preacher Man. You hurt my abuela's feelings the way you talked to her."

"You're correct. I shouldn't have done that. Please tell your abuela that I am sorry."

Chaparro stood mulling over Black's apology. "I think, maybe, that's not good enough, Mister Preacher Man."

"What else do you think you need?"

"I need . . . oh, what's that word, Hector? Somebody owes you because they did something that hurt you?"

"Compensation, jefe?" Chaparro's passenger suggested.

"Yeah. That's right! Compensation! Hey, Mister Preacher Man, you owe me compensation!"

"I'm not giving you a penny!"

"Oh, no, no, no. I don't want no money. I want a different compensation."

"What?"

"Your church . . . I asked around . . . In your church, you use peyote when you do your preaching."

"Someone told you a tale."

"A tale? Oh, you mean they told me a lie."

"Okay, yes. They told you a lie."

"That's too bad. Because that's the compensation I want. I want you to give me peyote. Not all of it. Just some . . . Let's say, half of what you have."

"I don't have any. You know that. You already looked. You'll have to find peyote somewhere else."

"I can't. That little cactus only grows along the Rio Grande. In Texas and Mexico. But you know that. You also know they only sell that little jewel to Indians like you. So, if you don't have none, you need to go to Texas and get some. We'll split what you bring back."

"Why would I do that?"

"Because if you don't, you will not preach around here anymore. I will make sure."

"Is that a threat?"

"No, Mister Preacher Man. That is a promise."

"I'm not leaving here . . . and I'm not going to Texas to get you peyote."

"That's too bad. You don't understand, there are other ways to stop your preaching."

"Like?"

"Like you could be dead!" Chaparro paused. "Think about that!"

"I've already thought about that, Chaparro. That's why I apologized. I admitted I was wrong. But I owe you no compensation. Even if I had peyote, I won't be sharing any with you.

Death threats don't bother me. I'm not surrendering to you either. I'm standing my ground."

"Even though it's four against one?"

"You need to look behind my trailer."

"Why?"

"Just look."

"Hector!" Chaparro shouted. He nodded his head toward the trailer.

The henchman trotted from the Chevy to peer behind the trailer. He immediately returned to his post. "There's a car and two trucks, jefe."

"So, you started a car lot," Chaparro spat. "What is that supposed to mean?"

"It means I may not be alone here. I told you. I'm standing my ground."

"Jefe . . ." Hector gestured toward the adobe building. "People could be in there!"

"I know that!" the jefe snapped. He shouted at Black. "My compadres and me need to talk."

"You can talk all you want. It won't change a thing."

"Maybe. Maybe not." Chaparro made a circling gesture above his head. "*Muchachos. Ándale!*"

A moment later the three Lowriders were gone.

Delgado emerged from the church. "That's it, I guess."

"They'll be back," Black said with certainty. "We need someone on the roof. Watch where they go and look for when they head our way again."

"Those engines are loud. We'll hear them when they drive back."

"They won't park close. That's why we'll keep an eye out."

Delgado shrugged. "Raphael's young. He can sit on the roof better than me."

Chapter Ninety-Six

Growing up in Albuquerque and having lived in Santa Fe for the last ten years, Abbie Fontana was not impressed with Las Palmas. It was alright for a small town. But shopping was limited to the essentials, and there was nothing unique to make the town stand out.

Dining establishments were horrendous . . . A Dixie Queen, a Mexican cantina, and a diner a block from the county courthouse. Housing was limited. There were tiny, single-family homes, a couple of one-story fourplexes, and very few places for sale. The only plus for the town was there was no real estate office. For sale signs listed Segovia and Santa Fe numbers.

Venturing beyond the city limits, Abbie noticed roads leading into the foothills. Following one, she found an impressive, two-story hacienda. This lifted the agent's spirits. Nothing said she had to live in the town proper.

Driving north to Cohino, she was amazed at the bustling tourist industry. Again, she was encouraged. Each visitor was a potential sale. Also, Cohino had two things Las Palmas didn't, a variety of eating establishments and the scenic railroad.

By the time she checked into the Las Palmas Inn that evening, she knew she would be a success in the new surroundings. There was also the added benefit of being close to Johnny Tapia, the man she loved. It didn't matter to her if she had to share her man with his family. She wanted to be available whenever he snapped his fingers.

Once she was settled in her room, she called the number Tapia had given her.

"Hello?"

"Yes, this is Abbie Fontana. Johnny told me to call this number."

"Okay."

"Could you tell him I'm staying at the Las Palmas Inn, room sixteen?"

The man spoke slowly as if writing the information down. *"Las Palmas Inn, room sixteen."*

"Right!" Abbie said, trying not to sound excited. "Do you know when he's coming?"

"He'll get there when he can," the man snapped.

"Oh," she said, surprised at the sudden rudeness. "Okay, well, thanks."

The response was a click when the man hung up.

Abbie prepared herself. She showered, overdid it on applying her make-up, then slipped into a new negligée and sheer robe. The outfit left little to the imagination. Turning the bedsheets down, all she needed was Johnny Tapia.

She made herself comfortable on the bed. All the lights were off. The HBO channel played a movie she had never heard of. It had been a long day, and she was more tired than she realized. She would have slept till morning if someone hadn't knocked on her door.

Abbie woke with a start. The alarm clock next to the bed read 11:12. Despite a nap of nearly three hours, there was no confusion on her part. She knew exactly where she was and who was knocking.

She sprang from the bed, then threw open the motel room door.

"Johnny!" she exclaimed. Her excitement evaporated in an instant. There was no Johnny Tapia standing in front of her. Instead, there was a man she had never seen before.

"Who are you?" she demanded.

"Johnny couldn't make it. I'm your date!"

"Oh, no!" Abbie tried to shut the door.

The man was through the opening before she knew it. His hand was on her throat, and he squeezed to prevent a scream. Pushing her backward, he kicked the door shut.

Forcing her onto the bed, he continued choking her.

Abbie clutched at the man's arm, trying to defend herself. Her struggles became more difficult. As her hands lost their grip, the dimly lit room grew darker. She could no longer breathe.

The last thing she remembered was the glow of the TV and the thought, "That's not the movie I was watching."

Chapter Ninety-Seven

Lincoln had moved a dining room chair next to the front window. The combination living-dining room was dark. The two Baca men were watching for the vampire's arrival. Simon sat on the sofa, his rifle leaning against the wall near him. Lincoln sat at the window, constantly peeking through the drawn curtain.

They had begun their surveillance not long after Lincoln finished his talk with the family.

"What time was it when your vampire started her rounds?" Simon asked, yawning.

"I don't know. I didn't see a clock. It was late enough that everyone's inside lights were off."

"Right now, are people still up?"

"Yeah. There are still lights on."

Simon got up and headed for the kitchen.

"What are you doing?" his son asked in a loud whisper.

"I'm just looking at the clock."

Armed with a flashlight, Simon turned it on for a few seconds to check the time. "It's almost eleven," he said when he returned to the sofa. "Way past my bedtime . . . How long are we going to do this?"

"I don't know."

"All night?" Simon asked, yawning again.

"I guess."

"Easy for you to say. You don't have work tomorrow."

Lincoln wasn't sure if his father was taking a dig at him for being jobless, or if it was an observation of his own plight.

"Yeah, I know." He stood and slipped on his jacket.

"Now, where are you going?" Simon asked.

"Outside. I need to walk around. All your yawning is making me sleepy."

"Sorry." The elder man closed his eyes. "Come get me if you see anything."

"I will."

Lincoln stepped through the front door, closing it quietly. He carried a flashlight and an ax. He knew how to swing an ax, and it became his weapon of choice. He hoped it would be effective against Mexican Vampires.

After walking completely around the house, the former firefighter chose an observation post at the corner of the building. The big tree near the other corner of the house was in full view. He squatted with his back against the wall.

Stuffing his hands in the jacket pockets for warmth, he felt something he didn't recognize. He pulled out the twig-like object and looked at it. It was a small bone. Montezuma had given it to him the last time they met. The hollow Eagle bone was a whistle he could use to summon the *viborón,* the Aztec king's giant rattlesnake.

Sticking it back into his pocket, he wondered if it really worked. Maybe even more importantly, he wondered if he would need it.

Chapter Ninety-Eight

The first thing Abbie became aware of was the need to cough. Her second realization was that she couldn't. Her mouth was taped shut. Her eyes flew open as she panicked. Sitting up, her instinct was to remove the tape. As she attempted to move her right hand to her face, she found it was bound to her other hand at the wrist.

She coughed and screamed, the sound muffled by the duct tape. She was roughly shoved backward.

"I'll pull off the tape, so you won't gag," the man growled. "But if you scream, I'll choke you, so you won't wake up. Understand?"

Abbie nodded, tears beginning to stream down her face. The tape was ripped away, and she coughed freely. She rolled onto her side to breathe better. The coughing gave way to gasps as she caught her breath. It took three minutes before her senses completely returned.

She was still in her motel room, on the bed. The newly christened real estate agent had never been choked into unconsciousness before. She had no idea how long she was out. She knew it was long enough for her attacker to tape her mouth and bind her wrists with zip-lock ties.

The man stood at the window peeking through the curtains. He turned to look at her when she grew quiet.

"Don't these people ever go to bed?" His voice was low and threatening.

"I don't . . ." Abbie cleared her throat, so she could squeeze out the words. "I don't know. My first time here."

"We'll go when the lot's empty."

"Are you going to rape me?" she whimpered.

"Please, Miss Fontana," the man said, a hurt look on his face. "Do I look like a rapist?"

She kept her eyes fixed on him, her speech still forced. "I don't know. I've never met one." She sat up again. This time he didn't push her back. "Who are you?"

He stepped to the nightstand and grabbed his roll of duct tape. Using his teeth, he tore off a long piece. Before she could stop him, he wrapped it around Abbie's head, covering her mouth again.

"No more talking!"

Abbie flopped backward onto the bed. A thousand questions swirled in her head. This man in her room . . . he wasn't there to rape her. Johnny obviously knew him. Did Johnny send him? Did Johnny know what he was doing? What was he going to do?

Every line of questions led to the same conclusion. This man was going to kill her. He was going to kill her because Johnny Tapia wanted her dead. Her now ex-lover somehow saw her as a threat.

Her mood alternated between fear of death and anger at Tapia for doing this. Plus, if this man was there to kill her, why didn't he just do it?

He was taking her somewhere else. He said they had to wait until the parking lot was empty. A new thought sparked hope. He was moving her because she was being kidnapped. Johnny didn't want her dead! This man, whoever he was, intended to ransom her.

Abbie Fontana felt a wave of calm wash over her. The fear lessened and her anger was diverted from Johnny to her assailant. There was always the chance he might still kill her, but he wouldn't see any money if he did.

She watched as the man moved from the window to her open suitcase. He dug through it, looking for something. Obviously, it would be the clothes she would change into. She needed more than the nighty she was wearing.

The man stopped digging and held up a pair of high-heeled shoes.

"You know, I like my ladies barefoot. I've never seen how well one of you runs in high heels. I guess we'll find out tonight!"

Run? Tonight? What was he planning for her?

The calmness she felt a few moments earlier was gone. She had no room for anger. Fear took over every fiber of her being.

Abbie's feet were still unbound. She jumped up and ran to the door, trying to scream through the tape.

No one would hear her.

Her bound wrists prevented her from grasping the doorknob. She was suddenly grabbed from behind. Her kidnapper slapped her across the face and threw her onto the bed.

"I see you don't want to cooperate."

The man grabbed the duct tape again. Abbie kicked furiously as he tried to bind her ankles together.

"Stop struggling," he said through clenched teeth. His anger was mounting. Fed up with her resistance, he struck her in the jaw with his fist.

That was the last thing Abbie remembered.

Chapter Ninety-Nine

Lansing attributed his second wind on feeling rejuvenated after his ride with Cement Head. The pressure of the day had dissipated. However, after pouring a whiskey and sitting in his reading chair, weariness crept over him. He took a sip of the brown drink, opened the book to the first chapter, and began reading.

He read to the end of the first page, then realized he was reading words, but no thoughts were sinking in. He took another sip of George Dickel and read the page a second time, concentrating harder. The second time didn't go much better than the first.

He fought the blurring words until halfway through the first chapter.

When his head jerked upright, he startled himself. He had dozed off. The western lay on the floor. He picked it up, trying to remember the story. Something about the end of the civil war, somebody gets shot . . . or was it two people got shot . . . or was it a man and his mule. He couldn't remember.

Setting the book down, he picked up what was left of his whiskey and downed it. The wall clock read 11:00.

He needed to go to bed. He needed a shower worse. Tina was in bed asleep when he came into the bedroom. He tried to keep quiet so as not to wake her.

He closed the bathroom door before turning on the shower. When he finished, he dried himself completely before stepping out.

His cell phone began ringing. He tried to grab it before it woke Tina.

"Lansing," he said in low tones.

"*Yeah, Sheriff, Deputy Peters,*" the night dispatcher said. "*Sorry to bother you so late.*"

"What is it?" Lansing was irritated on more than one level.

"We got a report of shots being fired."

"Where?"

"South of Artiga a few miles."

"Who did you send?"

"Jack Rivera."

"Were any law enforcement officers involved?"

"Not that I know of."

Lansing had his standing orders regarding officer-involved shootings. "I'll call, Jack. If he doesn't need me, I'm going to bed."

He ended the call, then quick-dialed Rivera's phone. "What's going on, Jack?"

"I'm not sure yet, Cliff. Evidently, a lot of shots were fired. Whoever called it in said it sounded like a war zone."

"Do I need to show up?"

"I don't think so. Phil called the State Police. They'll be there for backup if I need them."

"Sounds good. Call me if you need me."

"Sure thing, Boss."

"What was that?" a groggy Tina asked.

"It's nothing."

"What time is it?"

"Eleven-thirty. You need to go back to sleep."

"Okay." The teacher's head dropped onto her pillow, and she fell asleep immediately.

Wearing only his boxers, Lansing slipped his feet between the cool sheets. He leaned over and kissed Tina's forehead. He didn't remember falling asleep, it was so quick.

It wouldn't last for long.

Chapter One Hundred

Phil Peters gave Jack Rivera an update. The 9-1-1 operator got a call. Several people had been shot. Ambulances were needed. The address dispatch provided was familiar to the Chief Deputy. He had been there recently.

A quarter-mile from the property, Rivera passed four cars parked along the narrow shoulder of the country road. In the dark, he couldn't see they were decked out Lowriders. He connected the abandoned autos with the gunplay.

Rivera was the first emergency responder to arrive. Turning on the private drive, he had to swerve to avoid hitting a body. He stopped his car and got out. Checking the man's neck for a pulse, he could find nothing.

Returning to his car, he came to a stop a few yards from the adobe building. All the interior lights were on. The trailer, several yards from the church, also had its lights on. Four men holding either a rifle or a shotgun stood outside the church. No one tried to run away. The obvious leader stepped forward as the deputy got out of his car.

"Good evening, Sheriff," Jeremiah Black said.

"Thanks for the promotion, Mr. Black. I'm just a deputy."

"Oh, Deputy Rivera, isn't it?"

"That's right. We met a few days ago."

Rivera made a quick assessment of the scene. In another situation, he would have jumped from his car, his weapon drawn, and ordered the men to drop their rifles. They would be ordered to lie face down and he would keep his gun pointed at them until backup arrived.

The deputy didn't think it was wise to pull his gun from its holster. These men had been trading the lead with others very recently. Their adrenaline levels were probably high. Plus, one or more might be naturally trigger happy. Having another gun pointed at them might start the shooting all over again.

"You know, I would feel a lot safer if you and your friends put the guns down."

Black thought for a moment, then nodded. "Sure. That won't be a problem."

He and his men started leaning their rifles along the wall of the church.

"Actually," Rivera said. "Could you lay them across the hood of my car?"

The men looked at each other, shrugged, and placed their weapons on the patrol car. In the near distance, they all could hear the wail of sirens. A State Police patrol unit led the procession. He was followed by three ambulances.

Patrolman Rich Hidalgo was not as careful as Rivera. Not slowing when he turned off the road, he ran over the body the deputy had avoided. Hidalgo came to an immediate stop. The ambulances were forced to swerve around his patrol unit. The rocky, dusty property was quickly filling up.

Hidalgo hurried to the body to check for a pulse.

"Don't worry, Rich," Rivera shouted. "He was dead before I got here."

Hidalgo and six paramedics joined Rivera and his four suspects. The patrolman was curious why no one was in cuffs. The deputy assured him they had already been disarmed and weren't flight risks.

The medics checked the four Indian men for injuries. One man had a few scratches. Another had burned a couple of fingers from picking up a hot bullet casing. There was no indication any of them had been in a lethal gun battle.

"I take it you were attacked?" Rivera asked.

Black nodded.

"How many were there?"

"Six."

"Should we look for bodies?" a paramedic asked.

"Yes, but leave the dead bodies where you find them," Rivera instructed. "We need to get forensics in here."

"This is a pretty big crime scene," Hidalgo observed.

"I know," Rivera agreed. "It's more than my two forensic experts can handle. Can we get the State Forensics Unit in here?"

"I'll make the call."

Black approached the deputy. "You want all of us to stay here, right?"

"Yes. I need to get statements." No one would be released until the authorities had a complete picture of the incident.

"Gonna be a long night," Black observed. "I have coffee inside the church. Would you like a cup?"

"Sure. Why not?"

Chapter One Hundred-One

Lansing's cell phone began ringing. It took a long moment before he realized what woke him. The alarm clock display read 12:05.

"What?" The sheriff was angry at being woken and didn't care whose feelings were hurt.

"*Sorry, Sheriff,*" the dispatch officer said.

"What is it, Phil? Does Jack need me?"

"*No, sir. Deputy Cortez made a traffic stop and asked for your assistance.*"

"What the hell for?" Lansing demanded, sitting up and swinging his feet to the floor.

"Wha . . . What's going on?" Tina asked.

"Go back to sleep, hon."

"*Pardon me?*" Peters asked.

"Not you . . . What's so important that Danny needs me?"

"*He pulled over a Trailblazer . . . red.*"

"Oh?" Lansing was suddenly interested. "Where did he make the stop?"

"*Highway fifteen, five miles south of your ranch.*"

"Let him know I'm on my way."

"*There's something else. There was a woman tied up in the back.*"

"Was she alive?"

"*Yes.*"

"Thank God! I'll be there in ten."

Tina was sitting up now. Lansing had not attempted to keep his voice down. "Where are you going?"

Lansing was already pulling a clean uniform from his closet. "I think Danny Cortez just nabbed our hit-and-run killer!"

"Really? That's fantastic!"

"Yes, it is."

"Do you want some coffee?"

"No time, but thanks." He was out the bedroom door in less than three minutes.

"Call me, when you can," Tina shouted after him.

***

Lansing pulled up behind Cortez's patrol unit. He got out, flashlight in hand, and flashed the light into the backseat of the deputy's car. A man the sheriff didn't recognize quickly turned his head away from the beam. His hands were cuffed behind his back.

Cortez stood at the front of his unit. Next to him was a woman wrapped in a blanket from the deputy's trunk.

"Hi, Sheriff . . . This is Abigale Fontana."

"You can call me Abbie," she said, shivering.

"Put the poor girl in my jeep. She's freezing to death."

Still barefoot, Abbie stepped carefully walking back to Lansing's car. He had her sit in the front seat.

"Do you need to see a doctor?"

Abbie shook her head. "He knocked me around a little, but I'm okay."

"He didn't . . ." Lansing paused uncomfortably.

"Rape me?" she said, completing his thought. "No."

Lansing walked back to his deputy. "Have a name on our perp?"

"Paul Trevino . . . from Santa Fe. The SUV belongs to his mother. She lives in Segovia."

"Well, we need to get this highway clear. Call for a tow truck. Have them move that Chevy to the impound lot. Stay here until they move it. I'm taking Miss Fontana back to the office."

"What about my prisoner?"

"He can wait. We'll put him in a cell when you're finished."

Chapter One Hundred-Two

It wasn't until they reached the well-lit day room that Lansing got a good look at the victim. Despite the disheveled appearance and the smeared makeup, Abbie Fontana was a very attractive woman. He noticed a bruise had formed along her left jawline, probably from being punched.

"I had Deputy Peters start a fresh pot of coffee. Would you like a cup?"

Abbie nodded. "Before we start anything, do you have something I can wear?" She opened the blanket and gave the sheriff a quick glance at her meager attire, then covered up again. "If you don't, I have clothes at the Las Palmas Inn. Maybe you could take me over there?"

Lansing considered the request. He didn't know how long it would be before Cortez arrived with the driver. The sheriff wanted to be there when the two arrived.

"I can get you an orange jumpsuit. Other deputies will be here in a few hours. One of them can run you to your room then."

Abbie sighed, nodded, but said nothing, taking a seat at the table.

Lansing realized he was talking to a defeated woman whose world had just come crashing down. He hurried to retrieve the jail attire from a storage closet. When he returned, he handed the woman the jail suit along with a pair of inmate prison slippers.

"You can change in the lady's room," he offered.

"Thanks." She took the clothing and headed to the hallway.

"It's to your left," he instructed.

She took longer than Lansing expected. When Abbie returned, her face had been scrubbed, the cuffs were rolled up on the legs and arms, and her hair somewhat straightened.

"Did you need a bag for your clothes?"

"They're in the trash," was her angry response. "I'll never wear those damned things again."

She returned to her seat at the table. Lansing set a mug of coffee in front of her, then took a chair across the table.

"The man who abducted you . . . do you know him?"

"Never saw him before. But he knows me . . . he was going to kill me."

Lansing knew exactly how she was going to die. When the time was right, he would fill her in on who the man was. "How does he know who you are?"

"My ex-boyfriend sent him to get rid of me."

"Are you sure?"

"Of course, I'm sure," she snapped. "And you know who it is!"

"I do?" Lansing was surprised. "Who's your ex-boyfriend?"

"Johnny Tapia!"

"John Tapia the councilman?"

"Yeah. The one who's trying to take your job."

Lansing leaned back in his chair, dumbfounded by the revelation. The whole county would be rocked by the news. Tapia would need the opportunity to defend himself.

The sheriff also knew he couldn't make an arrest based solely on Abbie Fontana's claim. She might be telling the truth, or she might be a nut job. He had to tread lightly. People would accuse him of playing politics, trying to discredit his opponent.

Maybe when they interrogated Trevino, they'd get a better picture of what was going on. Lansing was 99.99 percent sure they had their murderer. Abbie still had marks on her wrists from the zip tie. On top of that, he had a survivor. Joy Baca would be the star witness.

"Miss Fontana . . ."

"Abbie, please."

"Alright . . . Abbie, do you feel like talking about what happened to-night?"

Her hesitation was brief. "Yeah, sure."

"Before we start, let me grab a tape recorder from another room. You don't mind if we record this, do you?"

"No, not at all."

The interview took an hour. Trevino arrived after she was finished.

What followed was the most intense week of activity that Lansing had ever experienced as sheriff.

Chapter One Hundred-Three

Squatting with his back to the wall, it wasn't hard to stay awake. The reason, Lincoln guessed, was because he stayed awake all night for five days. He was used to it. Of course, it could also have been that he slept twelve hours the night before.

Every ten minutes he stood and walked around. He needed to be prepared in case he had to run after the demon. Every few minutes he peeked around the corner, looking for the vampire.

There was no guarantee the girl would appear, especially at the tree where Lincoln first saw her. However, he couldn't think of a better place to look for her.

Doubt poked at him. What if this vampire didn't exist? What if she and Montezuma were both hallucinations? Maybe his tumor conjured up the whole thing. He pushed the thoughts away. He had to believe in himself.

He didn't have a watch, so he had no idea what time it was. It had to be well past midnight. It didn't matter. He would keep watch until dawn. He peered around the corner for the hundredth time.

A figure stepped out from behind the tree. Despite the darkness, the young woman was easy to see. She had the same inner glow Lincoln had seen in his visions. Without looking around, she started walking/floating toward the street. She seemed to move with a purpose as if she knew where she wanted to go.

Lincoln waited until she had moved a good distance from the house. He didn't want to alert her to his presence. He needed to wake his father.

Leaving the front door open, Lincoln rushed to the sofa. Simon lay on his left side, his right arm under his head.

"Dad!" he said in a hoarse, loud whisper. "Dad!" Carrying his ax in his left hand he grabbed his father's shoulder with his right and gently shook him.

"Dad! The demon just appeared. We have to go. She's walking down the street."

His father didn't respond. Stepping back to the open door, he tried to locate the girl. Blocked by the tree, he couldn't see her.

"Dad, we gotta go!" This time he shouted. "She's gonna get away!"

Simon refused to stir. Lincoln checked to see if the older man was still breathing.

He was.

Lincoln was on his own. He glanced at the rifle. It could be useful, but not in his hands. He would stick with his ax.

He ran out the front door without closing it. Stopping at the street, he desperately looked around. He couldn't see the girl anywhere.

"She might have gone around the corner," he thought. He ran down to the next street. It was empty. He ran back toward his own yard.

"Between the buildings! She must have gone between the buildings," he muttered. He ran to a spot where he could view between the first two houses. Still nothing.

Panic set in. He could cover more ground if his dad was there. But he wasn't. He began second-guessing himself. What if the ax doesn't work where a bullet might have?

He felt inadequate. Shoving his hand into a pocket, he felt the Eagle bone whistle. He pulled it out, looked at it, then put it to his lips and blew.

The only sound was his breath passing through the hollow tube. He looked at the whistle again, then blew a second time. The result was the same.

"Worthless!" he groused. Lincoln was about to throw the bone away when he remembered what Montezuma told him. Only the *viborón* could hear the sound!

Heartened at the thought, he began blowing again. He hoped the snake heard the call. If it did, he wondered how long before he would get there?

"Stop blowing that!" a raspy voice behind him ordered.

Lincoln whipped around to discover he was face-to-face with the *tlahuelpuchi*. The demon could hear the whistle. He had no idea where she appeared from.

"You!" the demon hissed. "You've come back!"

Chapter One Hundred-Four

"Yes, I'm back." Lincoln held the ax with both hands, ready to strike. Up close, the vampire was a beautiful young woman. Part of him wanted to spare the girl, but he knew what evil she could commit.

"Por qué?"

"English," he ordered. "Speak English!"

"Por qué . . ." She was angered at the command. "Why? Why are you here?"

"To stop you!" He swung his ax. She sidestepped the assault so quickly he didn't see her move. She was in one spot, then instantly in another.

"Stop me with your *hacha*? I don't think so."

"I know what you are." He took another swing, so hard he almost lost balance. She moved again.

"What do you think I am?"

"A demon . . . a vampire who feeds on the blood of others. I saw what you did to those children."

"I do what I do to live. I am no more evil than the coyote in a chicken yard. He takes a hen because he must."

"You are hurting others!"

"I don't have a choice!"

"And I don't have a choice, either. I can't let you hurt the people of my Pueblo." He attempted a third strike. It went like the first two.

"Before I was born, the ancient gods decided what I would become. My mother gave her life so that I could live. You cannot hurt me. I am protected by forces you could never understand."

"I will find a way to stop you!" He pulled the whistle from his pocket and began blowing.

"Stop!" the demon shrieked, in obvious pain. "Stop!"

She was suddenly standing in front of him, no longer a beautiful, young woman. The demon grabbed the whistle from his hand, her claw-like nails scratching his face, and drawing blood. She broke the Eagle bone and flung it on the ground.

That slight distraction with the whistle gave Lincoln the opening he needed. He swung his ax, burying the blade in the demon's chest.

The demon froze. She looked from her attacker to the ax in her chest and back. It let out a hiss of pain and anger, then grabbed the ax handle and pulled the blade from its chest. There was no blood and the gash disappeared. She ripped the ax from Lincoln's hand and threw it as far as she could.

Fear gripped the former fireman. He knew he wouldn't stop her that night. He turned and began running. He stopped after only a dozen steps. The *tlahuelpuchi* was now in front of him.

Before he could turn away, the demon knocked him to the ground. Stradling his chest with her knees on either side, she hissed, "You won't live long enough to stop me!"

With those words, she slashed his face and throat with her talons. Lincoln immediately grabbed his neck, hoping to stop the flow. She ignored his efforts to save himself, bending over to lick the flowing blood.

The *tlahuelpuchi* turned its head and spit. "Bitter!"

The demon stood, no longer interested in her victim. She transformed to her maiden form again. She looked down the street, then began moving in that direction.

Lincoln watched the dim light of the vampire-maiden disappear. He felt himself being wrapped in a warm, peaceful blanket. A veil of darkness slipped over his vision. He was overcome by a painless, even welcome oblivion. Then nothing.

***

The stench of Lincoln's blood filled Fernanda's nostrils. She shook her head and rubbed her nose. She could no longer find the scent of young children.

Since the first Pueblo baby, she had been much more careful. No more drinking blood until she was sated. Also, she never visited the same house twice. There were other pueblo houses further away. Her understanding of English improved daily. She knew she could move on. There was a big town to the north just waiting for her. She heard people speak of more cities to the south.

She would figure out a strategy. Her very existence depended on her guile. For now, though, she needed to feed, but it wouldn't be new blood. She had to visit a house for a second time. Plus, the night was nearly over. She would lose her protection of darkness.

As she passed between the darkened houses, she suddenly stopped.

Fernanda had heard the sound once before when she was a very young child. It wasn't a familiar sound, and she couldn't quite remember its source. The rattling that suddenly erupted, however, was loud and close. She wasn't afraid. Fear was mostly foreign to her. Only curiosity prompted her to turn around.

The head was huge, larger than her own. The fangs were long. The strike was quick!

Chapter One Hundred-Five

During Paul Trevino's initial interview that early Thursday morning, he came across as smug and confident. If asked why he would have said all the sheriff had on him was attempted kidnapping and possible assault.

His confidence began to wane when Lansing threw photos of his victims on the table in front of him. He said he had enough evidence to tie Trevino to two hit-and-run murders. The clincher came when the sheriff informed him he had left one victim alive . . . Joy Baca. She could easily identify him.

Trevino's self-assuredness crumbled completely. When Lansing asked him why he singled out Abigale Fontana for his next victim, he confessed everything.

He had been instructed to eliminate the woman by John Tapia. Tapia was afraid people would find out about his affair. Fontana was a threat and he needed her gone. Lansing wasn't completely shocked to learn Tapia and Trevino were cousins.

When asked why he would do such a horrid thing, Trevino eventually admitted he wanted to hitch his wagon to a rising political star.

Lansing had everything he needed to detain Councilman John Tapia. But he didn't want his office to make the arrest.

When the State Police Crime Lab arrived in Las Palmas the next morning, the sheriff requested a consultation. Included in the meeting was a representative from the county prosecutor's office. Lansing announced one of his deputies had arrested the hit-and-run killer the night before. He already had evidence to present to the prosecutor for an indictment, including a witness.

The lieutenant in charge of the Crime Lab was angry Lansing hadn't informed him about the apprehension before he left Santa Fe. Lansing assured him there was an entire crime scene south of Artiga that they needed help with.

Finally, the sheriff presented the last item on his agenda . . . John Tapia. The councilman had orchestrated the abduction and intended murder of Abigale Fontana, his former lover. He already had a taped confession made by Trevino earlier that morning. He needed James Lujan to draw up a warrant and have the State Police make the arrest. He didn't want the sheriff's office involved. It was a political hot potato.

The county prosecutor's rep said the State Police weren't needed. As long as the San Phillipe prosecutor issued the warrant, any county law enforcement agency could make the arrest. The Segovia Police department could handle the collar.

***

Trevino's arrest was kept under wraps.

Tapia's minions spotted the crime lab in Las Palmas, and his campaign went into full attack mode. The State had stepped in because of Lansing's incompetence. Radio listeners were bombarded with four new ads all day Thursday and Friday. When the sheriff didn't respond, even Lansing's staunchest supporters thought what was being said was true.

Saturday morning, James Lujan's office contacted Police Chief Ernie Solano. Initially, Solano was perturbed about an arrest warrant he knew nothing about. His attitude changed completely when he saw whose name was on the piece of paper.

John Tapia and his father-in-law, Matthew Franco, screamed bloody murder, blaming the arrest on Cliff Lansing. The whole charade was political. The sheriff pointed out he was sixty miles away, riding his horse when Tapia was hauled in.

The screams quickly dissolved into whimpers when the full scope of the warrant was revealed. John Tapia had cheated on his wife, then asked his cousin to kill his paramour from Santa Fe.

Despite denying that he knew Abbie Fontana, Tapia's personal secretary readily admitted Fontana had visited him that Thursday morning.

By Tuesday morning, Daniella Tapia had filed for divorce. Franco had fired his son-in-law and terminated all connections to the councilman. And John Tapia was no longer a candidate for the office of San Phillipe Sheriff.

***

The State Crime Lab didn't finish gathering the evidence on Jeremiah Black's property until late Friday afternoon. Six bodies were found. The victims had died from either rifle bullets or shotgun blasts. Weapons were found near their bodies. Additionally, all the weapons had been fired . . . an important point. The dead men could readily be tagged as the aggressors.

Jack Rivera interviewed Black and his three companions separately. Their stories were essentially the same. There was enough difference between the accounts to convince the chief deputy they were not rehearsed.

After the evidence was compiled and the interviews completed, Rivera recommended no charges be brought. The men acted in self-defense. That was fine with James Lujan. His prosecutors already had two big trials coming up. They had enough to do.

Jeremiah Black was told by different people he had screwed up. He had declared war on the entire Lowrider community. He had two choices . . . leave New Mexico or stay and be killed. He did some soul-searching because of the six dead men. The guilt weighed heavily, and he wanted no more bloodshed.

When Black was told no charges would be brought, he resolved to leave his church and go back to Oklahoma. He told Manny Hidalgo, the owner of the garage where he worked, his intention of quitting.

Hidalgo told Black there was no reason for him to leave. Chaparro and his little clique operated on the fringe of Lowrider society. No one would miss them.

His boss' opinion was bolstered a few days later when four, shiny Lowriders pulled into the lot. The owners got out and demanded to see Black. When he emerged from the bay, the leader of the group said they were there to thank him. Chaparro's group was considered a scourge. Black had done something others only wished they could have done. In the future, if the mechanic was harassed in any way, they needed to be told. They would take care of the pest. Additionally, they would put Hidalgo's Garage and Repair Shop as highly recommended to their friends.

That encounter made Jeremiah Black's decision much easier. He would stay.

***

No one could identify the teenage girl found dead between the Pueblo houses. She might have been Hispanic, but she had a lot of Native American characteristics as well. She was pretty. Her attire was a mismatch of ill-fitting clothes (recently stolen from houses she had visited.) There was no obvious cause of death. The Medical Investigator's office would need to make that call.

Her photo would be circulated but no one ever admitted to knowing her. No one ever claimed the body.

315

The Baca family knew who she was . . . or at least what she was. It would remain mostly a family secret. A select few . . . those who knew about the Mexican Doll, Izel, and what it represented . . . would share in the confidence.

Izel was found, nestled in the branches high up in the Baca's front yard tree. Joy carefully retrieved it and a debate ensued. Should it be destroyed or not. When all indications were that the *tlahuelpuchi* was no longer active, Izel was not considered a danger.

She was returned to the original owner, Tina Morales.

***

"How long have I been in the hospital?" Lincoln Baca asked.

"Four days," his sister said. "They had to give you a lot of blood. You almost didn't make it."

Lincoln tried to cough, but his throat was dry. He asked for a sip of water. Swallowing was hard. It was then he realized his face was almost completely covered in bandages.

"What happened?"

"You don't know?"

"The last thing I remember was running down the street, looking for you know what."

"Well, you found her. She sliced your face and neck with her long fingernails. She somehow missed your jugular vein, otherwise, you would have bled to death."

Lincoln touched the bandages on his face. His entire head hurt.

"Did I get stitches?"

"The nurse said you got two hundred and ten . . . I'm afraid you'll look like Frankenstein's monster. So, you don't remember how you killed the vampire?"

"The vampire's dead?" He was shocked and elated. "Are you sure?"

"The body of a girl was discovered two blocks from where you were found. She matched your description."

"H-how did she die?"

"No one knows. They're waiting on the autopsy to find out. That's why I asked." She paused. "You know, mom and dad are pretty pissed at you. Me too. Why didn't you tell us you had a brain tumor?"

"Because I didn't want people feeling sorry for me! I didn't like how people treated me when I broke my arm. This will be a thousand times worse. 'Oh, look! There's that guy with a brain tumor.' " He fought off his anger. "How did you find out?"

"Dr. Lopez told us when he ordered a new MRI. He wanted to see how far the tumor had progressed."

"So, what's the news?" Lincoln's tone was grim.

"It's gone!"

"What do you mean 'gone?' "

"It's not there anymore. He said he can't explain it. He showed us your other scans and pointed out the tumor. The new pictures showed it was gone!"

"It's gone! Really?"

Because of the bandages, Joy couldn't tell if her brother was smiling. His voice told her he was.

"Yes, big brother. Really!"

Epilogue

Cement Head and Little Orphan Annie loped along the bridle path enjoying the brisk air. Lansing and Tina had driven their horses to the mountains of Carson National Forest to escape the August heat.

"Tapia and Trevino are going to get convicted, aren't they?"

"Looks like it," Lansing nodded. "Lujan's team dug up a lot of dirt on both.

Tapia had a dozen women spread throughout the state."

"But he's being charged with ordering a murder."

"True, but his philandering speaks to his character. And it looks like Mr. Trevino has more trials in the future."

"Oh?"

"The two hit-and-run deaths in San Phillipe weren't his first, evidently. His wife walked out with their kids when he was living in Las Cruces. He went over the deep end. He assaulted one woman in a bar. A few days later she turned up dead. No one was arrested, but they're reopening that case. Then there is an unsolved hit-and-run death near White Sands, just east of Las Cruces. It looks identical to our cases."

"What about the dead girl they found at Santa Clara Pueblo? The one Joy Baca thinks is the vampire."

"They released the autopsy yesterday. They think she died from a snake bite. The inside of her body was full of hemotoxins that resembled rattlesnake venom. It had to be a lot of venom, though. Her insides were nearly dissolved."

"I thought it took a couple of days for rattlesnake venom to kill you?"

"I suppose . . . if untreated. But I have a problem with their conclusion. They found two holes on her torso, ten inches apart. They couldn't be from a snake bite. Too far apart."

"So, what do you think happened?"

"She was injected with venom by a hypodermic needle, twice. That's the only way that much venom could be introduced."

"What do the experts think about your idea?"

"Nothing. No one's asked for my opinion."

***

"Thanks for stopping by, Cliff," Ernie Solano said. "I wanted to get your opinion about dashcam footage one of my officers turned in."

He had Lansing step around his desk so he could view the computer monitor. Solano hit the enter key and the screen began playing the footage.

"When was this?"

"A week ago, Wednesday night . . . the evening you arrested Trevino. The officer was patrolling Highway thirty, just outside Santa Clara."

The replay continued with nothing appearing out of the ordinary. Solano touched a key and froze the picture. He pointed to an object stretched across the road further down the highway.

"What does that look like to you?"

"A log. Did someone dump a tree on the highway?"

"Keep watching." Solano started the picture moving again.

As the patrol car grew closer, the top of the "log" appeared to have a pattern . . . a distinct pattern, similar to the markings on a snake . . . and the pattern was moving. Before the patrol car reached the object it disappeared into the darkness, but not before they saw the end of the "thing." The tail had the lobes of the rattle on a rattlesnake.

"Wait! What did I just see?"

"I'll play it again in slow motion."

Solano started it from the beginning. Lansing leaned closer to the screen. When the rattle came into view, he asked the Police Chief to stop the video. He counted thirteen lobes.

"Damn! Can you imagine the sound that rattle would make?" Lansing looked at his counterpart. "This video is real?"

"As real as you and me standing here."

Lansing looked at the time stamp: 1:51 am.

"Where was it headed?"

"Into the Pueblo."

"How big is that thing?"

"We estimated thirty feet . . . Can you imagine the size of that bite?"

"Actually," Lansing admitted. "I can."

Author's Note

On a trip to New Mexico, my father, a geologist, related a natural, though unusual, phenomenon. Methane leaks in remote New Mexican canyons were known to be ignited by lightning strikes. These flames might last for years. Such leaks are not uncommon, e.g., Eternal Flame Falls, Western New York; Flaming Geyser State Park, Washington State; Condamine River, Queensland, Australia.

About the Author

Micah S. Hackler, originally from a small Kansas farming community, was the son of an exploration geologist. The family moved often, living in Colorado, Ohio and Oklahoma, just to name a few states. He always loved the Rocky Mountains. A family trip to Mesa Verde in 1965 started a life-long interest in the Pueblo Indian culture. He resolved to one day be a writer after consuming every novel written by Edgar Rice Burroughs. Dabbling as a play write in college, marriage, children and life in general delayed his plans. After graduating from LSU, he joined the Air Force and retired as a Major in 1993. It was upon retirement that he began writing in earnest, producing the *Sheriff Lansing* mystery series. The novels are set in modern day New Mexico and revolve around the exploits of Sheriff Cliff Lansing. Each story involves a mythology unique to the Apache, Navajo or Pueblo people. A widower, Micah is a father and grandfather and currently lives with his new wife, Olivia, in Spring, Texas.

Now Available!

MICAH S. HACKLER'S
Sheriff Lansing Mysteries
Books 1 – 10

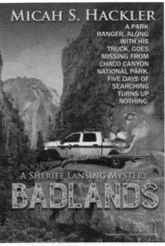

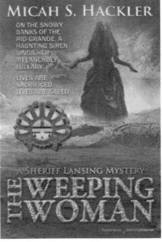

Upcoming New Release!

EAGLE FALLS
A Howard Moon Deer Mystery
Book 9
by
ROBERT WESTBROOK

Howie has been hired by Ryan Marlowe, an ex-governor of New Mexico, to discover why his 17-year-old granddaughter, Zia, committed suicide. Governor Marlowe, long retired from politics, is a friend and Howie is glad to be of help in what appears to be a straight-forward investigation. But when there is a second suicide, it's starting to look like murder, and Howie must discover what it was Zia knew that got her killed.

EAGLE FALLS is a tale of ambition and ego that takes Jack, Howie, and his daughter Georgie—now twenty-one—into the high-tech world of New Mexico's private space industry run by billionaires who, having won the treasures of the Earth, are now vying with one other to get to the stars.

For more information
visit: www.SpeakingVolumes.us

Now Available!

ROBERT WESTBROOK'S
Howard Moon Deer Mysteries
Books 1 – 7

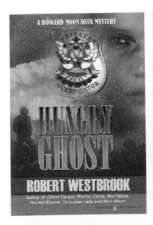

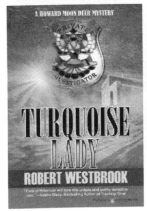
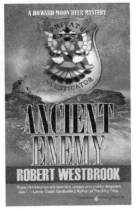

For more information
visit: www.SpeakingVolumes.us

Now Available!

AWARD WINNING AUTHOR
MARK WARREN

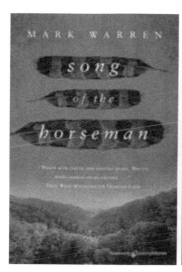 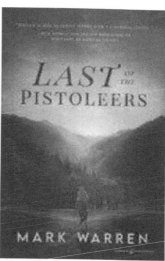

**For more information
visit:** <u>www.SpeakingVolumes.us</u>

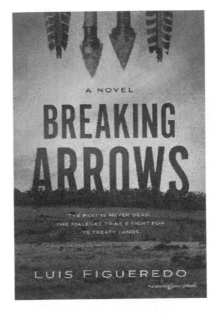

Made in the USA
Las Vegas, NV
16 March 2023